PERILOUS TRAILS: JACK'S ADVENTURE BEGINS

PERILOUS TRAILS: JACK'S ADVENTURE BEGINS

THE FRONTIER CHRONICLES
BOOK 1

MARK GREATHOUSE

WISE WOLF
BOOKS

WISE WOLF BOOKS
An Imprint of Wolfpack Publishing
wisewolfbooks.com
1707 E. Diana Street
Tampa, FL 33610

Paperback ISBN 978-1-957548-54-8
eBook ISBN 978-1-957548-98-2
LCCN 2024942620

Dedicated with love to my wife Carolyn, our two sons Mike and Matt, and the memory of my father, John F. (Jack) Greathouse

Christ is my firm foundation (testify)
The Rock on which I stand.

CODY CARNES, "FIRM FOUNDATION"

THE CAST

Jack O'Toole—*Fifteen-year-old son of Joseph and Anna O'Toole. He has two younger brothers and two sisters. The family strives to carve a life from the Texas frontier on the easternmost reaches of the Comancheria.*

Wild Horse (also Kobe)—*Fifteen-year-old son of a Penateka Comanche chief camped within the heart of the Comancheria.*

Blue Flower—*Sister to Wild Horse. She's a year younger than her brother and is her father's treasure.*

George Freeman—*A Black cowboy driving cattle north, later an Army scout, then Wyoming rancher.*

White Knife (also Tosahwi)—*Penateka Comanche shaman or medicine chief.*

Kate—*Jack's ten-year-old sister*

Buck—*Jack's five-year-old brother*

Eagle (also Kwihnai)—*Kiowa warrior.*

Colonel Steele—*Officer who replaces Colonel Loring as commandant at Fort Inge.*

Isaac Fisher—*An Amish farmer from Pennsylvania seeking new opportunity on the frontier.*

Sarah Fisher—*Isaac Fisher's wife.*

HISTORICAL CHARACTERS

Brevet Colonel William Loring—*Commander of a mounted rifle regiment assigned to Fort Inge near the southern reaches of the Comancheria. (Note: later serves as major general for the Confederacy.)*

Captain Gordon Granger—*Captain serving under Colonel Loring at Fort Inge.*

Buffalo Hump—*War chief of the Penateka Comanche, the southernmost band of the Comanche people in the Comancheria. He is father to Wild Horse and Blue Flower.*

Captain Nathan Benton—*Texas Ranger captain assigned to protect settlers from Indians in the Leona River region northwest of Fort Inge. (Note: Later serves the Confederacy as lieutenant colonel of the 36th Texas Cavalry.)*

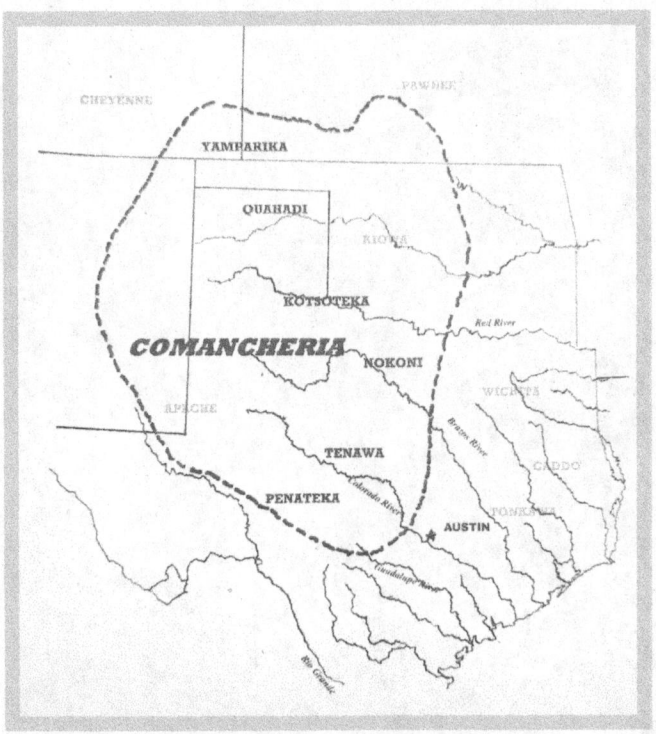

The Comancheria features six of thirteen recognized Comanche tribes: Yamparika, Quahadi, Kotsoteka, Nokoni, Tenawa, and Penateka. Other tribes are identified in gray typeface, all caps, including Apache, Cheyenne, and Kiowa. Note that the Sante Fe Trail followed the northern border of the Comancheria. (Map by Mark Greathouse)

YOU ARE INVITED

Dear Reader,

My story begins in 1855 in Texas. I was thrown alone and vulnerable by events beyond my control onto the Comancheria, the most dangerous part of the frontier, by a factor of 10x. I was only fifteen years old. What made it so dangerous? Comanche, for one thing. The Comancheria was a virtual no-man's land for White settlers.

This first book of my chronicles, *Perilous Trails: Jack's Adventure Begins*, offers more than my insights into this ruggedly harsh land and how I dealt with its challenges. It is a sneak peek into the courage, faith, endurance, and pure grit entailed by folks in conquering it. We young folks on the frontier grew up right quickly by necessity. From what older folks have told me, my story incorporates history not found in most school history books. This is my tale as driven by fate and guided by God.

I met up plenty with Indians. My first encounters were with Comanche, so you'll find me using some of

xiv   YOU ARE INVITED

their language throughout *Perilous Trails*. You will find that I provided a handy glossary of Comanche words toward the back of this book.

I'm a devout Christian, but I tried to understand the Comanche religion to better understand them. Their religion was based upon what is referred to as animism, in which every common natural item, from fish and animals to plants, trees, waterways, and mountains, was believed to have souls or spirits. The spirits and traditions connected with them guided the Comanche. Their passion for their spirits no doubt gave them their fearlessness as fed by the belief that they were protected in everything they did. Would they kill to defend their beliefs? Let's say that theirs was not a religion of love and forgiveness.

Could Indians like the Comanche become Christians? I have intended for my story in *Perilous Trails* to unfold at the intersection of faith and culture. Historically, it was not unlike Saint Patrick's conversion of the Irish to Christianity by folding many of their less-offensive heathen rites into the Catholic faith. The British derisively referred to the Irish as *Black Catholics*. Would this work with the Comanche? Well, it's part of the story I'm sharing with y'all.

As you follow my adventures, ask yourself whether you might be up to meeting the challenges I take on. Dangers? Privations? Hmmm. How might you have fared? Through it all, I first relied on the teachings of my family, then went on to learn from the raw and risky experiences I faced. I learned to trust in instincts forged from my biblical lessons.

To be straight here, I had no idea that my story was going to fill multiple volumes until I began to write it all down. I invite you to follow my often perilous adventures on America's western frontier.

Kindest regards,

John *Jack* O'Toole

PERILOUS TRAILS: JACK'S ADVENTURE BEGINS

PROLOGUE

PETER O'TOOLE FOCUSED on mending the fence post. His youngest boys, Samuel and Buck, laughed and squealed loudly as they chased each other around the yard. Peter didn't hear the laughs stop as the sound of unshod hooves reached his ears far too late. He felt the feathery touch of a coup stick, stood erect, and took an arrow full on in his chest.

The homestead swarmed with Comanche warriors. War whoops, cries, dust, and arrows filled the air.

Overcome with fear and seeing his father take a second arrow and tumble lifelessly into the Texas dust, Samuel ran screaming toward the shed. He'd never make it. Buck tripped, fell, and was swooped up into a savage Comanche's arms.

Mary emerged from the cabin at the first sounds of the commotion, and a Comanche war club dealt her the same fate as Samuel. Anna O'Toole and her daughter Kate cowered within the log walls.

Blood-lusting warriors stormed through the door and dragged the women outside. Young Kate fought and kicked but was helpless as she was swept up in the strong arms of the Comanche chief. His fearsome black warpaint and dark eyes caused her to faint. He draped her limp body across his pony and uttered fearsome war cries at the chaotic scene. With much taunting and whooping and hollering, Comanche warriors dismounted and strung up Kate's mother. Anna...poor Anna...was to meet a fate worse than death itself.

A torch was lit and thrown onto the cabin's thatched roof, sending flames and smoke high into the sky.

ONE
JUST FISHING

THE CRYSTAL blue vastness of a cloudless sky brought a smile to my face. Couldn't help it. I stood up to stretch and happened to look over my shoulder toward home. I reckoned my pa must have begun to burn something, because I could make out a column of smoke through the distorted waves of heat bouncing from the prairie. He'd be none too happy at my not being there to help, even though he'd told me mid-morning to go off and catch some fish for dinner.

I thought back a bit on what brought my family to this place they called Texas. I'd call it a godforsaken place only for its heathen Indians and the dangerous, nasty critters that lurked about. Lynx, mountain lions, bears, wolves, coyotes, javelina, and rattlesnakes could make themselves known from time to time.

The land itself was right pretty, with its verdant grassy prairies and rolling hills interspersed with stands of live oak, cacti, bald cypress, and juniper, as well as the pecan trees along the Guadalupe River. The hills were just big enough to bring back memories of our farm back in south-central Pennsylvania, a hundred miles or so west of Philadelphia. The forests back in Pennsylvania were a tad greener owing to the generally cooler climate and greater rainfall. In fact, my folks told us that they were more like the heathers around their home back in County Kildare, Ireland.

Our home back east wasn't far from a little farm town called Gettysburg. I occasionally made it to a local schoolhouse, but my tall, gangly physique, coupled with my Irish accent, tended to cause a couple of the local bullies to try picking fights with me. With my pa having drummed turning the other cheek into my head, I endured their taunts.

One day, about a half mile down the road from the school, a boy named Henry Smith confronted me. Henry, or *Big Hank* as they called him, was big for his age. Anyway, he strode up, put as evil a stare as possible in his eyes, and slammed my shoulder with his fist. A companion of his laughingly egged him on, so he hit me again. I guess I was done turning other cheeks.

I'm not sure where the force behind my fist came from, but I recall that my punch caught him square on his nose. There was a cracking sound, blood squirted everywhere, and he fell to his knees. He screamed out, "You busted my nose!"

I remember blurting out something like, "God have mercy on your soul."

Big Hank—not nearly so big now—whimpered through his sobs, "God nothin', I'm tellin' my pappy!" He shook one fist at me. "I'll get you! I'll kill you!"

I shrugged off Big Hank's threats and walked off just a tad proud of myself, but Pa wasn't especially happy when I told him. Pa believed in sparing the rod, that is, he never struck any of us. It wasn't that he was a nonviolent man, he just didn't believe that spanking or whipping were appropriate punishments. But my fighting did not go unpunished. The barn got a very thorough cleaning thanks to my efforts. I think Pa was secretly proud of me for sticking up for myself. It pretty much signaled the beginning of the end of my formal schooling. As to Henry Smith, I never heard from him or his pa.

Pa and Ma, Peter and Anna O'Toole, worked hard. However, successful farming simply wasn't my father's thing. He loved animals plenty more than raising crops. Our milk cow was treated like a queen, and our mule might well have been king. Pa, being a Godly man, his heart always overly-generous with folks. Travelers who passed by often overstayed their welcome thanks to my parent's giving hearts. Pa enjoyed preaching from the Bible pretty much any chance he got. Little wonder that its lessons stuck with me. He regularly hammered home to us that faith was meaningless unless you trusted God.

By the time my youngest brother Samuel was born, we'd endured two straight years of struggling to achieve a decent crop yield. All the praying in the world wasn't putting food on the table for our family comprised of my folks, me, and my two brothers and two sisters. Yep, I had a fairly sizable family. Pa and Ma pulled me from school to help, but it wasn't enough. They'd had enough.

At the time we left Pennsylvania for the opportunities Pa had heard about in Texas, Samuel and Buck were ages one and three respectively, and my sister Kate was eight years old and Mary only two years younger. My sisters stayed right close to my ma so as to learn all those housekeeping chores womenfolk were responsible for. Both my sisters could churn up some tasty butter, and I could never tell whether one of them or Ma sewed patches on my clothes so you could barely tell they'd been repaired. Ma said there would be a couple of lucky men in the girls' futures.

Family life was right pleasant, despite my tendency to tease my sisters unmercifully. They were scared to death of spiders. In fact, Mary nearly killed me one time when I dropped a big black spider onto her spool of wool. Spiders were nothing compared to snakes. Black snakes, garter snakes, copperheads, rattlers...didn't matter none. My ma and sisters were dreadfully afraid of those varmints. I could understand it with the poisonous snakes, but the others were harmless and could be counted upon to keep pesky rodents under control. Thanks to my pa's warnings, I exercised enough self-control to never tease my ma or sisters with snakes—dead or alive. Oh, and before I forget, I recall one of our hunts just before packing for Texas when my pa filleted a rattlesnake and fried it up. I nearly choked on the first bite, but found the meat decidedly delicious. It tasted sort of like chicken.

As I sat pondering how many bass I would fish from the Guadalupe this day, my mind wandered back again to the beginnings of what I call our Texas adventure. Yep, Pa sold the farm, loaded us and any worldly possessions worth taking into a wagon pulled by a team of oxen, and headed us for Texas.

Do you have any idea how far a team of oxen can pull a wagon in one day? Think twenty miles at most, usually ten or twelve. Do the math. It was about 1,300 miles to Austin, Texas. Figure that this included dealing with all manner of weather. We'd departed in the late summer of 1853, so the climate ranged from hot to warm, wet to nearly dry. The roads to Pittsburgh were passing fair, though would often become quagmires in heavy rain.

The family had to be fed, so Pa depended on what hunting skills we had to supplement the limited food supplies we'd managed to pack in the wagon.

At Pittsburgh, our rig was loaded onto a barge that took us via the Ohio River to Cairo, Illinois and thence the Mississippi River to Baton Rouge, Louisiana. There, we bought food supplies and once again embarked overland. This time, we joined with four other wagons also headed to Texas. I reckoned that the grownups figured there was safety in numbers. There were more guns to be sure.

In sum, the trip from our Pennsylvania farm to Austin took about six weeks. That was six weeks of living in pretty tight quarters. My sisters especially could get on my nerves, so I doubly appreciated it when my pa would give me responsibilities that got me away from my ma and the girls. Sam and Buck were too young to be any bother, and my sisters coddled them endlessly. I prayed they wouldn't become spoiled brats.

In Arkansas, we had a brush with a bear that I'd as soon forget. I was walking a few yards in front of our oxen when a mama and her two cubs crossed our path. We were the lead wagon, and she apparently reckoned we were headed on a path that threatened her cubs. She stood on her hind legs and shook her head menacingly. I heard my pa behind me cocking the hammer of his rifle. In a low voice, he told me to not move. I was quaking in my boots. Well, the bear must have decided we weren't much of a threat after all. She dropped to all fours and hurried her cubs off into the woods beside the road. Pa released the hammer on the rifle, and we all breathed a sigh of relief.

It was late October when we arrived in Austin. I recall my pa getting the deed to 650 acres and directions on how to get to the property. It was just under a hundred more miles to what they called our homestead. Pa bought a mare in Austin, and we tethered her to the back of the wagon. Dang, but it was a tough five days, especially knowing that the growing season had passed. We—mostly Pa and me—would be spending time building a two-room cabin, a shed for the mare, and clearing the area around the cabin as best possible. Ma and my sisters worked plenty hard trying to make the cabin a home. I think it was a huge relief for them compared to living from a covered wagon. Once the buildings were complete, Pa and I went about building a corral. I especially recall a brief conversation.

"You're a man now, Jack," he said, but with an earnestness I'd never heard before. "Boys grow up fast out here." He gazed at me as though allowing the words to penetrate my being.

"Don't make a difference, Pa," I responded a tad too nonchalantly.

He raised one eyebrow. "You heard me, son. You are a man. If, God-forbid, something happened to me, you'd be the man of this family. You have the brains, the skills I've taught you, the grit, and the strength of faith. You're fifteen years old and a man." His words were delivered with precision. Not stern, but serious.

What was I to say? "Yes, Pa."

He smiled, and we went back to sinking a post for the corral.

We had been leading the mare down to the Guadalupe River every day for a couple of weeks until a cistern arrived from Austin. I was so naïve. I had no idea how dangerous that two-mile walk from our cabin to the river actually was. It was this fear that drove my pa to insisting that I carry the Colt revolver I took with me fishing this day. In retrospect, the Colt would offer a rather puny defense against a raiding party of seasoned warriors. For all I knew, Comanche savages could have been scouting us pretty much every day.

I must say, Pa and I built us a fine home. His plans to raise cattle and horses were close to reality. The idea of breeding horses especially caught my imagination, and I was already dreaming on how one day I might have my own ranch to breed the finest horses on earth. But enough with reminiscing and dreaming. I shrugged myself back to reality. There were plenty of fish yet to be caught, but they'd have to wait for another day. Hoisting my day's catch of bass over my shoulder, I began the long walk back to the homestead.

The heavy Colt 1851 Navy revolver hung loosely in my waistband. It was a foot long and awkward to haul along, but, as I said, my pa made me carry the danged thing anytime I ventured away from home. Practice had made me a pretty-fair shot with the piece, so I expect that gave him confidence in me carrying it. My pa had already taught me to make my own loads, so ammunition was no problem. I must own up to rather preferring my pa's rifle. It was a .69 caliber Springfield Model 1842 smoothbore musket he'd brought with us from the farm in Pennsylvania.

Just the memory of the time when Pa let me bring down a majestic 12-point buck with that powerful musket was forever seared into the depths of my memory, not to mention that time with the bear back in Arkansas. I'd heard that the Springfield Armory was about to issue an improved rifled musket, and I longed to earn enough money from odd jobs to possess one.

But today had been about fishing, not shooting or hunting. As I mentioned, the walk from our homestead to the headwaters of the Guadalupe River was about two miles through what was purported to be dangerous territory, so it made perfect sense to respect my pa's advice and keep that Colt close at hand.

I was on familiar ground this day. I knew every nook and cranny of the river's shore for maybe a half dozen miles in each direction from my favorite fishing spot under the old cypress tree. It was a right pretty spot, soft bluestem grass on a bluff overlooking the river as it meandered southeastward. It was easy to throw in my line and pretty much guaranteed that I'd pull in a hungry bass. In fact, it was almost too easy, as it tended to make a body drop its guard, be complacent.

If my stringer of a dozen good-sized bass were to serve as evidence, the day's fishing had been exceptionally successful. I was feeling so happy-go-lucky that I nearly forgot to put my boots back on. It didn't take long to be reminded of my oversight, as the roughness of the rarely-traveled trail home was less than kind to bare feet. It felt at times as though the land was in a constant process of reminding me that I trod on hostile ground. I self-consciously said a prayer of thanks that I hadn't accidentally stepped on anything thorny. I took further solace in the thought of how a dozen fish would feed my ever-hungry family.

Oh, my name is John O'Toole. You can call me Jack. Pleased to make your acquaintance.

I must confess that my sisters also knew how to shoot. Did I say that we lived on land folks referred to as the Comancheria? Indians were supposedly everywhere, though I'd only seen a couple of hunting parties from a considerable distance. Maybe it speaks to the vastness of the region, that the populations of Comanche, Kiowa, and Apache were spread over such wide-open spaces.

I'd heard that if you were about to be captured by the Comanche, save your last bullet for yourself. It was said that the tortures they inflicted on their victims were worse than civilized folks could imagine. My pa once described them to me, and it made me sick to my stomach. I must add that no one seemed inclined to ever talk about the equally horrible atrocities levied by White folks on the Indians. I'd heard a story in Austin about the Hynes Bay Massacre back in 1852, where Texans wiped out nearly an entire village of Karankawa Indians. Seems there was nastiness, whether White or Red.

We were ever vigilant, especially when we learned that the Schultz family homestead several miles up north of us was brutally attacked by a large Comanche raiding party. Two children and Mrs. Schultz were killed, but Mr. Schultz and two of his sons fought the savages off. A passing cavalry unit later told us that the survivors gave up their ranching venture and headed back to safer environs east of Austin.

It'd be at least another couple of hours before sunset, and there were chores my pa was surely waiting for me to help with. He wouldn't be especially happy that I'd missed helping burn whatever it was he'd figured to dispose of. There was livestock to care for. We had grown our longhorn herd to nine beeves, and Pa was fixing to buy a stud stallion next year to mate with our mare.

I expect I'd walked maybe halfway home, when I first realized that the column of smoke was rising from where our house ought to be. Naturally, I began to run. If there was a fire, Ma and Pa would need my help.

AS I CAME CLOSER to the house, it struck me that there was no noise save for the occasional pop of burning timber. I instinctively pulled the Colt revolver from my waistband, threw caution to the wind, and ran faster. I scanned the still-distant scene ahead but saw no living soul.

Drawing nearer the cabin, I could see, much to my horror, that it was nearly fully consumed. Dropping the revolver and my stringer of bass, I took a couple more steps but was held back by the searing heat. I sheltered behind the shed that served as a barn for our mare. It struck me that our beeves were gone from the nearby pasture. Where were my ma and pa? Where were my brothers and sisters? Shielding my face from the heat of the fire, I stole a look inside the shed. Our mare was gone. I'd heard that the Indians stole horses so I wasn't surprised. A breeze had kicked up that would serve to speed the fire as it swallowed the dry timbers of my home. The scene overwhelmed me. I tried not to cry but couldn't help it.

Through a haze of tears, I was able to make out my Pa lying on his back in the dust in front of the cabin. Throwing caution to the wind and despite the heat of the fire, I rushed over to him. Blood seemed to be everywhere. Two arrows protruded from his side and another from his leg. As I kneeled beside him, I realized most of the blood was because he'd been scalped. I nearly threw up at the sight. I pulled myself together as best I could. I looked down at him. I so wished we could talk so I'd know what to do.

At that, Pa tried to open his eyes. It was as though a fog covered them as he struggled mightily to focus.

I dropped to my knees beside him.

Pa's lips moved ever-so-slightly as he tried desperately to talk. "Love...man," were the final words I was ever to hear from his lips. I sat there kneeling beside him, just taking in his now peaceful face.

I pulled myself up. Where was the rest of my family? Shielding my eyes from the sun and turning my back to the heat of the fire and the ash-filled smoky air, I scanned the area. The Comanche were obviously long gone. I felt light-headed but strove to keep my wits about me.

I wiped away the tears with my shirt sleeve and began a slow search. I finally found Mary a few yards away. She'd apparently tried to run only to have her head caved by a Comanche war club. Poor little Samuel lay nearby and had met a similar fate.

Kate and Buck were nowhere to be seen. Being that they were so young, it may have been God's will for them to have been taken captive. I'd heard that the savages would raise young White captives as their own. I could only hope they'd survived.

Pa and a sister and brother had been killed, and my other siblings were likely taken captive. Where was my mother? About this time, the remainder of our cabin collapsed in a heap of smoldering ruin. I could now see beyond it to one of the clothesline posts on the other side. There was Ma. I could see her now through the smoke.

I ran around the smoldering ruins of the cabin. I stopped a few feet from her, stung by the horror before me. Ma, my wonderful, full-of-love Ma, hung limply by her wrists that were tied to the top of the post. Her head hung to her chest, her eyes filled with the vacant stare of death. Anger began to share its place within me, along with grief, fear, and horror, as I slowly drew closer to her. She'd been tortured, and the Comanche had likely had their way before murdering her. My loving mother had clearly died an agonizing death. Words cannot begin to describe what torture was wrought upon her.

The idea of forgiveness was far from my mind, as I promised myself vengeance upon her killers. Revenge swelled in the very depths of my soul. I hadn't yet allowed the reality to seep into my puny teenage brain of how helpless I likely would be against dozens of Comanche warriors. I asked myself, "Is this what being a man is about?"

I found a shovel in the shed and tearfully dug graves. With everything burned, there was nothing to wrap them in as I gently and lovingly lowered the remains of my family into shallow graves. I found some sticks and was able to fashion crosses. Pa had carved the family name in the lintel supporting the front door of our humble cabin, and I was able to salvage it from the smoldering ashes and lay it along a row of rocks at the head of the graves. Upon finishing, I stood, doffed my hat, and recited Psalm 23. Tears? My eyes were now dry. I simply had no more tears to give.

Cold reality was in fact beginning to set in. What was I to do, and where was I to go? Could Kate and Buck be saved? I had the Colt revolver with a mere ten rounds of ammunition. The Comanche had taken my father's musket and ammunition along with any dry goods and food that took their fancy. I had no knife, as I'd neglected to take one with me when I left to go fishing. A second revolver had been in the cabin, but it had been burned beyond usefulness.

The cabin ruins were too hot to permit me to explore the cold storage space under the floor. From the look of the charred wood, I held little hope of anything surviving the heat of the blaze. I briefly lamented my lack of transportation, but that was pointless. Wherever I went would have to be on foot. As to food, the bass on my stringer might feed me for a couple of days. I still had my fishing pole, so that sort of determined that I'd be following waterways to keep from starving.

Using my now precious ammunition to hunt game was out of the question, as there was no telling how long it would take to rescue Kate and Buck, and I might have to fend off Comanche. I searched around the shed and was blessed with finding a small leather bag the savages had overlooked. Inside were spare flints from an old rifle and a piece of steel, a combination that would help me light a fire if needed.

Most folks would likely say that my next decision was plumb crazy. I could have headed southwestward to Fort Inge and sought the help of the US Army. But being downright certifiably demented with sorrow and vengeful anger, I decided to head back toward the Guadalupe River and the path northwest toward what I guessed was the living quarters of the Penateka band of Comanche. I was a scared kid substituting fear with an obsessive drive to wrestle my brother and sister from the clutches of the savages. I was pretty much blinded by that obsession, and I wouldn't be freed of its tentacles for some time. Heck, Kate and Buck were likely scared half to death and were probably already overwhelmed with the hopelessness of their situation.

I picked up the Colt revolver and my stringer of bass, took a final look at what had been my home, and began the trek back toward the river. I stopped after a few steps and took one more look back at the graves. Sighing, I continued my reluctant walk toward the river.

Pa and I had hunted together a few times, so I tried to recall what he'd taught me as we'd stalked game. Bottom line, that meant that I yet had an awful lot to learn about the frontier. Things like staying downwind of my prey, identifying and determining the age of sign, and doubling back to hide my travels were not yet in my frontiersman repertoire. It reminded me that my pa was a farmer first, rancher second, and never a frontiersman in the sense of depending on game to feed self and family. He passed on to me what he could. I would be fending for myself and learning hard lessons as I traveled among the dreaded environs of the Comancheria.

I hadn't walked but fifty yards or so when I came upon a dead horse. It had apparently been ridden by one of the Comanche, as it had symbols painted on its hide and feathers in its mane. I must have missed it in the blindness of running toward my burning home. The pony was long gone, and its rider must have escaped. The Comanche never left their warriors behind, but a dead horse was obviously another matter. Now, fortune smiled upon me just a bit. Lying under a nearby cactus was a knife apparently lost by the Comanche warrior. In the chaos of battle, he likely hadn't been able to find it. I picked up the knife and turned it in my hand. Its bone handle had been carved with images that likely meant something to its owner. For me, it was simply a godsend.

As I fondled the knife, it hit me that the savages had traded a dead horse for massacring my folks and siblings and taking prisoners. The anger at such injustice welled up within me. Why did there have to be hate and killing?

I took a final look around what had been my home. I'd vent my anger, have my revenge, and assuage my guilt. Maybe...just maybe...I would return to finish what my pa had begun. First, I had to rescue Kate and Buck, if in fact they were still alive. As I passed the shed, it occurred to me that anyone happening on this land might think it abandoned. I picked up a piece of charred wood from the cabin and wrote on the inside wall of the shed. "I am alive and will return." I signed my name, dropped the wood, and had myself a final cry, no tears, just sobs. How could this have happened? How could God have permitted this?

TWO
BURDENS

MY STEPS WAVERED SOMEWHERE between a reluctant trudge and an anger-driven stalk. It didn't take long to reach the familiar ground of my favorite fishing spot. I now saw that as an opportunity to stop and think. I needed to collect my thoughts. Worse still was a new emotion creeping into my very soul. I should have been there to help protect my family. My pa and ma and my sisters might still be alive. My brother and sister wouldn't be struggling in the arms of Comanche warriors. Guilt soon began to hang heavy within me. Anger...revenge...guilt. I didn't yet realize the terrible effect those deep feelings would have on the journey ahead. They were most unpleasant burdens.

I stared into the shimmering swift current of the Guadalupe River. It had a soothing, even numbing effect. I thought back to my pa counseling me. I visualized him standing before me, his shirt dusty from the day's work and one suspender hanging off his shoulder. Ma stood at the oven but turned an ear to what wise counsel he might deliver. He would flip through the Bible held in his strong left hand until he found what he was looking for.

I had been boasting about getting back at a boy who had been telling lies about me. Pa's finger landed on the book of Matthew. "Here we are," he said, clearing his throat. "Matthew 12:19-21. Beloved, do not avenge yourselves, but rather give place for wrath, for it is written, 'Vengeance is Mine, I will repay,' says the Lord." At that point, he looked sternly at me. You knew that he knew that Ma and my brothers and sisters—anyone within earshot—were listening. His habit was to clear his throat again for emphasis. "The Good Book continues," he advised, looking directly at me. "Therefore, if your enemy is hungry, feed him. If he is thirsty, give him a drink. For in so doing, you will heap coals of fire on his head. Do not be overcome by evil, but overcome evil with good."

I shook my head. Pa's words seemed to ring hollow in my current state. They ran off me like water over a duck's back. You'd better believe I was revenge-minded. The savages had stolen my family. They were going to pay. My pa's words faded, absorbed in that trio of anger, revenge, and guilt. I would find my little brother and sister and wreak my vengeance on the Comanche.

Yet guilt was weighing ever heavier to the very depths of my being. I should have been home, not fishing. At the least, I might have been able to kill an attacker. I might have been killed and scalped, but I would have gone down fighting.

All of a sudden, I felt hungry. I unhooked a bass from the stringer and filleted it with the Comanche knife. I was savvy enough to know better than to try and start a fire so long as a war party was in the area. When you're hungry, raw fish isn't so bad. I had a feeling that I'd be chowing down on worse.

With my hunger temporarily satisfied, I took stock of my situation. I had my Colt revolver, the Comanche knife, my fishing pole, and fish I'd need to eat before they went to rot. It was mid-September, and the nights were getting ever cooler. Nevertheless, I only had the clothes on my back. With any luck, I wouldn't have to deal with the coming cooler days and nights of fall and winter.

––––––––

I MUST HAVE FALLEN asleep as I awakened to a bright shard of morning sunlight full on my face. At first, I thought I'd had a nightmare. I wondered why Pa hadn't come searching for me when I hadn't returned home. It was only when I stood and saw the soot staining my shirt and the Comanche knife lying beside the Colt that the cold, hard truth of my circumstances set in. This had been no terrifying dream. For a moment, I considered going back to the cabin, but thought better of it. I needed to lay low in case those Comanche were still lurking.

I fixed a breakfast of—you guessed it—bass. The fish were beginning to get a tad ripe, so I prayed that eating one of them wouldn't make me ill. I reminded myself to next time dangle the critters in the river until I could feed on them. There was likely some way to dry the critters for eating later, but I hadn't a clue as to how to do that. I looked out from the south bank of the river. No friends or foes came into view. I belched and wretched up some fish. It was clear that I needed to expand my diet. I resolved to keep an eye out for berries. Meanwhile, I slipped down to the banks of the

Guadalupe and drank my fill from the cool running waters.

There was little point in delaying my mission further. I set my mind to following the river's edge and heading northwest toward where I calculated the Comanche captors of Kate and Buck might be encamped. By my reckoning, the raiding party wouldn't have ventured too far from their home, and it made sense for the savages to encamp near a plentiful water supply.

I did my best to use the brush and trees along the river bank as a protective shield, though I likely left behind me a trail that most anyone could follow. I had been thrown into the gaping jaws of dangers unknown, and I'd be learning as I traveled. Admittedly, it was my choice. I so yearned to save Buck and Kate. Anger and vengeance drove me, but deep inside, I felt as though rescuing them would relieve me of at least some of the burden of guilt that hung across my shoulders like an ox yoke. I recalled something in my pa's teachings about relief from heavy burdens, but it wasn't coming to me today in this place.

I hiked about what seemed like three miles or there-abouts and came upon ground stomped by horse hooves. They were unshod, so I reckoned they were Comanche ponies. Must have been at least a dozen. The river had narrowed here and it ran shallow-like over rocks. Ahead of me was a cliff rising among the reddish-brown rocks. It was maybe fifty feet high, imposing yet tempting to cross. I figured the Comanche likely waded upstream from here, as their ponies wouldn't be up to climbing the sheer face.

Being afoot and seeing places in the cliff face that afforded handholds and footholds to climb, I decided to give it a try. I'd be exposed briefly, but that was a risk I'd have to take. I looked both ways and cautiously ventured out. I held my Colt and ammunition over my head. I had ditched the increasingly malodorous stringer of bass. Dang, but the Comanche wouldn't even have to be downwind to smell that reeking, rotting...you get the picture.

I reached the north bank and was about to step into the shelter of riverside foliage and begin my climb. I placed my hand on a boulder to steady myself and, upon pulling away, felt a stickiness. I looked down at the palm of my hand. The stickiness was blood. The back side of the boulder was covered in more than blood. At its base —much to my horror—was a fawn. My heart sank, fearing the savages might have tired of Buck's squirming and fussing to get away and had bashed his defenseless body against the jagged rock. Seeing the fawn was a relief. I figured it must have fallen from up high.

At the thought of Buck and Kate, anger and vengeance once again welled up. I felt as though my very insides would burst with the poisonous venom of pure hatred. I would kill every Comanche I could see. I'd spare none. Women...children...elderly...even their horses and dogs would not be absolved of the vengeance I would wreak upon them.

What was I to do with the broken remains of the fawn? I was hungry. As I bent to pick up my dinner, I heard a low growl and found myself looking into the threatening gaze of a hungry coyote but six feet away. I expect that the scavenger figured me to be taking his dinner and wasn't excited about sharing. I was concerned that he might have brought company, and that wouldn't do at all. I swatted at him with my fishing pole, and he backed off some. I certainly couldn't risk shooting the beast. A gunshot might echo for miles.

I took my knife and separated a rear haunch from the fawn while keeping an eye on the coyote. I tied a piece of fishing line to it, slung it over my shoulder, and snarled at the coyote. He growled at me again. I gave the selfish beast one more poke with my fishing pole and began my escape up the wall. As I looked back, I saw that the coyote had been joined by a couple of his friends. They'd begun to feast ravenously upon the remains of the hapless fawn.

I climbed as quickly as possible up the cliff face to minimize my vulnerability. It was a tough climb. While there were plenty of handholds, the rock tended to breakup under my weight. I climbed like my life depended on it, which it did. Once at the top, I made my way among the trees and ducked behind some shrubs.

The foliage offered enough shelter that I felt comfortable resting and eating some of the raw delicacy I snatched from the coyotes. I admit that I was relieved that those varmints could enjoy their meal a distant fifty feet or so below me. Far as I could tell, there were no Comanche around. Then again, I didn't figure those varmints to be announcing their presence. I sure wasn't looking for dinner guests.

I really hadn't traveled all that far, but I found myself tired. Make that exhausted. I expect emotions were taking their toll on my body as well as mind. Some second thoughts entered my mind. Maybe, I should have headed to Fort Inge. Then again, would the soldiers have rescued Buck and Kate from the clutches of those savage Comanche? My pa had said something about the soldiers avoiding engaging with the Indians, so I reckoned my decision was the right one.

Anger, vengeance, guilt, and now fear entered my thinking. How was one fifteen-year-old boy going to rescue two children from what could be an encampment of a couple of hundred Comanche? Well, I would die trying.

Then, it struck me. I was alone. I had no one to talk with, no one to share my feelings and plans. Fear was coming on ever stronger as it displaced my bravado. Would the Comanche torture me? Would they kill me before taking my scalp? Who would know or care?

I threw up some of the raw meat. I was thirsty, but there was no way I'd be going back down the cliff any time soon. The coyotes had likely finished their meal, but they were a fate I wasn't up to tempting. Sleep overtook my tired bones.

THREE
ENDANGERED

OVER AND OVER, endlessly, Wild Horse practiced. The bow and arrow were an extension of his body. He was his father's pride. Buffalo Hump, war chief of the Penateka Comanche, smiled approvingly at his son's marksmanship. No varmint was safe from Wild Horse's arrows. His feathered shafts invariably flew true. He'd even begun practicing shooting from beneath the neck of his pony at a full gallop. Comanche warriors became one with their ponies. In fact, ponies were a measure of a warrior's wealth. It wouldn't be long before the teen would take his place among the hunters and warriors of his tribe.

Wild Horse's early years were under the tutelage of his mother and grandmothers. As a mere toddler, he'd been among his people when his father led their notorious march to the sea. He was too young to remember much, but the tale of triumph was repeated often enough at council fires that his head was filled with vivid details.

The Bluecoats had harassed his people in vain as they marched back from the coast. He rode a travois pulled by one of Buffalo Hump's ponies. His own father had been one of the few warriors lost in the attack. Runs With Buffalo had counted many coups before taking a settler's bullet. He vaguely recalled a time of grieving as his father was sent to the Big Father. Now, he wondered what sort of gods the White man worshipped? Could they be as powerful as the Comanche gods?

He heard tales of the Whites being liars and cheaters. Stories reached his people of tribes nearly destroyed by the White man's diseases. Yet, the white-skinned people kept coming. Their settlements sprawled along the edges of the Comancheria and beyond. Now, they were little by little encroaching on Comanche lands. The Comanche, like their red brethren of other peoples, had no property lines. They owned no land. They hunted and defended what had been theirs for centuries.

Wild Horse stood in the entrance to his teepee home. The buffalo hides gave him a warm assurance. He was taller than most of his fellow Comanche, perhaps barely more than six feet. He had a wiry, well-muscled build. This day, he chose to wear only breechcloth, leggings, and moccasins. He'd decided to go shirtless to better feel the warmth of the sun in these first days of autumn. Wild Horse slung his quiver of arrows over his shoulder and was prepared to enjoy a day of hunting. Of course, he'd gained permission from his father, who merely smiled and nodded approval. His best friend Buffalo Who Runs was joining him. They'd hunted together before and were good company for each other.

While the Comanche diet was varied, meat was a staple. This made hunting skills a critically important component of the life of any warrior to be. Hunting and fighting were man's work in the Indian culture. They were both defenders and attackers depending on which was necessary. Wild Horse would become a warrior within the year, joining the most-feared fighters on the frontier and horsemen without peer.

The Comanche victories over the Bluecoats were legendary in the council fires. The Bluecoats never seemed to learn how to counter Comanche tactics. While the warriors rode circles and lured troopers into traps, the Bluecoats would dismount and form battle lines that made them sitting ducks for arrows. In close quarters, clubs and lances were an easy match for swords and bayonets. There was a sort of ironic humor to the Comanche calling the sword-wielding White soldiers *long knives*. The sword was simply no match for a lance in close quarters.

The stories of the raid on the homestead rang as though alive in the young Comanche's mind. They had brought back two young captives. The Comanche women made them welcome, if beating them into submission was welcoming. A strange feeling swept over him as he watched the white-skinned girl and boy cower under the lashes and sticks of the Penateka women. Something about the beatings didn't quite sit right, and it gave him a queasy feeling deep in his gut. They were only defenseless children. Yet they were mild compared to tales of tortures inflicted by men on other men. It simply didn't seem honorable.

It bothered him that there appeared to be more and more Whites settling on Comanche hunting grounds. More Bluecoats came with the settlers. It looked to be an endless chain. There were so many that the Whites could even pay other Whites—the Bluecoats—to protect them and even to kill for them. Nevertheless, Wild Horse dreamed of the day when he could ride forth and join a raiding party. Soon enough, he'd be earning his warrior name. He'd count coup by touching his enemy, then kill and scalp his prey. No matter the wives and mothers grieving the loss of loved ones in battle, no matter how honorable. Wild Horse dreamed of great victories.

But this day, he was after *aruka* to feed his family. A big buck would be ideal. This was a big responsibility he was entrusted with. He felt honored to have been given the task. He glanced at his younger sister, Blue Flower, as he stepped toward the remuda of ponies at the edge of the encampment.

He and Buffalo Who Runs departed, riding their best ponies. Actually, they were their only ponies. The young braves needed the horses to haul their prizes back to their people. Surely, they'd bring home prizes. Wild Horse felt especially confident.

The lands between the Pedernales River and Guadalupe River were still teeming with game, especially *aruka*, the deer. Wild Horse was determined to bring down *aruka* with only a single arrow. There was no doubt in his mind.

As silently as possible, they walked their ponies along a dry creek bed, an arroyo meandering southward toward the Guadalupe. It was yet early, so they had plenty of time to find their prey. Sign was abundant, as droppings were plentiful at virtually any place that offered shade. The deer tended to rest during the warmer parts of the day, so it took a practiced eye to find them nestled in camouflaging foliage. Wild Horse had been on several hunts with his father and understood that patience was a virtue. It wouldn't do to spook their prey.

———

THE SUN WAS at its highest point when Buffalo Who Runs spotted a buck. Its rack of antlers had given it away as it lay among the prairie sage under a live oak tree. He crouched just high enough among the grasses to get a clear shot at *aruka*. He nocked his arrow, pulled back the bowstring, aimed, and was about to let fly when a tawny mass slammed into him. The jaws of the mountain lion clamped viciously around Buffalo Who Runs's neck and claws raked his body. The hunter had become the hunted and now prey.

Wild Horse had no time to think, only to react. He sprang into action to try to save his friend. Daring not shoot an arrow, as it could hit his friend, he pulled out his knife and leaped onto the back of the lion while making a deep cut in the beast's shoulder. He felt the blade slice through muscle and sinew. The lion released his prey and shook Wild Horse from him. He wheeled to face the new threat. He hissed. Saliva dripped from razor-sharp fangs as the lion crouched low to spring at the Comanche.

Buffalo Who Runs lay still in the grass. Wild Horse couldn't know whether his friend was dead or alive. As he stared into the lion's angry yellow eyes, his peripheral vision could see his friend bleeding heavily. The young Comanche's predicament was dire. His bow had been cast aside upon his leaping onto the lion to save his friend. His quiver of arrows was useless, at least for the moment. The knife? It had fallen from his grip and lay somewhere in the grass. The lion was crippled, but not much. Wild Horse wasn't likely to outrun the beast, and the idea of leaving his best friend to become a meal was unthinkable. On the other hand, neither was he anxious to feed the carrion of the prairies. Vultures and coyotes feasting on him held no appeal.

Wild Horse felt as the prey he'd hunted over many moons past must have felt, though few had the opportunity to face their hunter as he had now. He crouched with his hands held in front to ward off any attack and began to move toward the body of Buffalo Who Runs. Perhaps he could divert the lion's attention to his dying friend. It seemed to be his only chance at escape. He might even reach his bow and put an end to the lion.

The lion hesitated as though trying to decide whether the threat imposed by Wild Horse was enough to keep him from his fresh kill. He distractedly licked at his shoulder, glanced at the body of Buffalo Who Runs, and then turned with a deep guttural growl. He bared his fangs and hissed again. His eyes seemed angrier and yellower than ever. As if this were not enough to send chills of cautionary fear up the spine of Wild Horse, a female lion appeared. The lioness slunk up alongside her mate and sniffed at his shoulder.

Dismay? Hopelessness? Wild Horse was in a serious predicament. He began to hum the Comanche death song, as he was sure his end was at hand. His visions of joining Comanche raiding parties and tribal hunts were about to become fleeting dreams.

The male began to gather his hind legs under him, coiling a hundred and fifty pounds of muscle to spring while his mate sniffed at the inert body of Buffalo Who Runs. As Wild Horse chanted louder, the lion paused as though frozen in time. It barely gave the Comanche youth time to thrust his arms up in self-defense as the big cat leaped upon him with claws and fangs bared. The Comanche managed to fend off the lion's initial attack, but not long enough to catch his breath. Yellow eyes sized up their prey. Claws had already shredded the skin of the Comanche's chest and arms, and deep gashes were gouged into his thighs. The mountain lion sought the neck of his victim to make his kill.

The lion backed off for but a moment to gather himself to renew the attack. It cocked its head at the death chant wailing from his victim's lips. The viciousness in the cat's eyes spoke all-too-loudly that the kill was at hand. Muscles tensed under its tawny hide as he prepared his final leap.

FOUR
RESCUED

I HEARD A STRANGE SOUND. It was a chant such as I'd never heard. I was downwind from it, and it couldn't have been more than a hundred yards ahead. A snarl joined in the noise as though singing some demonic duet. It was easy to figure that danger lurked. The chant stopped abruptly and a scream followed.

I'd been hiking stealthily all day from one cluster of trees and brush to another. By my reckoning, I was at least thirty miles from what had been my home. I was ever mindful that prying eyes could be lurking, watching my every move, and likely laughing at my ineptness. Well, I wasn't laughing. Whatever was out there could easily be a threat to me.

I drew the Colt from my waistband and pulled back the hammer. Waving it in front of me, I began moving cautiously toward the sounds, soon figuring to have closed something like half the distance to the source. All of a sudden, I saw the biggest—in fact, the only—mountain lion I'd ever seen leap into the air. My hand seemed to take a life of its own as the Colt barrel pointed in the direction of the cougar and my finger squeezed the trigger. My bullet plowed through the beast's hindquarters. I didn't have a clue what the danged lion was leaping at, I just instinctively fired at the danger. If I had taken the time to reason it out, I don't know that I would have shot at the beast. It could have been attacking a deer for all I knew.

A cat-scream shattered the air. The lion turned toward me, the new threat. It charged at me, and I fired again. By some stroke of fortune, my slug hit him between the eyes. The cougar was dead in mid-flight. Its momentum carried it past me. One claw-bared paw caught my forearm, leaving a trio of gashes behind. Ignoring the pain in my arm, I crouched defensively and swept the area with the muzzle of the Colt. I saw the lion's mate running away as fast as her paws could carry her. I swung the gun back to where the mountain lion had met its fate.

As the smoke began to clear, I found myself staring down the barrel of my revolver at a young Indian. He was sorely wounded. Rivulets of blood ran down his chest and thighs where he'd been raked by the mountain lion's razor-sharp claws. He stood helplessly, mouth agape. He hesitated as if to run, but seemed held fast by something lying on the ground near him. The young Indian looked up at me with pained and pleading eyes, yet there seemed an undertone of defiance despite his obvious distress.

Part of me wanted to pull the trigger. This was an Indian, after all. And he was most likely a Comanche. He might even have been with the raid on my home. Anger, vengeance, and guilt were roiling within me. He was unarmed...vulnerable. My family had been vulnerable, and the savages had brutally murdered them. I found myself sweating. It was as though time had frozen. I stood looking down at the Colt revolver in my hand, the aroma of gunsmoke still hanging in the air. My finger on the trigger wanted to squeeze it back. Mercy and death battled within my mind.

Ma and Pa had striven to drive Christ's teachings into me. By that measure, I was to resist hate, anger, vengeance, and fear—all those emotions that this scene had brought to the forefront of my senses. Was God throwing a trial before me? Trials could be constructive or destructive, depending on whether we listened to our Maker.

"*Kobe...Pena...teka...*" The young Indian tried to speak. I couldn't understand his gibberish. Already weakened from loss of blood, he dropped to his knees.

If my faith was ever to be tested, this was surely the great test. I lowered the muzzle of the Colt. I began to stuff it into my waistband, but the barrel was too hot. I cautiously walked over to the Indian. The look of fear on his face caused me to stop and reconsider. It was as though he was resigned to dying but not by my hand. My eyes locked onto his.

"*Kobe,*" he repeated and tried to point toward a cluster of trees.

It was then that I saw two ponies a hundred yards or so from us. They were hobbled among the nearby grasses. *Kobe* apparently translated to wild horse.

As I tried to decide what to do next, the young Indian fainted. I approached warily. Much to my dismay, I discovered the body of another Indian. He was apparently also a young man, but it was hard to tell. The lion had mauled him badly. I found myself in quite a dilemma. To save the one who still breathed or not?

Added to the mix was the pain from wounds in my head and on my arm.

The young warrior was unconscious, so he presented no immediate danger. I contemplated the likelihood that the two savages had come from the very band that took Buck and Kate prisoner. If so, showing mercy to this Indian just might gain me an ally toward securing their release. I surprised myself that I'd exercised reason—a strategy, if you will—in the midst of this chaos.

My Colt had finally cooled sufficiently, so I stuck it in my waistband. I put my hands under the young warrior's shoulders and dragged him to the shade of the trees near the horses. I grabbed a blanket from one of the ponies and lay the Indian upon it. Then I went back to check on his friend. The Indian was dead, so I searched him for anything useful toward my own welfare as well as for caring for the one that yet lived.

Upon returning, I began to try to stop the bleeding by strapping the dead Indian's clothing tightly over the young Indian's wounds. It wasn't much of a solution, but it did stop the blood loss. There was even enough to staunch the bleeding of my own wounds.

I gave a passing thought about the mountain lion's mate. The lioness had not reappeared. No matter. I couldn't worry about it. I fetched the male lion's carcass. It seemed even heavier than the Indian. I built a small fire using fire-making materials that I gathered from the dead Indian. Flint and steel were reliable, though nothing like striking a match. I was glad my pa had taught me how to make fire. I skinned enough of the lion to enable me to begin preparing parts of it to cook. This entire situation had made me especially hungry. I speared a couple of pieces of lion meat on a stick and held it over the fire. Now and then, I glanced over at the Indian, but he was still unconscious.

His words yet hung in my mind. *Kobe* was wild horse. I wondered what *Penateka* was. Was that his name? I vaguely recalled someone referring to the Comanche tribe by that name. I reckoned I'd have time to learn a bit more. I had found myself grudgingly committed to aiding this wounded heathen. Nevertheless, parts of me—deep within my very soul—still wanted to kill him. Yet, I was showing mercy. Such was my dilemma. I had saved his life, and by virtue of that act, it was no longer my choice to take it. If he died, it would have been the cougar's doing, not mine. Had I killed him now, it would have been murder by any measure.

I began to gnaw on the lion meat. The hot juices lingered deliciously on my lips. It wasn't beef steak, but it was downright scrumptious to my starving tastebuds. The combination of coming down from the excitement of killing the mountain lion and helping the young Indian, combined with my full belly, made me a tad drowsy. I was giving serious thought to catching a wink when I saw the Indian open one eye.

I was sitting on my haunches, so I turned to face him. I forced a smile.

Panic swept across his face. He tried to rise but collapsed back onto the blanket. His eyes searched for his weapons before finally coming to rest upon me. He glanced at the makeshift bandages covering his body and gave me a pained but inquisitive look.

I smiled again and raised my hands with palms open to him as a gesture of peace.

At that moment, we both heard the sounds of coyotes that had found the remains of the Indian's friend. In truth, it had likely helped keep the varmints from what remained of the mountain lion carcass but a few feet from us.

"Jack," I said, pointing to myself.

The Indian pointed toward where his friend had died. I sensed that he wanted to recover the body.

I stood and grabbed what remained of the lion carcass. I headed to where the body lay, drawing my Colt as I walked. The cowardly coyotes backed off, nipping and snarling. They were apparently in no mood for a trade. I hoisted the remains of the cougar and tossed it at the four coyotes. They appeared none too happy, but went to work on it after only a brief hesitation. I grabbed the arm of the dead Indian and dragged the body back to the cluster of trees. Amazingly, the coyotes hadn't yet ripped the body apart.

As I approached the trees, I quickly became aware that my Indian friend had found where I'd hidden his bow and arrow. He was seated under the tree with an arrow nocked in the bowstring and pointed at me. I dropped the arm of his deceased companion. I sighed resignedly. I repeated giving him my open palms as signs of peace. "Jack," I said, pointing once again to myself.

The Indian winced as a sharp pain swept through him.

In that moment, I swiped the bow and arrow from his hand.

He looked up at me with what I interpreted as some feeling between anger and fear but was then once again overcome with pain and fell back on the blanket. I found myself at a loss as to what to do next. We both desperately needed water. I had crossed a creek before coming upon the mountain lion attack. Dare I venture off? No telling what he might do in the few minutes I'd be absent. He'd already found his bow. What if he found the strength to mount his pony and go warn his encampment? I'd have to take that chance. I snatched the leather bota bag from the pony. It wouldn't hold much, but it was handy. I grabbed my Colt and the Indian's bow and headed for the creek. Naturally, I kept a wary eye out for coyotes and that lioness.

When I returned with the bota bag, the Indian was still asleep. I eased up slow-like and gently touched his shoulder. It was warm, so I figured he might be running a fever from his wounds. They could be infected. His eyes flickered, and I put the bota bag to his lips. As the water poured over his lips, he tried to grab the bag, but it pained him too much.

The Indian looked up at me pleadingly. He struggled to speak through still-parched lips. Bending his elbow as far as he could, he pointed a finger at me. "Jack... tosa." He then pointed at himself. "Kobe...Penateka... Co...man...che." The words trailed off as he fell back with exhaustion. "Paa." He gestured toward the bota bag.

I put the bota bag to his lips again. He coughed enough to send spasms of pain from his wounds. I could see through the makeshift bandages that he was still bleeding. Apparently, paa meant water. I had no idea what tosa meant.

My knowledge of the Comanche tongue was growing. Horse—I gathered that was his name—tried to speak once again. He made a wavy motion with his hand. I took it to mean travel.

"Kobe," I said, pointing to his pony.

He moved his fingers in a random manner and moved his head side-to-side. "Puuka," he said, pointing to the horse. Then, he painfully pointed to himself. "Kobe," he said.

I figured he meant crazy or wild. I chose wild. "Wild Horse," I said. "*Kobe*," I repeated and pointed at him.

"*Ana o'a hi'it*," he said, pointing to his mouth. He moved his jaw as though chewing.

I picked up a still-warm piece of mountain lion meat from the embers of the fire and handed it to him.

Wild Horse smiled hesitatingly as he took a bite. His eyes went wide. "*Pia wa'óo*," he declared. He made a clawing motion with his free hand.

Pia wa'óo was apparently the Comanche phrase for mountain lion. I nodded affirmatively and pointed to myself.

"*Unha haksi nahniaka?*" he asked, pointing at me. I hadn't a clue as to what he was saying, so I guessed that he was asking my name. He apparently didn't understand my earlier attempt to tell him.

I pointed to myself. "Jack."

The Comanche chewed thoughtfully and shrugged. It was a decidedly painful shrug. "*Eetu?*" He struggled, but managed to make a motion like a bow and arrow.

"No," I said, shaking my head. I drew the Colt from my waistband. "*Pia wa'óo*." I said forcefully while pretending to shoot.

Wild Horse's eyes went wide. "*Tomoobi umaru!*" he said emphatically. Later, I'd figure that was as close as his language came to expressing thunder. I suppose my Colt sounded like thunder to some ears.

I could sense from his efforts to communicate that Wild Horse was feeling better despite his wounds. However, I could tell that he still had a fever.

He looked pleadingly at me. "*Kobe...numunuu.*" He pointed to his horse and then made a sign that I took to mean people.

"Penateka Comanche?" I queried.

"*Numumuu*," he repeated and pointed to his bandages. He was begging to return to his people.

I felt a moment of truth coming on. It was clear that Wild Horse needed help far beyond what I could offer.

He pointed to his quiver of arrows and motioned to bring them to him.

I shoved the Colt back into my waistband and walked over to the quiver. I thought about whether I was doing the right thing. Was I being a naïve idiot? I took a deep breath of resignation to my fate and laid the cluster of deadly missiles beside him.

Wild Horse drew a single arrow from the quiver. "Jack...*eetu*," he said, gesturing at the arrow as he presented it to me. "*Kobe numunuu*," he repeated. He made a sign for me to stay in this place, then made the travel sign again.

It was clear that he knew that to live, he needed to ride to his people for help. I sensed that my saving his life from the mountain lion had created some sort of honor debt. The arrow was intended to show that I was protected and trusted. A voice within me—maybe it was God himself talking—told me to trust my instincts. I'd come this far in saving the Comanche's life, it was not for me to stop now.

———

GETTING Wild Horse mounted on his pony was easy compared to securing the body of his friend, the translation of whose name I never learned. It had something to do with what he called *tasiwoo*, apparently a buffalo. Wild Horse was nearly as tall as me, though not so thickly muscled. Wirey best described him, to my judgment.

My new friend was obviously in considerable pain but

managed to sit the pony pretty well. I handed him his knife and his bow and arrows. This was a leap of faith I would never have imagined taking, especially as he eyed me through his pain with some inner conflict he had yet to resolve.

Mercy had triumphed for the present over my lingering anger and desire for vengeance, not to mention the intense guilt at not having been present to defend my home. Among the swirl of emotions was the ever-present hope that Buck and Kate were safe and I might free them. I ignore Wild Horse's apparent uncertainty.

"*Numunuu*...Comanche," I said as I gestured at Wild Horse to depart.

"Jack...*pia wa'óo*," he responded with his fist gently placed against his bandaged chest. The mounting onto the pony had caused some of his wounds to bleed, but he put up a brave face. I had no idea what might be going through his mind. Were his intentions honorable? Would he bring his entire village upon me? I only had eight rounds of ammunition remaining, seven if I didn't count the last one for myself if overwhelmed in an attack. That would hardly be enough to fight off a Comanche raiding party. But the die was cast. I would have to rely on my instinct to trust the young Comanche. I could only pray that when and if he returned, he would come alone.

Meanwhile, I was committed to making some sort of camp arrangement in this godforsaken piece of the hills of the Comancheria. I had water, enough mountain lion remains to last a couple of days, and the means to fashion a shelter. I said a prayer that some roving band of Comanche or even some other tribe would not venture near. And I hoped and prayed that his wounds would be treated and, mercifully, he'd return.

FIVE
TRUST

WILD HORSE HELD TIGHTLY to his pony's mane and kept his legs clamped as solidly as he could to its sides. The pony carrying Buffalo Who Runs followed on a long lead, though it was unlikely to wander off. The ride from the scene of the mountain lion attack was ever behind him. Roiling through his mind was what to do about the White boy who had saved his life. He was unable to put a name to the concept, but he was realizing that he'd created a life debt. He knew of no word in the Comanche language to express it. Wild Horse owed his life to one of the detestable Whites, the invaders, the killers of his people.

After several hours, the young Comanche finally reached the edge of his village. He was barely able to stay on his pony. His mount instinctively headed for the remuda, where Wild Horse half-slid and half-fell to the earth. As fate would have it, the warrior guarding the remuda of ponies was nearby. Moon Walker ran over to the ponies. He quickly realized that Buffalo Who Runs was dead. He wondered for a moment how the dead

Comanche had managed to find his way to the encampment but then saw the badly wounded Wild Horse lying in a heap. Realizing his chief's son lay badly wounded before him, he lifted the young Indian and headed on the run for Buffalo Hump's teepee.

"Aaiyee! Aaiyee," hollered Moon Walker as he approached the teepee.

Upon hearing the shouts, the old war chief emerged from his teepee, where he'd been smoking a pipe and relaxing.

Moon Walker didn't stand on the formality of an invitation and carried Wild Horse into the teepee. He lay the Comanche youth on the nearest blanket.

A fully surprised Buffalo Hump followed Moon Walker inside. In but moments, he'd assessed his son's wounds.

Moon Walker explained that the two had arrived at the pony remuda just a few seconds ago. Buffalo Who Runs was dead from an attack by *pia wa'óo*. Given the seriousness of Wild Horse's wounds, he was at a loss to explain how the young Comanche had been bandaged, much less mounted his pony and returned to the encampment. He swept his hands in a gesture to convey that some sort of magic was at work. Moon Walker was convinced that the mighty hands of the Big Father had been at work.

Buffalo Hump listened distractedly as he began removing the makeshift bandages from Wild Horse. Despite his having lived many moons and seen many horrific wounds in battle, he was shaken by the terrible wounds inflicted by the *pia wa'óo*. He didn't yet have time to ponder what Moon Walker was telling him. His son and his son's friend had gone hunting and now returned to his teepee with one dead and his son on death's door.

Infection had already begun to creep its evil tentacles into the most serious of the wounds. Buffalo Hump directed Moon Walker to fetch the shaman. As the warrior exited the teepee to find the medicine man, Buffalo Hump turned and began to chant a song of grief over his stricken son.

Blue Flower, Wild Horse's younger sister, heard the commotion that began to ripple through the camp. She'd been down at the creek washing. When she heard her brother's name being shouted, she ran as fast as she could back to camp. By the time she arrived, *Tosahwi*—or White Knife—was hovering over her brother and applying various herbs and ointments aimed at staving off the infection and aiding healing. He sewed the worst of the wounds with thin strips of buckskin.

Blue Flower entered the teepee and was immediately embraced by Buffalo Hump. He held his daughter back, assuring her that White Knife would save her brother.

White Knife stepped back for just enough time that Blue Flower glimpsed her wounded brother. Her hands went to her face and tears flowed at the horror she saw. She parted her fingers to look again, but White Knife had completed his work and covered Wild Horse with a blanket.

The medicine man, also a Penateka Comanche chief of some repute, arose from tending to the young Comanche. His eyes found those of Buffalo Hump and spoke volumes. They were hunter-warriors and understood the risks to be faced among the hills of the Comancheria. The reality they faced was that there was slim hope of recovery.

White Knife's gaze shifted to Blue Flower. He instructed her to bring water and make a broth to keep Wild Horse's strength up. Like Moon Walker, he wondered how the young hunter had bandaged his own wounds and made it back to the encampment. There was a very real sense that something magical, and therefore powerful, was at work. Now, they'd see whether that same magic healed Wild Horse's wounds.

Blue Flower exited the teepee and motioned to the White girl gathering firewood. She made a sign to bring water from the creek.

Kate dropped an armload of sticks beside the teepee, grabbed some gourds, and headed for the creek. Her long blond hair had been cut short by the Comanche women, and what remained of her clothes were torn and dirty. There was barely enough material to preserve what modesty remained. She glanced around as she walked to the creek, but her young brother Buck was nowhere to be seen.

Blue Flower waited impatiently for the water so she could begin to cook up the broth. She'd already begun cutting onions and slicing strips of buffalo meat for flavor. Once Kate arrived with the water, Blue Flower added a fistful of ground corn to the mix. As the broth heated over the cooking fire in the center of the teepee, its aromas wafted throughout.

———

I WAITED AS PATIENTLY AS I could. Each hour that passed brought a new sense of vulnerability. What if this Comanche, this savage, returned with a war party?

"*Puuka*," I whispered. Then, "*Kobe*." The Comanche word for horse and the Comanche's name rolled around in my thinking. I'd put aside my anger, hatred, commitment to avenging the death of my parents and siblings at the murderous hands of the Comanche to save some savage Indian I didn't even know. What force caused me to be at that place at that moment? How on earth had I been so accurate as to kill the mountain lion and save the Comanche? What was it that kept me from killing the savage? Well, the last question wasn't so hard to answer. Like it or not, my years of Bible-learning had kicked in. I had time on my hands. I thought back on my pa reading from the book of Daniel. I think it was the ninth chapter. *"To the Lord our God belong mercy and forgiveness, though we have rebelled against Him."* Guess there was no question that my thinking had been rebelling against God's ways.

Not knowing what to do with myself, short of surviving, I ventured out to the remains of the mountain lion. There wasn't much left. Parts of the beast were strewn about as I sought tangible reminders of my encounter. What the coyotes hadn't eaten, other varmints had picked clean. I settled for a set of fangs and as many claws as I could find.

By the third day, I managed to catch a couple of small fish at the creek and even nabbed a bullfrog. Roasted over a small fire, the tiny fillets and frog legs might as well have been some sort of highfalutin delicacies.

I was ever alert for any sign of Indians, and the image of that lioness seemed forever stuck in my mind's eye. My arm hurt. The wounds were mostly superficial, but I was wary of possible infection. I kept both the revolver and knife handy.

I passed much of the time using the tip of my knife to make holes in the mountain lion fangs and claws such that I might ultimately string them for a necklace. I wondered as to what the Indians must do to drill holes.

———

THE THIRD DAY under the care of his sister brought Wild Horse out of the delirium. He'd consumed enough broth that he was beginning to feel as though he might drown in it. His infections had subsided, and wounds were mending well. He was beginning to think on how to sneak from the encampment and return as promised to the White man who'd saved his life.

He was sitting up when Buffalo Hump entered the teepee.

Buffalo Hump observed the questioning expression emblazoned across his son's face. It was so obvious that a deep question was lingering. "What troubles you, my son?"

"*Pia wa'óo, ap*," he responded, but it was clear that the mountain lion wasn't what he was really concerned with.

"*Pia wa'óo?*" queried Buffalo Hump. "That is past. What truly troubles my son?"

"Does saving a life create a debt?"

The chief's eyes widened. This was a very heavy question from a fifteen-year-old who had yet to engage in battle journey on a vision quest or count coup. Buffalo Hump sighed deeply. "You ask if you owe debt to one who saves your life?"

Wild Horse nodded.

The old chief was beginning to put together pieces of whatever puzzle was involved. Had someone saved his son's life? Is that how Wild Horse had been bandaged and sent home? Is that why the *pia wa'óo* hadn't finished the kill. If he had eyebrows, Buffalo Hump would have raised them. As was the custom with many Comanche, most of his body hair—including eyebrows—had been plucked. "You ask of a life debt, Wild Horse? Is honor." He wasn't sure he wanted to know more. If his son had been saved from death, why wouldn't his son's savior have accompanied him to the Penateka Comanche encampment? Was it someone from an enemy tribe, a dark-skin, or a white-skin? He sighed. "Did someone save you from *pia wa'óo*?"

"No, *ap*." Wild Horse knowingly lied to his father. It was an unconscionable act.

Buffalo Hump found himself both taken aback and hurt as Wild Horse's obviously deceitful denial plunged into him like a knife. His son was quite clearly not telling the truth. He excused his son's behavior as being caused by the pain of his wounds. Wild Horse simply was not thinking straight. He sighed, patted his son's hand, and exited the teepee. He would eventually learn the truth. Buffalo Hump was beginning to recognize that his son was a thinker. Perhaps he'd place him under White Knife's tutelage and teach him the ways of the shaman. That decision would be for another day.

No sooner had the chief left than Blue Flower entered with a roasted rabbit on a skewer.

Wild Horse looked relieved at the combination of not having to tell his secret to his father and being presented with solid food. The *tamu* was far preferable to broth. He began to gnaw ravenously on the rabbit meat.

"Father not happy?" Blue Flower asked.

"You are too nosy," responded Wild Horse. He handed her the skewer and grasped one of the nearby support poles to the teepee. He struggled but managed to get to his feet. The stretching of skin brought considerable pain, but he did little more than wince and bear it.

"You not get up!" His sister was insistent.

"You not *ap*...or *pia*." Referring to their mother especially hurt, as she'd died a couple of years back, and it still pained Blue Flower. It was a nasty retort by any measure. "Is Buffalo Who Runs honored?"

Blue Flower was still smarting from his hurtful words. "Still buried in mountain," she finally said. The mountain was filled with the sorts of crevices in which the Comanche placed their dead. They were preferable to scaffolds or trees. She thought on how the mother of Buffalo Who Runs had cut her arms in mourning over the loss of her son. Buffalo Hump had assured her that her son's death from a mountain lion was honorable. Her son had been no coward.

Wild Horse took a tentative step. "Me see." He desperately wanted to honor his friend by visiting the burial site. However, he had a dual purpose. He wanted to see how close the horse remuda was. There would be no moon on this night, and he sought to return to the White boy as promised. "Jack," he whispered to himself as though reinforcing the image. He lurched toward the opening to the teepee. He nearly fell, but Blue Flower's quick reaction kept him upright.

"Wild Horse not ready," she reprimanded him.

He shook himself loose from her grip and stepped outside. He shielded his eyes from the sunlight and turned to look at her. She had been nursing him full-time, and he was appreciative. He gave her as loving a smile as he could muster before turning and limping toward the crevices in the cliff where the Comanche buried their dead.

He passed by his favorite pony. His only pony. Tonight, he would put caution—and pain—aside. A life debt had to be repaid. Wild Horse would have to overcome his own hatred and fear of the Whites. He'd heard words from the council fires. The Comanche leaders worried that their way of life would be forever corrupted if not ended. Unlike tribes to the north that didn't yet understand the immigration onslaught to come and the mentality of the Bluecoat generals to kill Indians, the warriors of the Comancheria understood that they must eliminate the White threat.

Despite the strong talk of killing all the White invaders, something about it failed to sit well with Wild Horse. He stopped just long enough in his limping walk to the burial site of Buffalo Who Runs to call to his pony in a low guttural voice, "*Puuka...puuka.*" The pony snorted and lifted his forelegs as though in recognition. "*Puuka,*" Wild Horse repeated. "Tonight, we ride."

ON HIS WAY back from paying homage to his friend, Wild Horse passed the young White woman who served Blue Flower. She gave him an angry look before diverting her eyes. It was not permitted for an enslaved woman to look upon the Comanche men. He wondered where the young boy had gone. His sister said that one of his aunts had taken the male boy in. As with full-blood Comanche boys, he'd learn the ways of the Comanche for many moons before being given over to the men—if he lived that long.

Blue Flower had mentioned that the boy they now called Prairie Dog refused to eat. They would have let him starve but prevailed upon the White girl to feed him. The young boy was nevertheless stubborn and frequently felt the wrathful scolding of Wild Horse's aunt as well as the far less tolerant Comanche boys. Prairie Dog was teased unmercifully over his white skin.

It struck Wild Horse that Jack might be interested in the captive Whites, though he didn't make the connection that they might be of the same family.

Upon entering the teepee, Wild Horse was

confronted by Blue Flower. He feinted to his left, but she moved to block his path. He attempted to step to his right, but she blocked him again. His reflexes weren't up to playing this little game. "What is it, sister?"

Blue Flower stared intensely into her brother's eyes. "Who bandage Wild Horse?"

"*Tosahwi*," he tossed out White Knife's name, deflecting her question. He knew what she was really asking.

She placed her hands on her hips. "Not *Tosahwi*."

Wild Horse once again tried to move around her. "I must lie down."

"Who, brother?"

"Me...okay?"

Blue Flower shook her head. "Secrets not good," she admonished.

"You not *pia!*" Wild Horse was becoming angry that she was behaving like his mother, then regretted his words. They both still grieved the loss of their mother, and he'd hurt her once again by referring to her.

Blue Flower's face turned sad, partly because he had thrown the image of their mother at her.

"Sorry," apologized Wild Horse.

His sister offered an exasperated sigh, gave him a gentle hug, and stepped aside. She figured that he would eventually tell her. They never kept secrets, so he wouldn't hold out for long.

Wild Horse limped over to his blanket. He'd grown up close to his sister and truly detested the very idea of deceiving her. He wanted to discuss life debt but feared her reaction. The two had shared their feelings about the Whites and their Bluecoat soldiers, yet neither of them had ever imagined being beholden to a White. He knew that he would eventually have to tell her, but not until he had figured all this out himself.

———

I FIGURED to give my Comanche friend one more day before once again venturing out on my quest to find Kate and Buck. This time of staying in one place had the effect of cooling my emotions a bit. I resented this in a way, as I truly wanted to hate the Indians. I'd heard some men say that the only good Indian was a dead Indian and even begun to believe it until I saved that savage's life. Dang it!

Laying under the stars was a humbling experience. The work on the homestead had given me little time to take in the grandeur of the giant sky lit with thousands upon thousands of stars. I was grateful that it hadn't rained despite distant thunderheads and especially given no cover save for layers of switchgrass and branches that I'd managed to gather to fashion a very humble shelter. I still had one piece remaining of what I loosely called mountain lion steak. I stared into my little cooking fire, mesmerized by the flames while listening to the sizzle of the meat. A hoot owl called in the gathering darkness as the sun dropped below the horizon. A few coyotes barked their evening chorus. I eased back into my shelter, asked for a blessing on my meal, and took a bite of mountain lion steak. It was doggone chewy.

SIX
LIFE DEBT

WILD HORSE'S EYES OPENED. He didn't move a muscle as he slowly scanned the teepee interior. He heard the mostly droning sounds of sleep. Buffalo Hump would occasionally snore. Blue Flower breathed softly. The embers from the fire cast a dim light within the shadowy walls of the teepee. Unbeknownst to anyone, he'd managed to gather pemmican and fruit that he secreted away in a deerskin sack. He even managed to secret away a small amount of the salve White Knife had applied to his wounds. Any moves that stretched the skin around his still-healing wounds now caused more discomfort than pain.

He silently grabbed the sack, picked up his bow and arrows, and managed to tip-toe from the teepee without disturbing anyone. He nearly tripped over the White girl who was sleeping just outside the teepee entrance. Wild Horse noted how peaceful she looked in the light of the stars. He wondered why some people had white skin but shook off the thought. He must focus on the task at hand.

Now free of the teepee, he trod silently onward to the remuda. He stopped fifty yards away and froze in place. He waited until the warrior guarding the ponies had to answer nature's call. Thankfully, it didn't take long, and Wild Horse was able to sneak over and slip a rope halter over his pony's head and lead him from the encampment. The pony made nary a sound, as though it sensed something secretive was afoot.

Wild Horse gave some thought to stampeding the entire remuda but decided against it, fearing that would rouse the encampment. The young Comanche also considered bringing along a second pony, but he feared that would raise suspicions that there was indeed someone else who had helped him. Blue Flower would surely have reached that conclusion.

Once free of the encampment, Wild Horse grabbed a fistful of his pony's mane and swung himself onto its broad back. Pain shot through his entire body as his muscles resisted the challenge. He sat a moment to take stock of himself. No wounds had been reopened, and his legs seemed to quickly become reaccustomed to the pony. He reminded himself of his father's constant reminders that Comanche were the best horsemen on the plains. When a Comanche rode, he was one with his pony. Wild Horse took a deep breath and nudged his mount southeastward.

Now the he was truly alone and on his way to where he'd left Jack, he could more fully concentrate on this life debt notion that apparently had been created. It deeply troubled him that this life debt was to a white-skinned boy. He was determined to keep it a secret as long as possible.

Wild Horse sensed that his people would discover at first light that he was missing. Knowing his father, he figured the chief would awake to feelings of curiosity, anger, and concern, while Blue Flower would be seriously upset given their conversation of the previous night. With at least a four-hour head start, he felt confident that he could reach Jack before any search party caught up with him. He made it as difficult as possible to follow him as he hid his trail by occasionally doubling back and by riding his pony through the waters of the creek.

The young Comanche stopped once to rest his pony and drink water from a spring. He also dismounted and walked a couple of times more to rest his horse. By his calculation, time was on his side. How he would deal with Jack once he found him was an entirely different matter.

As the sun reached its zenith high in the sky, Wild Horse smelled the faint aroma of smoke.

———

I HAD GIVEN up on the young Comanche. I began to gather my meager worldly possessions to resume my hunt for the savages that kidnapped my brother and sister and massacred the rest of my family when I heard the whinny of a horse. I looked at my Colt revolver and ducked behind the shelter of the live oak. I peered out from one of the tree trunks. My jaw just about dropped to my boots as Wild Horse appeared.

The Comanche looked a sight different from when he'd left four days ago. I noted first thing that the makeshift bandages I applied had been replaced by someone far more skilled than me. His color had also begun to come back, so it was clear that he was healing.

"Jack," he called out in a low voice.

"*Kobe*...come in." I lowered my revolver and

motioned him into the campsite. I smiled so as to appear more welcoming.

As he approached, his eyes caught the fact that I had assembled my possessions in preparation to depart. With disappointment written all over his face, he motioned that observation with his hands.

I was helpless to respond. He'd caught me not trusting that he would return. Thinking fast, I crouched low and pretended to be hunting.

That seemed to work, as Wild Horse thought on it and smiled. He slid slowly and just a bit painfully from his pony. He took a moment to gather himself before he stepped toward me with his sack extended in front of him. He stopped a couple of feet from me and opened the bag. The aroma of food was especially welcome. I could have eaten just about anything at this point, but the venison jerky gave off a distinct aroma that brought saliva rushing to my lips.

I smiled broadly and motioned him to sit.

He shook his head. This apparently was not yet the time to share a meal. He made a motion pointing to the northeast, as if we were to head in that direction. He signed with all his fingers that he might be followed.

I was a bit more than disappointed that we wouldn't yet feast on the jerky.

He pulled a small package from his sack and unwrapped it. It contained some sort of strange-smelling substance. Wild Horse pointed to my arm and made a motion as though he were applying it.

I unwrapped the makeshift bandage from my arm. There was no infection, but it looked pretty doggone ugly. In fact, downright angry.

My Comanche nurse grabbed my hand and began to apply an herbal salve to the wounds on my arm.

I immediately sensed a soothing feeling. I began to rewrap my arm, but Wild Horse stopped me. I nodded that I understood.

He pointed to his pony. *"Puuka,"* he said.

"Yes, horse," I replied.

He made a sign that I was to mount his pony.

I made a walking motion with my fingers and pointed to first him and then me. "Walk," I said.

Wild Horse smiled. He reached into his bag and drew out two pieces of pemmican and two of venison jerky. He gave half to me and began to eat the other half. "Pemmican," he said, gesturing with the treat. He then lifted the piece of venison jerky. *"Aruka,"* he explained, making the sign of deer antlers with his hands. He then turned to what I presumed was to the northeast and took a couple of steps. "Walk," he said and smiled at having learned an English word. "Jack, walk."

I halted abruptly.

Wild Horse looked questioningly at me. I walked over to the shelter and brought out the fangs and claws of the mountain lion. I hadn't had a chance to string them, given I had nothing handy to string them on, but I had prepared them as best I could. I extended them to him as a gift.

"Pia wa'óo," he said with a totally amazed expression on his face.

"Yes," I said. What was I thinking? Here I was, giving a gift to my sworn enemy. If this was God's way of teaching forgiveness and humility, it was one heck of a lesson. *"Pia wa'óo,"* I said. Between *pia wa'óo, puuka, aruka,* and a couple of phrases, I was actually learning some Comanche language. While waiting for Wild Horse's return, I had time to think on how we might communicate. It was clear that a relationship of some sort was brewing, and I'd have to reserve my wrath for the savages that actually attacked my family.

It had begun to occur to me that Wild Horse was helping me only because I'd saved his life. I guessed that it had to do with honor among his people. It didn't take much to extend that thought to wish there was more such honor among my own people. Honor was surely there. My pa was an honorable man.

Wild Horse accepted the gift, but I could tell that he was concerned about not having a reciprocal gift. He smiled uncomfortably.

"Walk," I reminded him.

Uncomfortable as the lack of reciprocity must have been for him, he began to head off to the northeast with pony in tow.

I was curious as to how he chose the direction we should follow. To the south lay Fort Inge and the Bluecoats he feared, and there were far too many Whites due east. I gathered that to the northwest lay his own people's encampment.

———————

WILD HORSE MADE every effort to hide our trail, sweeping away footprints, doubling back occasionally, and taking us through creeks when available. We had trudged wordlessly for perhaps twenty miles when we came upon a small stream that seemed to satisfy whatever Wild Horse was looking for. We watered his pony and sat under a live oak tree while consuming more of the food he'd brought.

I tried my best to communicate with my hands. I used my fingers to indicate many people and then waved them slowly in several directions to ask where they were. With a stick, I drew figures in the Comancheria dust.

Wild Horse nodded. *"Numunuu."* He pointed due west from where we sat. He looked deep into my eyes as though grabbing at my very soul, clasped his hands together, and pointed to me and then to himself.

I reckoned that this meant that we had some sort of bond.

My new Comanche friend seemed encouraged that I was understanding him. Wild Horse took some of the mountain lion claws and placed them between his fingers like he had claws. He swiped in the manner of the mountain lion and then pointed his finger in the fashion of a gun. He pointed up with both hands in what I'd call a supplicating gesture. I figured he must be referring to his god or great spirit or whatever the heathens called it.

I nodded that I understood.

"Jack..." Wild Horse was at a loss for words. He pointed to the shelter of some rocks that overlooked the stream. He motioned for me to stay there. He stood, pointed to himself, and made a travel motion with his hand. He made the sign of *numunuu*, the people. He pointed to the sky where the moon would be in a couple of hours and raised two fingers. He pointed back to where we were standing.

"Numunuu," I responded.

A broad grin creased Wild Horse's face. He pointed to his pony. *"Puuka,"* he said and raised two fingers. He was going to get us a second horse. In a way, I suspect it was more than about faster travel, but a way to reciprocate the gift I gave him.

"Horse. Penateka Comanche horse," I ventured.

He nodded vigorously and smiled.

Now, I had a big question to communicate before my

friend departed. I pointed to my skin. "*Tosa*." I used the Comanche word for White man. I gave the sign of the people with my fingers, then showed only two fingers. "Two," I said.

He nodded cautiously and raised two fingers. "*Tosa*, two," he repeated.

I wrapped my arms around my body, trying to communicate that the two *tosa* were my family. I displayed three fingers and said, "Family."

Wild Horse repeated, "Family." His face turned sad as he shook his head. It would clearly be a tall order to rescue the *tosa* from his encampment. "*Puuka*...horse," he said, nodding. He stood as though to leave. Before heading to his pony, he paused as though a question lingered. He pointed to the necklace around my neck.

I had forgotten about the necklace that my sister Kate had made and gifted to me a couple of years back. I had become accustomed to it hanging around my neck, such that I barely noticed it. It was comprised of long ivory-colored beads and featured a silver cross. While Wild Horse looked on curiously, I touched the cross, put my hands together as though praying, and pointed to the heavens.

Wild Horse nodded and mimicked my signing, apparently appreciating that we both worshipped some great deity.

"*Taa Narumi*," he said. Satisfied, he mounted his pony. Before leaving, he pointed to the sack and made a motion to his mouth that it contained more food. He held two fingers to remind me that he'd return with a second pony.

I figured *Taa Narumi* must have been the Comanche Big Father. As I thought on that for a split second, a brilliant idea came to mind.

As he was about to press his heels into his pony's sides, I called out, "*Kobe!*"

Wild Horse pulled up and looked back at me.

As I walked toward him, I unfastened my necklace. "*Tosa,*" I said. I touched my hair and then pointed at the sun.

"*Ohapitu,*" guessed Wild Horse with a questioning expression.

I assumed *ohapitu* meant yellow, as in yellow hair. My sister's hair was blond. I hoped and prayed that was what he meant. "*Tosa ohapitu,*" I repeated for emphasis and handed the necklace to him. I pointed to me and said, "Jack," then I said, "*Tosa ohapitu*...Kate."

Wild Horse appeared uncertain for a moment and then nodded. He put his heels to his pony and was off.

I watched him disappear from view, praying that the necklace found its way to my sister. With any luck, it would send a message that I was near. Then it occurred to me that she might think Wild Horse had lifted it from my dead bones. I shook off the thought. My new Comanche friend should be able to communicate to her that I'm very much alive.

———

I WAS ONCE AGAIN THRUST into a dilemma, but hadn't the time to cogitate on it. I was apparently being put upon a path not of my choosing.

Come morning, I awakened to the thunderous sound of hoofbeats. If it were Comanche, it would have been the entire nation. I cautiously peeked from my shelter. To my relief, consternation, and concern, the deafening roar was being created by a herd of buffalo. I was much relieved that Wild Horse had chosen a sheltered place for me, amazed by the sheer power of the lumbering beasts and anxious as to the possibility of Indian hunting parties. My greatest challenge was gasping for air amid the choking dust kicked up by perhaps a thousand hooves.

A huge bull paused at the entrance to my rock shelter. He blinked before being nudged along by the herd. That was about as close as I ever cared to be to a bull buffalo. Dang, but he was huge! It was hard to believe that the Indians could kill them with arrows.

The herd eventually passed, and I cautiously emerged from my shelter. I waved my hands as best possible to clear the air from the dust combined with the pungent, earthy aroma of buffalo. There were no Indian hunting parties that I could see.

———

WILD HORSE RODE BOLDLY into the Penateka Comanche encampment. The first faces he saw were of women and children, but the alert went out rather quickly. The young Comanche sat straight and proud.

He rode directly to his father's teepee.

The curious murmurings of a dozen warriors mixed with several women and children coupled with a loud snort from Wild Horse's pony brought Buffalo Hump from the teepee. Upon emerging, he laid an angry glare on his wayward son. "Where you go, Wild Horse?" He didn't await an answer, but held up two fingers. "Search two suns!"

Wild Horse slipped from his pony's back. He stood tall before Buffalo Hump. "Home now, *ap*." He was respectful but definitely not submissive.

Blue Flower had come running from her chores when

she heard the commotion and now stood behind her father. She gave Wild Horse a sisterly *now look what you've done* look.

Buffalo Hump turned to Blue Flower. "Take pony," he told her. He turned back to his son and delivered an emphatic motion to get inside.

As Wild Horse walked past his father into the teepee, Buffalo Hump gave his gathered people a look that told them to disperse, that he had important business to tend to. He entered the teepee and directed Wild Horse to be seated.

The young Comanche obeyed.

"Wounds healing," observed Buffalo Hump as he stood opposite his son with his arms crossed.

Wild Horse nodded. He looked up. "Yes, *ap*."

"You tell where you go." Buffalo Hump was getting right to it. There was no beating around the bush.

"East." It was a smart remark that Wild Horse quickly regretted.

The chief brought back his hand as though to strike him but thought better of it. His days of old, when he led his warriors against the *tosa* villages and ranches, were ever-more-frustrating dreams of the past, as the *tosa* seemed to come in an endless stream. Changes were afoot, and he didn't yet fully understand them. It would be the young Comanche men who would have whatever destiny awaited thrust upon them. Buffalo Hump gave an exasperated sigh. "Secret not good. Truth strong."

It was good advice, and Wild Horse knew it.

Buffalo Hump gazed deeply into his son's eyes. They told him not to press, that the secret would eventually be revealed. "You talk with White Knife. Go now," he said and waved his son to leave him.

White Knife was a shaman, an old war chief who held powerful medicine in the eyes of the Penateka people.

Wild Horse was immensely relieved. His secret was still intact. He exited the teepee quickly before his father could change his mind. As he hurried past a couple of teepees and came upon the pony remuda, he saw the yellow-haired girl tending his pony. He dared not be seen talking with the captive, yet he felt a strange sort of obligation. His eyes scanned the area. The people had gone back to their work and no one seemed to be paying attention. He eased over to a tree about ten feet from the girl.

Kate didn't notice his presence, as the task of currying the pony was a relief compared to the back-breaking chores she was normally given.

"Jack," whispered Wild Horse.

Kate froze. She looked around. Where had the sound of her brother's name come from?

"Jack," he whispered again.

She saw him half hidden by a tree. The combination of typical Comanche dress and bandages made Wild Horse something just short of a fearsome sight.

Wild Horse could come no closer or say no more without arousing attention. It wouldn't do to be seen close to a captive *tosa* girl. He pointed at her. "Kate," he said. He tossed the necklace at her feet, turned, and headed for White Knife's teepee as fast as he could.

Kate's eyes widened at the sight of Jack's necklace at her feet. That the Comanche savage knew his name must mean that her brother was alive and somewhere near. Hope lifted her heart. Perhaps her fervent prayers would yet be answered. Did she dare share the news with Buck? His youth made him susceptible to blabbing things meant to be secret. She decided to keep it secret for now.

———

WHITE KNIFE HEARD footsteps outside his teepee. "Come in, Wild Horse."

The young Comanche paused. How could the shaman have possibly known it was him? He shook his head. Was this the magic White Knife was reputed to have? He took a deep breath and entered.

"Welcome, young one," said *Tosahwi*. "Please sit." White Knife made the unusual act of offering his pipe to Wild Horse.

To refuse would dishonor the elderly medicine chief. Wild Horse held the pipe aloft ceremoniously as he'd seen adults do, put it to his lips, and took a drag. He choked and coughed.

Tosahwi laughed heartily. "Too young to smoke pipe... too young to have secrets." He was wasting no time getting to the purpose of their meeting.

Again, Wild Horse was amazed at how this shaman knew why he was visiting. "Old one, do you know my secret?" he asked respectfully and handed the pipe back.

White Knife thought a moment and looked at Wild Horse as though digging into the young Comanche's very soul. "You talk with *tosa*."

Wild Horse's face gave him away. *Tosahwi* had touched a nerve.

The medicine chief nodded. "No secret," he said with a knowing smile.

"You know life debt?" asked Wild Horse.

Of course, *Tosahwi* understood life debt. "Save your life." It was a statement, not a question.

Wild Horse nodded. "From *pia wa'óo*," he added. The wounds were still quite visible under the bandages on the young Comanche, thus validating his story. "*Tosa* shoot *pia wa'óo*. Save Wild Horse."

White Knife remained silent. Deep inside, he was drawing upon the wisdom of many years. Perhaps this wasn't such a bad circumstance. The smoke from White Knife's pipe wafted aimlessly through the air between them. But his thoughts were far from aimless. He handed the pipe back to Wild Horse. "You smoke," he directed.

Once again, Wild Horse ceremoniously held the pipe aloft. This time, he didn't take so deep a draw upon the pipe. He had to clear his throat, but he didn't cough.

"Do as *Taa Narumi* tells you," counseled the shaman.

This was big medicine being given to Wild Horse. *Taa Narumi* was the Big Father, the head deity of all the Comanche nations. "Am I in debt forever?" asked Wild Horse.

Tosahwi nodded. "Yes, my son. *Taa Narumi* has given this to you. He will lead you to truth."

The concept of considering truth was new to Wild Horse.

"Truth sets Comanche free," advised White Knife. He had no idea as to its parallels in the White man's faith. It was as though it was a common human concept. "You go now. I talk to Buffalo Hump." As an afterthought, he smiled reassuringly and added, "*Tosahwi* keep secret."

They smoked the pipe for a few rounds more, and then Wild Horse departed. Upon exiting the shaman's teepee, he nearly ran over Blue Flower. He said not a word but gave her a look as though he were a man on a mission.

Blue Flower watched him pass and took note of his purposeful stride. She dared not say a word.

Wild Horse suddenly stopped and pivoted back toward her. "What do you hold?"

She dangled the necklace with the cross.

"That belong to *tosa*."

Blue Flower was doing the calculation in her head. *Tosa* necklace to *tosa* woman. Whatever Wild Horse was up to involved the *tosa*.

Frowning angrily, he snatched the necklace from her. He walked over to where Kate was tanning a deer hide and dropped the necklace at her feet. "Jack," he whispered. With that, he headed for his father's teepee.

Buffalo Hump greeted his son with a smile. "You talk with White Knife?"

"Yes, *ap*." Wild Horse grew serious. "He say listen to *Taa Narumi*."

His son's words gave no comfort to the chief, but he felt as though there was a higher power at work. He nodded. "Wild Horse follow *Tosahwi* words."

"I leave at rise of sun," said Wild Horse.

Buffalo Hump nodded. He'd have to be satisfied for now.

———

"WHERE YOU GO?" Blue Flower had awakened just before dawn as she suspected her brother would be venturing off early. She wore her hair in bead-decorated braids framing her dark eyes, classic, high cheekbones, straight nose, and full lips that set her beauty apart from other Comanche women. Even at only fourteen years old, her shapely form could not be hidden by the buckskin dress with its colorful beadwork designs. "What is *tosa* necklace?" Her curiosity had weighed upon her all night. "Secrets not good." She smirked.

Wild Horse rolled his eyes. "You ask too many questions."

She glared at him.

"White Knife give me quest." He figured that should put an end to her questions, though not her persistence.

"Me follow," she threatened.

"No follow," insisted Wild Horse. "Anger Buffalo Hump. Anger *Taa Narumi*."

"Does father know you go?"

Wild Horse nodded.

"And *tosa* woman?" She obsessed.

He shook his head. "Do not hurt *tosa* woman. Be sure *tosa* boy safe."

Her brother's sudden concern for Whites was like a slow torture. She did not understand. Their mother had been killed by the White's disease. How could he be so insensitive? *Men*, she thought. Blue Flower turned and began to walk off but stopped and turned back. "Wild Horse, travel safe." She touched his cheek gently with her hand, smiled lovingly, and then went inside the teepee.

Wild Horse stood stunned by her sudden change in demeanor. He shook his head and headed for the remuda, where he placed a halter on his pony and another on one of Buffalo Hump's lesser-used ponies.

His thighs were still wrapped with bandages, but most of his other wounds had nearly healed. He carried an extra blanket for Jack and plenty of food. In addition to his bow and quiver of arrows, he carried his knife, a war club, and a lance. He figured to be ready for most any circumstance.

Wild Horse had taken the shaman's counsel to heart. He had begun to think of the obligation of the life debt as an opportunity to learn more about the *tosa*. Perhaps the knowledge would help in battle someday.

———

I TRIED to make my campsite as comfortable as possible. The stampeding buffalo had alerted me to its vulnerabilities, not the least of which was one side being wide open. The buffalo had sure torn up the ground around my humble shelter. It opened toward the east, so the afternoon sun afforded a good deal of shade. A cooling breeze gave me a case of drowsiness, and I expect that I nodded off.

The hoofbeats of at least two unshod ponies stirred me from my afternoon nap. Sure enough, Wild Horse appeared. While he had a beautiful pinto mare in tow, I found myself impressed with his bearing and weapons. He had transformed into a young Comanche warrior. He wore leggings, beaded moccasins, and, much to my pleasure, a lion claw necklace.

Upon dismounting, he grabbed the tether of the pinto and led her to me. "Jack *puuka*," he said as he handed the reins to me. He stroked the pony's neck and motioned me to do the same.

I instantly decided to call the mare Paint. "Jack...Wild Horse...Paint." I said, pointing to each in turn.

Wild Horse smiled and patted the side of his black pony. "*Tuhibitu*," he said. He pointed to his own black hair and to my black belt to indicate the color.

"Black," said I, smiling. "*Tuhibitu*...black *puuka*," I repeated. Dang, but we were making progress as to communication.

"*Kohto*," said Wild Horse as he began to grab kindling for a fire. "*Ana o'a hi'it*."

I knew that moment he was ready to eat.

Wild Horse made a sign that he'd traveled far and very cautiously. He feared being followed or worse. Worse being happening upon enemies. Unbeknownst to me, he worried that his sister would follow him. He pointed to the landscape torn up by the buffalo. "*Tasiwoo.*" He pointed his fingers of both hands downward and made a running motion.

I nodded vigorously and signed that there had been many and had come close. I think I was getting pretty good at this signing thing, but it lacked what my pa called nuance. The buffalo were a reminder that I dared not forget how wild and unpredictable this country was. The attack on my home remained an even more powerful reminder. I struggled to shake those thoughts loose as I sought some sort of friendship with this young Comanche savage. For now, my purpose was to save my sister and brother from captivity, though I felt a growing sense that something more was brewing between Wild Horse and me.

The fire was plenty hot, and we cooked venison that my young Comanche friend had brought with him. It was delicious.

I had been holding back on asking him about my necklace and my sister Kate. "*Tosa ohapitu...Kate?*" I asked.

Wild Horse smiled broadly. "*Tosa ohapitu,*" he repeated. He touched his heart.

I took Wild Horse's sign to mean Kate was okay. "*Tosa ohapitu...*White woman, yellow hair," I said, adding the translation to English.

"White woman, yellow hair," he repeated and smiled again.

"Is she safe?" I knew as the words fell from my lips

that Wild Horse wouldn't understand. I decided then and there to teach him English. I tried to think of something to indicate safety. All I could do was resort to a happy facial expression, figuring that happy equaled safe.

My friend nodded vigorously. "Wild Horse...family," he added. "Blue Flower family...Kate family."

I was overjoyed at the simple fact that he had remembered the word family. Maybe I was making progress. In any case, it was apparent that Kate was with Wild Horse's family. I hadn't a clue as to who Blue Flower was, but I reckoned to eventually find out.

Wild Horse pointed to Paint. Seemed it was time for me to climb aboard.

The mare was calm as can be. My Comanche friend had chosen well. I know I'm referring to him as a friend, though I'm using the word guardedly. After all, he was a Comanche, and they were known for their savage ways. It didn't occur to me at the time, but I likely should have taken into account the savage ways of the Bluecoats. I had no idea as to some of the horrors White soldiers had inflicted.

I was aware that the Karankawa tribe of Eastern Texas had practiced cannibalism, but the White man's diseases had mostly wiped them out. I also wondered whether my father had any idea that the land he bought in Texas was cheap because it was on the Comancheria? Did the government know it was putting us in danger?

Wild Horse broke my philosophical spell by grabbing my arm and pulling me toward Paint.

I patted Paint's nose to get acquainted, grabbed a handful of mane, and swung myself onto the mare's back. I thanked God that she stood steady. She didn't even flinch.

Wild Horse smiled and nodded approval. He made a circle motion.

I grabbed the rope dangling from the halter and pressed my heels into Paint's sides. She whinnied and began to move forward at a slow walk. I gently pulled the rope to my left, and the mare dutifully turned left. I gave Wild Horse a big grin.

The Comanche nodded approvingly.

"*Kobe*, good," I said.

"Good," he repeated.

I spent the next hour striving to establish a man-horse relationship with Paint.

———

AFTER MY RIDING LESSON, Wild Horse and I spent the rest of the day with me scribbling words and he symbols in the dirt around our campsite. He seemed to be a willing student, absorbing English words like a sponge. I was never one to enjoy school, but I found myself actually delighted in teaching him. He was quickly dispelling my notion that the Red man was an ignorant race. I made a mental note to one day straighten out folks who thought that way. Shucks, maybe they were the ignorant ones. That's a tad harsh. It's more like they had never made the effort to get acquainted with the Indians.

I was fast realizing that fate or God's will was leading me down a path that transcended the anger and vengeance that consumed me after the Comanche attack on my home. Fear of the Comanche, as based on stories and rumors, had likely made me more susceptible to a hatred of the race. Now, God had placed Wild Horse in my life. The question remained whether I could forgive him and could I forgive his people.

In the Ten Commandments, we are told, *Thou shall not murder, shall not commit adultery, shall not steal.* The Comanche had violated all of these upon my family. Forgive? My pa taught me that forgiving a sin didn't excuse the sinner from punishment. I recalled that the worst sin in his mind was any disrespect of my mother. Yep, learned that lesson right quick. He never struck me, but punishments were never pleasant. But back to Wild Horse. As we were able to communicate better, we also seemed to more fully understand each other's thoughts.

Inevitably, our rudimentary conversation got around to the question of how I happened upon him and the mountain lions.

"I search for my sister and brother," I told him.

Wild Horse gave me a questioning look.

"You ask why?"

He nodded. "Why?" he said, delighting in using an English word.

I swallowed. No, it was more of a choke than a swallow. "Comanche raid my home. Kill mother, father, sister, and brother. Take sister and brother captive. Burn house...steal horse." I didn't have to mention torture and scalping. Nor did I reference my Ten Commandments...yet.

Wild Horse pointed to me. "You?" he questioned.

"I was away fishing. I came home after the raid."

My Comanche friend sat silently, as though absorbing my story. Unbeknownst to me was the fact that just a few days ago, he had been hearing warriors boast of the raid on my home. His fervent hope was to join such raids, especially as the son of a Comanche war chief. His realization that I was a victim of his people had opened his eyes just a tad. "Jack search for sister and brother?"

"They are my family," I responded. "I walked west

toward setting sun to find my sister and brother and kill Comanche."

His eyes widened. "Many Comanche, one Jack." He shook his head. "Not wise," he added.

"Anger blind," I said, covering my eyes and shaking my head ruefully.

Wild Horse nodded. Then asked, "Why kill *pia wa'óo*, mountain lion? Why save *Kobe*?"

We hadn't dealt with English words like instinct or mercy yet. I shrugged, then said, "You human in danger." I pinched my skin and then reached out and pinched his. "Human," I repeated.

"Human," he replied.

"It was will of my God," I tried to communicate that my saving him was God's choice, not mine. I pointed up toward the sky. "*Taa Narumi*," I added. He had taught me the Comanche name for Big Father, so I loosely applied it here. I drew a cross in the dust between us, pointed to myself, and pointed once again to the sky. "God," I said.

Wild Horse nodded. "Me hunt deer with friend Buffalo Who Runs. *Pia wa'óo* kill my friend. Wild Horse try to save. No run faster than lion, so must fight. No bow...no arrow...no knife." He grew excited as he recounted the story, making hand gestures to emphasize each phase of the mountain lion's attack. "Fear *pia wa'óo*." He didn't have a word for lioness, so he held up two fingers. "Two *pia wa'óo*."

He had my full attention.

Wild Horse cupped his hand to his ear. "Thunder," he said, seeking to describe the report from my Colt revolver. "Wound *pia wa'óo*, save *Kobe* life." He smiled gratefully. "Jack kill *pia wa'óo*." A look of consternation came over Wild Horse. He looked at me dead-on. "Wild Horse owe life to Jack," he said quite firmly.

I realized that he was saying that he was in debt to me. As I understood it, this was a life debt that couldn't be repaid unless he saved my life in turn. This seemed barbaric to me. It was an uncivilized concept to my way of thinking. I looked him square in the eyes. "No owe life. Wild Horse friend."

He flinched. He didn't seem able to grasp the concept of me forgiving him his debt. "Jack save Wild Horse life," he reiterated.

I grasped his hand. In that motion, it occurred to me that to cement our budding relationship, we must be blood brothers. I released my grip, took out my knife, and made a motion to make a cut on our arms and intermingle our blood.

Turned out Wild Horse wasn't quite ready for that obligation. He was still dealing with the life debt and keeping secrets from his people. He shook his head. "No," he said respectfully and reinforced the decision with the palms of his hands pushing away.

I sensed that it had been a long day. We'd made great progress in understanding each other. I hoped that hearing of my grief and anger from his people's attack on my home gave him a new perspective on the divide between Whites and Indians. My bedroll beckoned.

SEVEN
INTERLOPERS

BEFORE THE FIRST shard of sunlight struck our hiding place, I was awakened by a sobbing sound. Startled, I struggled to open my eyes only to see a silhouette hovering over me.

"Jack," came the whisper through great sobs.

"Kate?" Was this some cruel dream? I sat up.

"*Tosa*," came another female voice.

"Jack, it's me."

By now, Wild Horse had fully awakened. He was startled to see that the population of our campsite had doubled overnight. He jumped to his feet.

I threw caution to the winds, arose from my blanket, and embraced my sister. Oh, but it felt so good to hold her close. Such a relief that she was alive.

"Blue Flower!" Wild Horse was angry that his sister had appeared. He stood with arms folded over his puffed-up chest. "You...go now...take *tosa*." He was spitting mad!

Just as obstinately, his sister placed her hands on her hips. "No!"

It took but a moment to figure Wild Horse's reasoning. He feared for the life of my brother, Buck, if it were discovered that Blue Flower had left camp with the White girl. This was a matter of life or death, and his sister had created an unnecessary peril.

"*Tosahwi* be angry! *Ap* be angry!" admonished Wild Horse.

Blue Flower's stance softened. She now knew her brother's secret. But what of the *tosa* girl? And, more importantly, who was this other *tosa*? Who was Jack?

Wild Horse took a deep breath, as he sought to gather his wits. "Jack, this my sister, Blue Flower," said a calmer Wild Horse. "She young," he said as though it were an excuse for her behavior.

I figured to further defuse the situation and help my Comanche friend deal with his sister. I turned to my sister, now sniveling and desperate to escape the clutches of the savages. "Kate, you are protected. To save Buck, you must go back with Blue Flower."

"What of Mary and Samuel? Mother? Father?" she pleaded. She had no idea.

I put on as compassionate an expression as I could muster. There was really nothing that could soften the blow. "They are gone, Kate. I buried them."

To my surprise, she didn't cry. Her expression turned almost stoic for a split second. She hesitated, looked me in the eyes, and then hugged me very tightly. "Thank God you're alive, Jack. Save Buck and me from these savages," she pleaded.

"Kate...I saved Wild Horse's life. Careful how you talk of his people. He knows some English."

"You are with the savages?" she asked incredulously.

"No. Teaching them. It's God's will."

"Did God's will attack our family?" There was a touch

of anger and resentment in her response. I understood. But I was struggling with God's help to get past those feelings.

Wild Horse stepped in. "Must go," he said to Kate.

"Bear with this a while longer, Kate. I'll get you and Buck free of the Comanche."

Kate hung her head, shrugged, and sighed resignedly.

Blue Flower watched the interaction between Kate and me. She must have felt some sort of compassion, as she gave me a barely perceptible smile before reluctantly heading to her pony. She would obey her brother. She dared not incur the wrath of Buffalo Hump. It was still early enough to make up a plausible excuse for being away from the camp with the captive *tosa* girl. She and Kate mounted their ponies. Blue Flower gazed once more at me as though sizing me up. Trying to figure out the *tosa*. She and my sister nudged their ponies to a walk and were soon departed.

Wild Horse and I breathed sighs of relief. We'd been trailed and found by two young women. What if they had been Kiowa warriors? Our vulnerability was made clear.

"Must be more careful," I said.

"*Hoikwa*, now. Make new camp," advised Wild Horse. He decided that we would hunt and make a new camp further away from the Comanche encampment. He smiled. "We find *tamu*." He smiled broader. "Or *Tasiwoo!*"

Rabbit or buffalo was quite a contrast. I laughed at his Comanche humor. Importantly, it relieved the pressure created by the morning interlopers. We resolved to be extra cautious.

We began to gather our meager possessions. To say we were traveling light would have been an exaggeration.

I FOLLOWED Wild Horse's lead for about two miles through some very rough countryside for both humans and horses. Hills arose around us as we wended our way through draws thick with an ever-changing patchwork of live oak and juniper forest and broad savannas interwoven with bluestem grass, Indian grass, tree mottes, the ever-present cacti, and shrubs. I prayed he knew where he was going, because I was clueless. I got to thinking there was a method to this, as his Comanche mind sought to ensure that we wouldn't be tracked so easily again.

All of a sudden, Wild Horse halted. *"Aruka,"* he whispered, pointing ahead of us.

I strained my eyes to see what he had discovered. It took me a couple of minutes to sort out *aruka* from all the natural ground cover. There it was. Dinner...breakfast...and more. A partially-hidden twelve-point buck stood standing majestically among some junipers. He hadn't seen us. He gave not the slightest sign of awareness of our presence.

Wild Horse nocked an arrow, aimed, and shot before I had a chance to take another breath. The shaft found its target. The hunt was brief but successful. Wild Horse immediately urged his pony on. Upon reaching the dead buck, he quickly dismounted. There was no point in attracting any undue attention as he efficiently field-dressed our prey and hoisted it over Tuhibitu's rump.

I was impressed with my new friend's dexterity. We would eat well, and the hunt had turned out to be but a momentary interruption. Quick as could be, I was once again following him through meandering trails. The downside was that we could barely communicate, but the upside was there were no sounds save the breathing of us and our ponies to give us away.

We rode for what I guessed was nearly thirty miles. Every hour or so, we stopped and rested our ponies. The landscape was dryer, so there were fewer watering holes or streams. We walked our ponies as much as possible.

It was nearing dusk when Wild Horse pulled up along the shore of a stream that was a tad bigger than others.

I'd later learn that the Whites called this the Pedernales River. They pronounced it *Perd-năl-ĕs*. Go figure. I set to work building a fire while Wild Horse butchered the deer. I was impressed at the way he worked with his blade, though tempered that with memories of the same sort of knife used for scalping.

Wild Horse cut some venison steaks for dinner but also cut strips that he stretched on a rudimentary contraption that he made with sticks so the meat would dry. He saw my curiosity and smiled. "*Pemmican* good," he said. With that, he pulled some from his bag and showed me the *pemmican* we had been eating on our ride. "Blue Flower make," he added.

I hoped he could make his own *pemmican* as tasty as his sister's.

He dragged what remained of the carcass up a natural trail a goodly distance from our campsite. There was no telling what varmints it might attract.

With my trusty Comanche knife, I carved a stick into a serviceable spit upon which to roast our venison dinner. The crackling of the meat juices combined with the growing chorus of wildlife. It was what my pa called *right peaceful*.

We continued our English language lessons as we chowed down on the roast venison.

BY MY GUESS, it was long about midnight when we heard a ruckus out where Wild Horse had deposited the deer carcass.

"*Kutseena*?" I whispered. I recalled the coyotes.

He listened another moment. "*Isa*," he whispered back. He spread his hands to indicate that *isa* was bigger than *kutseena*. He brought his bow and arrows closer and laid his lance within easy reach.

"*Isa* is wolf," I translated as I kept my hand on my Colt revolver. I reckoned that I just might have to expend a bullet if necessary.

"Jack sleep. Wild Horse watch." He volunteered to take first guard duty on our humble campsite.

It was late, and I reckoned I might yet get a couple of hours of shuteye. There was no telling what adventures might yet find us.

EIGHT
ALPHA WOLF MEDICINE

COLD. Wet. Warm breath. I'd been dreaming of Wild Flower. She was a mighty pretty Comanche maiden. Bold and feisty, too.

Cold? Wet? Warm breath? I opened my eyes. A pair of pale blue eyes stared back at me. I blinked. Those pale blue eyes were set in a large hairy face...no, not hairy... furry. The biggest danged wolf I had ever seen was hovering over me, sniffing, nudging at me with its cold nose. To be honest, I'd heard the beasts howl a few times but never actually seen one.

What to do? I dared not move a muscle, much less alert Wild Horse. He had called it *isa*, and danger was implied. No matter what it was called, it was far too close to me for comfort. I prayed that it would lose interest. Hadn't the deer carcass been enough?

I ever-so-slowly slid my hand to the grip of my Colt.

The wolf froze.

I froze.

The beast actually made a soft whining sound, almost as though he was talking to me. He nuzzled me again.

I prayed like my life depended on it. For all I knew, it did. I glanced over at Wild Horse. He'd fallen asleep. So much for his sentry duty.

The wolf backed away and turned toward the path that led to the deer carcass. He was even bigger than he'd seemed while hovering over me.

I pulled myself up to a sitting position with my trusty Colt now firmly in hand.

The wolf took a step toward me and then turned back, looked back over his shoulder, and began a fast walk up the path. He stopped again and looked back.

Something kept me from shooting the varmint. I sensed that he was asking me to follow him. I was tempted to awaken Wild Horse but wasn't so sure that I wanted to deal with his reaction. Besides, I had this hair-brained idea that I was to follow this *isa*. Was this God's doing? I quietly slipped on my boots, stuck the Colt in my waistband, and headed toward the wolf.

As I began to follow the wolf, it struck me that this was truly weird. Why on God's given earth was I following a wolf? I had no idea as to the true nature of wolves. They were wild animals after all. I rethought awakening Wild Horse. He was undoubtedly taught about the nature of wolves by his Comanche people. But the wolf would not hear of me turning back. The one time I paused, he whined loudly in protest.

We finally arrived at the scene where Wild Horse had deposited the remains of the deer. We were likely no more than two hundred yards from the campsite. Lying beside the carcass was a wolf with an arrow protruding from its side. Instantly, my hand went to my gun. Where there was an arrow, there must be a bow with an Indian behind it. I scanned the surrounding woods. There seemed to be no immediate threat. I kneeled beside the female. She was barely breathing. The wolf watched closely as I stroked her gently. There were scrapes in the arrow shaft where the male had bitten it in his vain attempt to remove it.

Was I to be killed by an Indian's arrow or a wolf? Thus far, the wolf had given no indication of any intention to kill me. Still, his behavior was exceedingly strange. Wild Horse likely would have told me that wolves could be friendly, social, and highly intelligent. But what had drawn this particular beast to seek the help of a human, the very creature that sought him for his luxurious fur or shot him for his killing of domestic livestock?

I desperately yearned to get back to Wild Horse and inform him of the Indian threat, as evidenced by the arrow, but dared not leave the wolves. I looked up at the big male. He was likely what was called an alpha male, for he was surely big enough to lead a pack. The wolf cocked his head as though asking for my help.

I prayed. What to do? The female would surely never survive with an arrow in her. I had no choice but to remove it. It was her only hope of survival. I broke off the tip of the arrow, took a firm grip on the shaft, and yanked it out. The female yelped and the male leaped back with a start. I gently stroked the female and whispered soothingly. "It's alright, girl. It's alright." She was in no position to protest and quickly calmed down. To my delight, her breathing soon became stronger. The arrow must have nicked a lung. It would surely have killed her eventually.

The male cautiously eased over to me. He licked my hand as I continued to stroke the female. I took it as a signal that my work was finished, so I backed away and stood. I picked up the arrow and began to walk back to the campsite. I looked back a couple of times, and the wolf was tending to the female that was very likely his mate. How did the beast know to come to me for help? Why hadn't the wolf torn me to shreds? I hoped Wild Horse might give me a clue.

————

I STAGGERED MORE than walked into camp to find Wild Horse busily preparing pemmican from the venison he'd dried. I stood a few feet away, just staring at him.

He didn't look up as he was busily mixing crushed venison with wild berries. "Where Jack go?" he asked nonchalantly.

It occurred to me that he had not tried to follow me, though I'd left plenty of sign on the path to the deer carcass. "*Isa*...wolf," I said, holding the arrow behind my back.

He finally looked up at me. "*Isa?*" He laughed. He was certain that I was joking.

I brought my arm around and thrust the arrow toward him.

An expression of total awe swept his face as he abruptly stood.

I handed him the arrow, pointing to the tooth marks.

Wild Horse took it in his hands almost reverently. He examined the marks left by the wolf's teeth and the now-dried blood. He scanned the rest of the shaft and lingered on the feathers. "Kiowa!" he announced emphatically.

I had heard of the Kiowa tribe and that they were often allies and just as often bitter enemies of the Comanche. They'd been known to attack Whites as well.

They were easily as savage as any tribe on the Comancheria.

"*Isa?*" Wild Horse questioned.

How was I to communicate that a wolf had fetched me to tend to its wounded mate? I tried using our trusty drawing-in-the-dirt method interspersed with a mix of English and Comanche.

His increasing expression of concern weighed heavily on me.

Out of the corner of my eye, I spotted some paw prints beside my bedroll. I pointed to them.

Wild Horse looked as though he'd seen a ghost. "Leave this place now," he announced. "*Taa Narumi* tell us," he stated, invoking the spirit of his Big Father. I had no idea that the wolf stood as a strong spirit of courage and strength in the Comanche culture. *Isa* was big medicine.

I was sure that God likely would have advised the same.

"Kiowa know we here. Bring many warriors," he said mostly in sign and drawn with a stick in the dust at our feet.

My Comanche friend was telling me that we'd be dead and scalped—if we were lucky enough to be killed first—if we stayed here.

We hastily began gathering our belongings. He'd just about finished making the pemmican, so he wrapped the fixings in buckskin and packed them away to finish later. It didn't take long before we were mounted on Tuhibitu and Paint and wending our way westward. We rode exclusively in the waters along the bank of the Pedernales River so as not to leave a trail that would be easy to follow. It was slow going as we picked our way around rocks and dealt with occasional pools of deeper water.

Our lives depended on it. Wild Horse knew that the Kiowa usually ranged to the northeast of his Penateka Comanche people, so he was intent on gaining separation.

WE HAD likely traveled a little better than twenty miles before I could sense my companion beginning to relax. We had arrived close to the headwaters of the Pedernales.

Wild Horse pulled up alongside a motte of live oak. "Camp here," he said. He looked back at from where we'd come. "Safe now," he added. Safety was certainly debatable.

After making camp and satisfying our hunger, we sat quietly beside our small cooking fire. The evening air had gotten chilly, a sure sign that autumn had arrived. We'd be sleeping under blankets this night.

Wild Horse finally expressed a thought he'd apparently been chewing on as we traveled. "Talk of *isa*," he asked me to repeat my story.

I appreciated the opportunity to tell the story without the pressure of running from the Kiowa threat. "*Isa*... wolf...lick my face." I dared not tell him of my dream about Blue Flower.

Anyway, I made the licking motion.

He gave me an incredulous expression.

I continued, "Follow *isa* to *aruka*." I drew a deer in the dust and a path leading to it. "*Isa* mate have arrow in side." I drew the female wolf with an arrow. It was mighty humble art, but Wild Horse understood. "I pull arrow. *Isa* live."

The whole tale of being called by the wolf and saving

its mate was apparently super big medicine for Wild Horse. "*Isa* powerful spirit. *Isa* in Jack," he concluded, pointing to me. He didn't for a moment question my story. The evidence of its truth was pretty danged solid.

I wondered what might have happened if the wolf had awakened Wild Horse? Worse yet, what if the wolf had never sought human help, and we were killed by marauding Kiowas? Questions lingered, but they were conjecture, and we only had time for reality. Wild Horse seemed to have a deeper respect for me by virtue of *isa's* spirit. Combined with the mountain lion, there apparently was powerful medicine surrounding me.

Seeming satisfied, Wild Horse renewed his effort to finish making the pemmican.

I could see that my new friend was deep in thought. As I stared into the fire, my thoughts went back to my loss of family, my pressing need to rescue Kate and Buck, and why God had placed this heathen savage into my life.

"We go to Penateka Comanche camp," Wild Horse blurted.

He had definitely broken my train of thought. "Comanche camp?" I asked, wondering why he'd possibly expose both of us to what I perceived as danger.

"Strong spirit," he said, pointing to me. "Talk with *Tosahwi*."

Apparently, I was to meet his shaman. The strong spirit of *isa* concerned Wild Horse, and I reckoned he wanted to seek the shaman's counsel.

We decided to take turns keeping watch. This would be especially important given that we'd be doubling back toward the range of our Kiowa enemy. I fell asleep rather quickly beside the dying embers of our cooking fire. It seemed as though I'd barely slept when Wild Horse woke me from another dream of his sister. This time, that danged wolf had snuck into my dream, so I welcomed my turn to keep watch.

Wild Horse smiled knowingly and whispered, *"Isa,"* as he bedded down in his blanket.

I hadn't dared mention my dream of his sister as I feared he might take offense. Then again, he might have seen her smile at me. Something was cooking in that Comanche brain of his.

NINE
THE DROVER

WE HAD AWAKENED AT SUNUP, enjoyed as hearty a breakfast of berries and venison as we could, and began our trek to the encampment. We rode easy, keeping an eye out for the Kiowa.

I had been following Wild Horse's lead for perhaps a half dozen miles when something indescribable loomed ahead of us. It was a mountain. But no, on closer inspection, it turned out to be a huge pink rock. I'd never seen anything like it in my brief life. Huge? It was the biggest doggone rock my mind could ever conjure up. There was certainly nothing to compare back in Pennsylvania.

Wild Horse pulled up. "Strong magic," he warned.

I didn't argue. There was something about that rock that could be taken as magic, as holding some strong power in the Comanche mind.

"Rock sing, take people," he expanded on his warning of magic.

I sorely wished our communication was a lot better, as there must have been some story about this incredible chunk of what I presumed to be granite.

Wild Horse pointed southeastward. "We go this way." He was giving the rock a wide berth as though fearful of its power.

Who was I to argue? We were getting ever-better acquainted, though I felt that I was learning more about his culture than he was mine. It seemed as though God was sending me a message to understand the Comanche. Deep within some inner recess of my mind, I was still dealing with the devastation the savages had wrought on my family. I wasn't sure how long I might yet wrestle with that dilemma. I settled in for what was likely a long ride.

We'd ridden no more than another two or three miles when a cloud of dust appeared on the distant horizon ahead of us. I figured it was another herd of buffalo.

Wild Horse saw it too and pointed toward a rocky outcropping ahead to our right. It didn't seem likely that any buffalo would scale its heights.

We tied off our ponies to a mesquite branch clinging for dear life to a rock halfway up and hiked to the top. It was a great vantage point. We sat snacking on pemmican and trying to figure out what was kicking up so much dust.

"Wild Horse, those are cattle, not *tasiwoo*." We were seeing a herd of longhorn beeves being driven to market somewhere north. I figured whoever was driving them was pretty brave driving through the Comancheria.

———

I CAN'T SAY we were especially concerned about watching our backsides. We were both engrossed in the scene before us. A cattle drive wasn't an everyday occurrence on the frontier.

I heard the click behind us of a hammer being cocked.

Wild Horse heard it too and froze.

"What are you two lookin' for?" A deep voice resonated from where we'd left our ponies. "These Indian cayuses yours?"

We turned simultaneously to face one of the blackest humans I'd ever seen. I was frightened half to death. It could easily have been one of those dreaded Kiowa sneaking up on us, but this seemed worse.

Especially important at the moment, the Black man was pointing the muzzle of his rifle in our direction. That didn't bode well.

We stared at him, two scared-to-death teens near wetting our pants...or breechclout.

Suddenly, the man began to laugh. It wasn't just any laugh, but a deep belly laugh. His white teeth dazzled in the sun as contrasted with his dark skin. "Why," he gasped, "you be just kids." He looked more closely. "Dang, an Injun an' a White boy!"

I reckoned our best chance was for me to explain. "We thought the dust was buffalo, mister."

"Y'all git yourselves down from there."

I was relieved that he had released the hammer and put up his rifle.

In but minutes, we stood in front of the man. He was a big man and his boots, chaps, and shirt were pretty much coated with the whitish dust of the trail. Even his horse towered over our Comanche ponies.

"What are you boys doin' out here?" he asked, eyeing Wild Horse suspiciously.

I could see that he was curious about a White and an Indian being together on the frontier on what appeared to be friendly terms. He seemed distracted, too. I figured he must have been looking for strays when he came upon us. "It's a long story, mister," I ventured in as firm a voice as I could muster.

"Ain't got time for long stories," he responded. "You alright?" he asked, looking directly at me.

"We are friends who strayed far while hunting." I had decided not to get into my personal tragedy, mountain lions, wolves, or Kiowa threats. I figured a little lie about hunting would end the questions.

He laughed again. "You hunting with that Colt?" He'd seen through my story like water through a sieve. He had discounted Wild Horse's bow and arrow, but no matter. "My handle is George Freeman." He extended a hand to me.

I shook it and glanced at Wild Horse standing beside me.

George turned to Wild Horse, shrugged, and extended his hand.

My Comanche friend hesitated but shook George's hand. There I was, witnessing a Black man shaking hands with a Red man.

"The boss will kill me for hanging out here much longer. Got strays to catch," he said, removing his hat and wiping the sweat from his totally bald head. "Are you boys alright?" he repeated.

"It's a long story," I said.

"Trail boss will be bedding the herd right soon. Y'all camp here an' I'll double back later." He smiled broadly, then hesitated. "Lucky you boys didn't run into the Kiowa war party we met up with yesterday. We run 'em off. Killed three or four." He mounted up without awaiting any response from us. "Y'all be sure to stay here." There was that broad, white-toothed grin again.

I must admit, it was a relief to know that the dreaded Kiowa had been sent packing. I could sense the relief in

Wild Horse. Apparently, the Indians would take a couple of days to recover from a defeat. Guess they needed time to grieve for their dead, pray to their spirits, and get remotivated. That was fine by me. I stuck with thanking God.

George gave us a wink, turned his horse, and headed toward the herd of cattle.

We let loose a breath of relief.

As the cowboy faded into the distance, Wild Horse set about arranging our campsite. The rocks made a nice shelter, though he warned me to be on the lookout for rattlesnakes. The critters liked to bask on the warm rocks. Soon enough, cold weather would be setting in, and the snakes wouldn't be so active. As I understood it, they didn't hibernate like bears, but they might nest with other reptiles. That was fine by me. We sat silently awaiting George's promised return.

"Man dark," observed Wild Horse.

I nodded.

Wild Horse broke into a broad grin. "No hair." He laughed, making a slicing motion at his hairline.

I was beginning to appreciate my companion's sense of humor. Regardless of the circumstances that brought us together, we seemed to be moving toward some sort of friendship. I simply could not feel angry or vengeful with Wild Horse. I could feel a trust developing. I was unable to hold him to account for what happened to my family. It could even be that he'd prove to be an ally in freeing Kate and Buck.

———

GEORGE RODE into our campsite a bit after sunset. We heard him before we saw him. The creak of leather, jingling of his outfit, clopping of hooves on rock, and an occasional cuss word urging his cayuse on preceded his arrival. "Hail the camp," he said laughingly.

"Come on in, George," I said in a now more confident voice.

He dismounted and led his horse over to Tuhibitu and Paint, where he simply dropped his reins. There was a certain friendly swagger to George. He lifted a sack from his saddle horn and strolled over to our fire. "What y'all cookin' up?" There was that smile again with its blaze of white teeth, brilliant even in the growing darkness of evening.

"Got some pemmican to share," I ventured.

"Pemmican?" He chuckled. He placed his sack near the fire and opened it up. Three beef steaks, potatoes, and corn emerged in his huge black hands. He even brought coffee fixings. "Talked with cookie, and he whipped up some victuals for you boys," he said tauntingly. He even pulled out plates, tin cups, and forks. George had thought of everything.

We were speechless.

"Thanks kindly, George," I half-mumbled through saliva drooling from my lips. What could I say? "Pull up a rock and join us."

Wild Horse sat amazed at the Black man's thoughtfulness and generosity. Between George and me, he was getting a lesson that he might never ever have received but for the attack by that mountain lion.

We made small talk as we cooked and prepared to devour George's bounty. We were just about ready to chow down when George spoke up. "Ain't you offering a blessing to our Savior?"

I sheepishly looked at the sizzling, juicy steak on my

plate while turning three shades of red from my embarrassment.

Wild Horse began to reach for a steak.

I placed my hand on his arm to stop him. I pointed skyward. "*Taa Narumi*...God." I invoked the name of his Big Father and my God.

George and I bowed our heads while Wild Horse looked on in wonder. He was sure getting insights into a side of us Blacks and Whites that he'd never experienced before.

"Lord bless this food we are about to eat. In your precious Son's name, Amen." It was short and sweet, but it likely mattered not to God except that we thanked Him.

Over the next half hour, I spilled the story of what happened to my family, meeting up with Wild Horse, our subsequent travels, and how I was determined to free my brother and sister. Now and again, Wild Horse would contribute in halting English. I think that impressed George. We didn't mention that Wild Horse was taking me to talk with his shaman about the wolf.

"What of you, George?" I asked.

"First things first, men," he said as he reached over to the sack.

I was basking in the respect he'd just put on us by referring to us as men when I saw an apple pie appear from George's sack. "Oh my!" I blurted.

Despite nearly-full bellies, we managed to pig out on that pie. I watched in amazement as Wild Horse licked the pan.

George laughed and settled back against a rock. "I'll make my story short, but I expect I owe it to y'all to share it." He drew back his shirt sleeves to reveal scars around his wrists. "I was born a slave back in Carolina," he began, speaking slowly so Wild Horse might better understand. "I was maybe your age when the master hired him a nasty overseer. He chained an' even whipped us. I promised I would escape first chance I got." George's story had already gripped us. He drew pictures in the dirt to better explain.

I already sensed an impact on Wild Horse as he listened intently. I understood that the Comanche kept captives as slaves and were known to beat them. Enslavement was common among the tribes. "Chains and whips?" I asked.

"An' worse," continued George. "One night, it was thunderin' and lightnin' like crazy. Rained so heavy you could have cut it with a knife. It was my chance, and I escaped in the darkness and blinding rain." George took his stick and drew in the dirt a map of his escape. "It was a chance God led me to take."

I could see that reliving his past had quite an impact on him. It was affecting Wild Horse, too. The scars he'd revealed on his wrists had been dealt him by other men. I could only imagine the scars that might be on his back, much less his soul. Wild Horse and I carried scars from the mountain lion, but they could never compare.

"That overseer, he set the dogs to followin' me, but they lost my trail in the rain and swamps. I just kept runnin' for my life." He erased the map. "I snuck onto a flatboat on what I learned was the Ohio River. Got to a place they called Cairo an' headed northwest by foot along the Missouri River."

I couldn't help but interject. "We passed through Cairo a couple years back, George, but headed south." As I said it, I realized that an escaped slave wasn't going to head south. "Er, go on," I said apologetically.

"That's alright, young'un," he said. "I fell in with

some trappers, but the fur business wasn't for me. I next hooked up with some Pawnees who thought I was something special owin' to my black skin. That's when I shaved my head. There weren't no sense temptin' them Indians." George chuckled. "After about a year with the Pawnee, where I learned bits of their language and ways, plus got my first horse, I happened upon a cattle drive. It looked like fun, so I parted ways with the Indians and offered my services to the trail boss.

"The facts that I was human, could ride a horse bareback, and spoke enough Pawnee to be of value, must have convinced him to hire me. The trail boss's extra bonuses were that I knew the territory well enough to mostly ride point, and I could sing old spirituals to calm the herd at night." George smiled. "That's pretty much it. Now, I'd best be heading back."

"Thanks kindly, George. Glad you found your way," I said.

"Seems so," he responded. "When I happened on you young men, I expect I saw a bit of myself in you. 'Course, you ain't Black." He laughed, flashing those white choppers once again. George got up, grabbed his sack, shook our hands, and headed for his horse. As he grabbed the reins, he paused as though he'd nearly forgotten something.

What George did next will be forever burned within my soul.

George reached over his saddle and drew out a Springfield Model 1855 rifle musket. "You might find this handy, Jack. I grabbed it from a dead Kiowa. I expect you might know that it uses a .58-caliber hollow-base Minié bullet. Some soldier must have lost it, the Kiowa found it, an' you just might find it handy."

I was speechless, he was handing me my dream rifle. It was like a gift from God.

George waited patiently for me to come back down to earth from my euphoric dreaming and placed the rifle in my hands. He glanced at Wild Horse, who looked on in amazement.

"Bless you, Mr. George Freeman," I said.

"Oh, and these may be handy," he added as he handed me a bag full of Minié bullets and primer strips. "Good luck...Jack...Wild Horse. God bless." He mounted up and headed his horse back toward the herd.

Wild Horse seemed quite taken with the entire experience. "Strong medicine, Jack. We see *Tosahwi*."

TEN
MEETING THE SHAMAN

I THINK Wild Horse was just a tad envious of my new rifle. I must admit that I couldn't put it down. I barely slept after the drover departed—as it wasn't very comfortable to sleep wrapped around a rifle.

Breakfast consisted of the few leftovers from the previous night's feast. As we packed up, we kept looking out to see whether George might return. We were packed and mounted up on our ponies by the time the sun crested the eastern horizon. Wild Horse was intent on reaching the Penateka Comanche encampment. He appeared obsessed with what the shaman might think of the strong medicine he'd been witnessing.

From what Wild Horse was able to communicate to me, we had a long day's ride and then some ahead of us. I was pleased that we'd mostly be on horseback, as the landscape was very rugged and would have been a considerable challenge on foot. As it was, we rested our ponies by dismounting and walking every other hour or so.

Where our route permitted, I walked or rode beside

Wild Horse. He was picking up English faster than I was learning Comanche, so we could communicate better each day.

We were walking together along an arroyo when I asked, "What will your shaman want to know?"

"Not know White Knife questions," he responded. "Might take long time to answer," he added.

I wasn't up for any snap judgments from a Comanche medicine man, so that worked for me. There was apparently a lot of what Wild Horse called strong medicine at work, beginning with the mountain lion, then the visit from the wolf and chance meeting with the Black drover. This was all working on my Comanche companion's mind. To me, it was simply God's providence.

———

FROM WHAT I could gather by the sun being high overhead, it was nearing midday. We stopped in the shade of a motte of live oak trees for a brief rest and a snack of pemmican. It was fairly high ground, affording us a view of the surrounding area.

All of a sudden, Wild Horse motioned to be silent. He pointed off to our left.

I followed where he pointed, and my eyes grew big as saucers.

About a hundred yards off and as yet unaware of our presence was an Indian in full fighting regalia. His pony was following on a long tether, and I could see colorful symbols painted on it. He wore a roach headdress, buckskin leggings, and a breechcloth. Along with a buffalo-hide shield, he carried a war club. His lance and bow and arrow were hanging on his pony.

"Kiowa," whispered Wild Horse. He drew his bow

and nocked an arrow. This was apparently a situation of shoot first and ask questions later. Silence was critically important, as the warrior was not likely to be alone.

To my reckoning, he must have been a scout looking for enemies that his war party might find worthy of attacking.

Wild Horse drew back the bowstring, aimed carefully, and let fly the arrow with a barely audible twang. His arrow caught the Kiowa warrior through his neck near the collarbone, and he fell to his knees with nary a sound. Wild Horse motioned me to bring our ponies as he moved toward the Kiowa.

I came upon Wild Horse as he had knife in hand and was lifting the still-breathing warrior by the hair in preparation to scalp him.

"No," I cried out. "No scalp!"

Wild Horse paused. All of the instincts fed by years of Comanche tales around council fires told him to take the Kiowa's scalp.

"He's alive!"

"Kiowa!" sneered Wild Horse and angrily touched the knife to the warrior's hairline. A rivulet of blood appeared along the edge of the blade.

"No," I repeated as I reached out and pulled his arm from the warrior's head. I came dang near close to cutting myself on Wild Horse's knife. "*Isa!*" I said firmly. I drew upon what I prayed he'd understand, the power of the wolf. More importantly, I hoped he'd recall my saving the wolf's mate.

The Kiowa's breathing was weak. He was looking at me pleadingly as he sensed a reprieve from certain death. His weapons and shield lay too far away to give him a fighting chance, and the arrow protruding from his neck was causing considerable pain.

Wild Horse looked at me angrily.

"Do you know of lion and thorn?" I was grasping at a way to explain myself beyond God's mercy.

My Comanche companion looked at me quizzically. He was still a tad annoyed at me for stopping his scalping of the Kiowa but was holding off likely owing to his respect for my strong medicine.

I hurried to tell a very brief version of the fable about the lion. "Man finds lion moaning in pain with thorn in its paw. Man removes thorn. Lion is thankful and later saves man's life." That was the very short version of the far more elaborate tale of *Androcles and the Lion*, but it would have to do.

I seized the opportunity afforded by Wild Horse contemplating my story and I grabbed the sack with the poultices from his pony. I went over to the wounded Kiowa warrior and motioned Wild Horse to move aside, which he did very reluctantly. The arrow had fully penetrated through the mostly fleshy part of the warrior's neck, so I proceeded to break off one end and pull the shaft out. The Kiowa winced with pain but made barely a sound. The Kiowa warrior looked at me in rapt amazement, as though trying to figure me out. I guess he was wondering why I was helping a sworn enemy. I applied the poultice to the wound and wrapped it as best I could.

Wild Horse watched me as his initial annoyance was replaced with a certain awe in his expression. He was obviously impressed by whatever powerful medicine had possessed me and was curious as to what I had in mind as my next move.

"Let him go," I directed.

Wild Horse moved toward the warrior threateningly with the knife still in hand. My words ran fully counter to all he'd been taught.

I blocked him. "No...he free. No danger," I said in English, figuring that the Kiowa would not understand me. This was more than about biblical mercy. I was counting on the warrior reacting like the lion and telling his war party to leave us be.

Wild Horse shook his head and shrugged. "Strong medicine," he mumbled resignedly as he urged the Kiowa scout to mount up and leave us. As the wounded Kiowa rode off, Wild Horse looked at me curiously. He was still trying to figure me out. "You take thorn from Kiowa?" he finally said. I was behaving unlike any White he'd ever been told about.

I nodded. "Kiowa like lion. Let's get going." I didn't want to take the chance that my mercy to the savage would backfire. We still had many miles ahead of us.

———

THE SUN HAD SET, and Wild Horse had no intention of riding into the Penateka encampment at night with me in tow. He explained that I would spend the night in a well-concealed spot overlooking the Guadalupe River. From what I gathered, we were about a mile from his people.

"Me go alone. Talk to White Knife. Talk to my father." He gave me the remaining pemmican. "Wild Horse return at rising sun." He didn't waste any time settling me in and heading to his people. He did leave Paint with me. I hoped I wouldn't need the poor mare. Escape wasn't in my thoughts in any case. A speedy rescue of Kate and Buck remained foremost in my mind. The less time they spent in the hands of the Comanche, the better.

I reckoned Wild Horse was going to clear the way for my visit with the chiefs. As he rode off, I got to wondering how we would deal with Blue Flower and my own sister and brother.

The night was crystal clear, and the sky seemed even bigger than usual. It seemed as though a million stars were trying to light the place up like it was high noon. They reflected in the waters of the river far below me. Seemed God was putting on a light show just for me. It gave me time to reflect on the past few days since the tragedy at my home. I really hadn't grieved my loss and wasn't sure whether I ever would.

I became aware that I was having to grow up very fast. I got to wondering whether anyone had happened upon our ranch and discovered the horror of what had happened. Of course, they wouldn't know what became of me or Kate and Buck, though they'd observe the fresh-dug graves. I kicked myself for not having the presence of mind to leave a more detailed message on the shed wall. I was so caught up in vengeance and rescuing my sister and brother. Maybe I should have headed to Fort Inge. I'd never know what outcome that choice might have brought. I could only hope that Wild Horse's venture back to his people would come to a good ending.

———

WILD HORSE KNEW that his personal constitution, his ever-expanding knowledge in a changing and challenging world, was going to be tested. He trusted that his father Buffalo Hump's counsel to seek the wisdom of White Knife still held. He surely had to wonder whether Blue Flower had spilled the beans about the White boy.

The young Comanche was relieved that no one took notice of his entering the encampment. Even the sentry simply ignored him as a fellow Penateka Comanche. His status as Buffalo Hump's son wasn't even a concern. He rode to the remuda and tied off his pony with the rest. He looked about before heading to his father's teepee. It was a matter of honor and respect that he would see his father first. He stepped over the White girl sleeping soundly at the entrance and entered. In the dim light of the fire, he saw his father and sister seated and in some sort of animated conversation. Upon his entry, they turned with surprised expressions writ large across their faces.

"Wild Horse return, *Ap*," he said, bowing slightly toward Buffalo Hump.

Blue Flower stood and began to leave, whispering, "*Tosa*," as she stepped past her brother.

"Sit, *Kobe*," invited Buffalo Hump.

"I cannot stay, *Ap*," responded Wild Horse, as he sat opposite his father but with a facial expression that spoke volumes as to the anxiety dwelling within him. "*Tosahwi* say big medicine." Wild Horse hesitated but finally shared his adventures of the past few days. He especially focused on the strong medicine of the *tosa* to whom he owed his very life.

Buffalo Hump nodded resignedly yet proudly. He recognized that his son was growing and gaining knowledge that one day might make him a great chief among his people. He had been confident that Wild Horse would eventually come clean about the secret, though he was surprised that it involved a White boy. "Wild Horse speak with straight tongue. Powerful medicine. See *Tosahwi* for counsel." He smiled and waved his son to go.

Wild Horse walked past Blue Flower as he headed to *Tosahwi's* tent.

"Where you go, brother?"

"Strong medicine." He smiled at her. "Talk later." As

he walked past, he couldn't help but smirk over his privilege of seeking counsel with the powerful medicine man and war chief. As a woman, Blue Flower would never share such favor.

After making the young Comanche wait a few minutes outside his teepee, the shaman emerged. One look at Wild Horse's face and White Knife hastened to invite him in. They sat on opposite sides of a small cooking fire. "Strong medicine?" he questioned the teen whom he was beginning to think of as a protégé.

Wild Horse proceeded to tell of Jack and all they had encountered. He concluded with, "Wild Horse talk with *Taa Narumi*. Only see power of White god."

White Knife lit a pipe and passed it to Wild Horse. "This *tosa* strong medicine. This *tosa* different." The shaman was reluctantly recognizing that Jack was not behaving like other Whites. "Sleep now. Take *Tosahwi* to Jack at rising sun." He rightly reckoned that the encampment might not be ready for a visit by a White man, regardless of age or circumstances. There was already brewing trouble with the Bluecoats and a band called Texas Rangers.

Jack smoked the pipe and handed it back. He arose, nodded to White Knife, and departed.

He had barely walked a half dozen steps when he encountered Blue Flower. She had been waiting patiently. The look on her face and knowing smile revealed that she had been eavesdropping on his talk with the shaman. "*Tosa* strong medicine, brother." She seemed to revel in Wild Horse's secret being revealed.

He put his fingers to her mouth. "No talk."

"Blue Flower and *tosa* girl know," she teased.

Wild Horse stalked past her and headed for his father's teepee.

Blue Flower followed at his heels, taunting him with snickering sounds.

Kate had awakened and sat at the teepee entrance. She was curious as to the commotion. Seeing Wild Horse, she feared something happened to Jack. If so, hope would be lost and she was resolved to dying...even to killing poor Buck if need be to save him from the heathen savages.

Wild Horse stopped so suddenly that Blue Flower nearly ran into him. He looked down at Kate and pointed to Jack's necklace around her neck. He gave her a smile but said nary a word of reassurance as he entered the teepee. Kate took it as a signal that her older brother must be alive.

Blue Flower followed her brother into the teepee, giving Kate a hard look and motioning her to lie down and go back to sleep.

Once inside, Wild Horse saw that Buffalo Hump was asleep. He turned to his sister. "Sleep now. Talk tomorrow," he told her. He didn't wait for a response but went straight to his blankets. He was resolved to get up before Blue Flower and lead White Knife to Jack.

IT HAD BEGUN to grow chilly, so I wrapped my blanket over my shoulders. We had decided not to make a fire so as to keep my location as secret as possible. At some point, I must have dozed off, because I awakened to Wild Horse calling. I was so well hidden that even he was having a tough time finding me.

"Wild Horse," I called out. "Over here." I stood and waved my arms.

Wild Horse rode in with his chin high and wearing

fresh buckskins. In fact, he looked quite regal in his Comanche finery. I could barely see any of the hideous scars from the mountain lion attack weeks ago. Of course, the necklace stood as an ever-present reminder. He brought company.

His older companion wore a serious expression and sat his pony tall and proud. A headdress of many eagle feathers graced his head, and his near-white buckskin shirt and breeches, as well as moccasins, were beaded with beautifully intricate designs. I saw no weapons save for a knife. From his nose to his forehead, a black band was painted across his face, making his penetrating eyes especially stand out as he gazed at me. Those eyes. I felt just a bit of an involuntary shiver. He held a carved feather-decorated pipe in one arm set across his lap. Clearly, this was a very important person.

Wild Horse motioned me to come near.

I glanced at my Springfield rifle lying on my blanket, then down at the Colt shoved out of habit in my waistband. I drew the Colt and placed it beside the rifle as a sign of peace before approaching Wild Horse.

"This *Tosahwi*," he said.

He had brought his shaman to see me.

White Knife had yet to move a muscle. He sat imperiously on his lofty four-legged perch as though judging me and deciding whether to sully himself by dismounting and engaging at my level.

Wild Horse turned to the shaman. "Jack," he said while pointing to me.

Finally, White Knife dismounted. Even that seemed almost ceremonious. Maybe it was partly because he was older and his joints were stiff, though it was more likely his attempt at acting like a visiting dignitary. His very being oozed power and influence. Yet, I could feel a sense of a brewing jealousy.

As we stood facing each other about six feet apart, Wild Horse spoke to the shaman in Comanche. Whatever was said, Wild Horse nodded and set to work building a fire.

I motioned White Knife to enter the campsite. He didn't budge, just stood with a penetrating stare.

Finally, Wild Horse had a fire going, laid a couple of blankets, and invited White Knife to sit with us before the fire.

The shaman seemed to relax at last as he sat cross-legged with us. His facial expression revealed that he was still sizing up the White boy.

I reckoned he must have been done with sizing me up. I was about a head taller and carried more muscle, though all those feathers told that he'd likely been quite a great warrior in his day. I looked to Wild Horse for guidance.

"Jack kill *pia wa'óo,* save *Kobe* life," were White Knife's first words. He'd even worked in a bit of English.

I nodded.

White Knife lit the pipe, took a puff, and passed it to me.

I took a slow pull on the pipe and passed it to Wild Horse. We did this passing of the pipe for the next few minutes as we sat in silence.

"*Isa* magic," White Knife said, as though he'd been cogitating on the words for hours. Wild Horse had told him of my meeting the wolf.

We passed the pipe around a couple of more times. By now, I had it figured that the shaman had come to see me outside of the encampment so that my visit wouldn't stir up the people. I reckoned it was his way of maintaining control and power.

"Free Kiowa," the shaman said just a little disconcertedly. His accompanying nod indicated to me that he understood whatever explanation Wild Horse had delivered.

White Knife's eyes had been riveted on me for what seemed like better than a half hour. Finally, he turned to Wild Horse with an instruction. "Jack talk."

Wild Horse turned to me. "Ask questions, Jack," he counseled in near-perfect English.

My mind immediately went to thoughts of Kate and Buck, but I knew better than to blurt that concern out. I really hadn't given thought to what might be said in meeting an actual Comanche medicine man. I pointed to him and then back at me. "*Isa* and *pia wa'óo* strong medicine," I ventured.

To my relief, White Knife nodded. He raised his eyebrows. For the first time, he actually smiled. His teeth weren't all that pretty, but the smile was a sign of some sort of mutual respect. I'd apparently struck a chord with him.

"Power of strong God," I said, pointing up to the heavens.

"*Taa Narumi* strong," he responded.

I calculated that it wouldn't be a good idea to get into a battle over the power of our deities. There was no question in my mind that it was no contest. I glanced deferentially over at Wild Horse and nodded to White Knife. "Jack kill *pia wa'óo*, save Wild Horse life, talk with *isa*, and hold power over Kiowa. Strong medicine. Jack want peace with Penateka Comanche, no fight *numunuu*." I expect it could be said that I was laying my cards out on the table to make a play for freeing Kate and Buck.

However, that apparently wasn't the deck we were playing with just yet. White Knife was sizing me up, so he could report back to Buffalo Hump at their council fire.

White Knife stood abruptly.

Wild Horse and I immediately stood. I gathered it was out of respect.

I glanced questioningly at Wild Horse, who nodded almost imperceptibly in return.

The shaman locked his dark eyes on mine, nodded, and surprised me by reaching out his hand.

I shook it. White Knife had quite a grip. Maybe it was his way of letting me know he was old but tough.

"We return tomorrow," he said to me. He motioned Wild Horse to join him. They mounted up and were soon on their way back to the Comanche encampment. As they rode off, Wild Horse looked back at me and gave a reassuring smile. White Knife had apparently been impressed. How much, we'd have to wait and see.

NO SOONER HAD Wild Horse and the shaman disappeared into the early morning mists when a muffled sound startled me. I quickly deduced that it wasn't an animal.

"Jack?" It was a soft female voice floating at me through the haze.

Straining to hear, I leaned in the direction of the voice. I had heard it before. It wasn't Kate's.

Like some magical apparition, Blue Flower appeared with a white pony in tow. She stood about twenty feet from me and gave me a smile that sent mixed signals. It was simultaneously innocent and flirtatious.

There was no way I was going to risk my trust with Wild Horse. "Blue Flower, go," I ordered firmly.

"How strong Jack's medicine?" she cooed.

Dang, she couldn't be more than thirteen or fourteen years old. I was in danger of treading on ground I dared not travel. I laid a stern stare on her. "Blue Flower, go... now!" I demanded. I sought to be as firm as possible with my fifteen-year-old voice.

She was about to speak when an arm grabbed her from behind and carried her off. It was White Knife. He and Wild Horse had suspected they'd been followed, so they doubled back. The shaman smiled at me as he dragged her away in his powerful arms. She kicked in protest initially, but quickly gave in. Even the chief's daughter dared not resist the shaman.

The entire episode with the shaman's visit and now the temptation of Blue Flower had stressed me out. I decided to try to relax. I lay down on my blanket with my rifle. Soon enough, I fell asleep. I wasn't sure when or what the shaman's advice to Buffalo Hump might be, much less the outcome.

———

I WAS ONCE AGAIN AWAKENED by the sound of hoofbeats. This time, it was one horse. I quickly drew my Colt. These hoofbeats were from a shod horse.

"Well, I'll be hornswoggled, Jack. You boys couldn't hide a trail if your lives depended on it." George's broad smile preceded him.

"George?"

"Yep. That's me," he responded with an even greater white-toothed smile and walked into camp with his horse in tow.

"What happened to the cattle drive?"

"Them Tenawa and Noconi Comanche blocked us. They demanded beeves that my trail boss wasn't about to give up. It was a sort of standoff. They kept threatening to attack, and we couldn't risk giving up our defensive position protecting the herd. My trail boss was just about to give in when a company of cavalry showed up."

"Then what?" I asked.

"The Comanche decided it wasn't worth fighting over. My trail boss gave them one longhorn as a token gift. I think some call it saving face," he said, chuckling.

"Saving face?" I asked.

"So no one appears to lose. There are no hard feelings."

"Oh. Did the drive continue?"

"Sure did," he said with a grin. "This Captain Granger, who led the Bluecoat mounted rifles, was looking for a scout. I was tired of the trail drive. The trail boss promised he'd get my pay to me, and I joined up with the cavalry."

"How'd they figure you could scout?"

Now, George laughed heartily. "I threw some Pawnee language at them. Guess they figured that if I could speak the language, I could scout like them."

"Where are they?"

"About a half mile back."

Now, it was my turn to smile. I sure didn't need a bunch of Bluecoats messing up my negotiations with the Penatekas. "Well, I'd be steering them due south, George. There's a big Comanche encampment about a mile east of here. They are the people of my friend Wild Horse. The Bluecoats could be a problem."

"These the Comanche that've been raiding homesteads?"

"Afraid so, George," I responded.

"Captain Granger has orders to punish them."

I wasn't certain how close the cavalry unit really was and time was wasting. "George, it could risk the lives of my sister and brother who are held captive. I'm trying to get them out safely. A battle would likely not end well."

George nodded and pondered the situation. "Come to think of it, my scouting instinct tells me to head due south. Let me know if you see anything, Jack. God bless." He smiled and headed his horse back to the Bluecoats at an easy trot.

About the time George disappeared from view, Wild Horse rode up. He looked at the shod prints in the dirt and gave me a questioning look.

I laughed. "It was our friend George. He's scouting for the Bluecoats but will direct them away from the Penateka camp."

Wild Horse shook his head at my seeming to frequently be in the right place at the right time. "Strong medicine, Jack."

"Any word from White Knife?"

He shook his head. "They have council tonight," he informed me. "I bring food." With that, he dismounted with a sack of food in hand.

"Do you know of my brother?"

"Boy safe," was all Wild Horse would say.

Kate was old enough to hold up pretty well under the circumstances, but Buck was just a small, vulnerable child. I sighed resignedly and stoked the fire. I was famished after surviving the last couple of days mostly on pemmican. We ate well.

"Wild Horse must sleep in own teepee tonight. You safe." It appeared that Buffalo Hump would deliver his decision tomorrow after considering the advice of White Knife and the Penateka Comanche subchiefs.

"Must free my sister and brother," I insisted.

Wild Horse shrugged. "We know tomorrow."

I wasn't encouraged. It began to occur to me that Kate and Buck might be sort of bargaining chips, trade goods for the Comanche. "What of Blue Flower?"

"Buffalo Hump punish her."

I had no idea what sort of punishment a Comanche chief might mete out to his roguish daughter, especially for flirting with a *tosa*. He'd have to set some sort of an example for the tribe.

"Is she alright?"

Wild Horse laughed and nodded. "You big medicine to her, Jack. You right to stay away from Blue Flower."

I took that as a sort of friendly warning.

Wild Horse departed under a full moon. I could hear the yips of coyotes and howls of wolves off in the distance. I was sure that plenty more critters lurked in the darkness, but I felt reasonably secure with my fire, the Springfield rifle, and my trusty Colt revolver. Whether human or beast, I'd put up a fight against any threat.

I lay for a bit thinking on what might be going on at the Comanche council. What might they be coming up with? I drew the blanket a bit tighter. While the days were still warm enough to bring sweat to your brow with any significant exertion, the nights were increasingly chilly.

I fell asleep pondering Wild Horse's culture. From our limited communications, it had begun to occur to me that they were pious toward their many gods, seemed to care for their parents, respected their elders, obeyed tribal laws, and followed traditional customs. Yet there seemed an almost simplistic innocence to their culture. Their warlike nature seemed counterintuitive. I too worshipped my God and had respected my parents. I never knew my grandparents but held a certain reverence for older folk. Far as I knew, I obeyed the law. What was the difference between Wild Horse and me? I fell asleep before I figured it out.

———

I HAD BEEN BLESSED with another clear night and awakened to shimmering rays of sunlight dancing across my face. Shedding my blanket, I stretched and basked for a few precious minutes in the sun's warmth. I looked about and grabbed a stick to stir the dying embers of my campfire.

I was about to begin a prayer of thanks when I heard the sounds of unshod ponies on the rocks leading up to my lair.

"Jack!" called Wild Horse.

"Welcome, Wild Horse." I was excited at the prospects of the day. "Are we to visit your father?"

He silently dismounted from Tuhibitu.

I quickly realized that he had a pony in tow with a pack tied to its back. His bow and arrows, war club, and lance were hung across the pony's back. It became readily obvious to me that he was prepared to travel, not engage in bringing a *tosa* into the Comanche encampment. "What happened?" I finally asked.

Wild Horse brought out food and began stoking the fire. He appeared to be carefully weighing his words. "Not good, not bad," he finally revealed.

I gave him a decidedly inquisitive gaze.

He wouldn't look me in the eye but went about

preparing food. Finally, he looked up at me. "You hungry? *Ana o'a hi'it?*"

Of course, I was hungry, but the uncertainty of the council outcome was killing me.

He began to cook strips of buffalo meat and had even brought eggs. "We eat, then talk."

Breakfast was soon ready. We remained silent through breakfast, occasionally exchanging anticipatory glances.

We finished eating, and Wild Horse began to extinguish the fire. It was becoming ever clearer that we weren't staying here. Where might we be going? It seemed clear from the supplies he brought and his body language that we wouldn't be visiting his people's encampment.

At last, Wild Horse sat and motioned me to join him.

I locked my eyes on his as I stood opposite him. I paused, then sat across from him.

"Sister Kate and brother Buck safe," he said reassuringly. "No hurt *tosa*."

I shrugged. "Is problem?"

He nodded. "*Tosahwi* problem."

"White Knife has a problem?"

Wild Horse nodded again. "He want trade."

The reality looked to be that the shaman was a greedy son of a gun. I figured that out straightaway, plus it seemed clear that the old man feared what seemed to him to be my strong medicine. "Ransom," I responded.

"What ransom?" asked Wild Horse.

"Ransom is when hold *tenahpu* or *wa'ipu* for trade." I actually had the presence of mind to mix in a little of the Comanche he'd taught me. I reckoned he'd better grasp the difference between humans versus inanimate objects by referring to holding kidnapped men or women. "Trade is blankets and beads," I added.

"Ransom bad?" Wild Horse sighed.

I nodded. "Ransom bad."

"White Knife say go to Bluecoats. Trade for blankets and guns. Then he free *tosa* girl and boy."

"Your father agreed?"

"Buffalo Hump fear power of shaman."

The reality of the Comanche culture was hitting me hard. These were indeed primitive people thinking in simple, even crude, terms. Maybe my earlier instincts to punish them for taking away my home and family wasn't so far off. Then again, that wasn't a very Christian thought. But even Christ told that sin ought to be forgiven, but sinners are still punished. These thoughts raced through my young but rapidly maturing mind. Obviously, my Springfield rifle and Colt revolver were a rather feeble means for punishing a hundred or so armed savages. What happened next shouldn't have surprised me so much as it did.

The sound of an unshod pony brought both Wild Horse and me to full alert. Emerging from the trees was Blue Flower.

Before we could get up, she'd ridden right up to us. She spoke nary a word.

Wild Horse was speechless. How bold of her, how disrespectful of her father's explicit orders.

Blue Flower motioned me to come to her.

I glanced at Wild Horse for approval.

He looked as though he was still too surprised to say anything and simply nodded.

I stood perhaps a yard from her as she looked down from her pony.

Blue Flower smiled and motioned me closer. From a

pocket within her buckskin shirt, she drew a beaded necklace. "Kate," she said. It was apparently a gift from my sister.

I felt relieved that it wasn't a gift from this sister of Wild Horse. That would surely have screamed complications. "Thank you," I said. Unthinking, I placed my hand gently on her pony's withers.

She responded quickly by backing the pony away a step.

I guess touching a Comanche girl's pony was just a tad too intimate.

Blue Flower offered a demure yet suggestive smile. "Jack, strong medicine." With that, she turned and headed away.

Through it all, Wild Horse had remained silent. Finally, he stood. "Blue Flower strong *wa'ipu*. Like *pia*." He was warning me. His sister was a strong woman like her mother.

I nodded to indicate that I understood. "My *pia* was strong," I said as an afterthought. In fact, she was very strong to have endured raising five children and a husband she loved despite him repeatedly failing at his livelihood.

He thought a moment on my words, then headed for his pony. "We go to Bluecoats," he said, turning to the task at hand.

"You agree with ransom?" I queried.

Wild Horse looked at me. It was quite clear that he held my medicine in deep respect, and there was this consideration of the life debt. These were surely coloring his point of view. "*Taa Narumi* speak to White Knife. Buffalo Hump listen. Decision made. I must agree."

I sensed reluctance in his voice. That had been the longest string of words I'd yet heard Wild Horse utter.

My response was almost reflexive. "My God says ransom wrong." I was effectively pitting the one and only God against the Comanche Big Father. Given the supposedly strong medicine I'd been exhibiting thus far to my Comanche companion, God's will was winning out. I reckoned my bargaining chips were strong in this contest.

Wild Horse sighed and mounted his pony. "We go."

Obviously, we weren't going to have an in-depth discussion of God versus Big Father at this point in time, but it was a long ride to Fort Inge.

ELEVEN
BLUECOATS

WE BEGAN TRAVELING south through some of the roughest country in this part of Texas. From what I recalled my pa telling me and allowing as best I could for where we'd traveled, I reckoned the fort was maybe seventy miles or so distant. Allowing for alternately walking and riding our ponies, it would likely take at least three or four days. We'd have to be constantly on the lookout for enemies.

In addition to the varmints with claws and fangs, we had to be wary of Kiowa and Apache raiding parties. A new dimension I'd been unaware of until Wild Horse mentioned it was what he called the brown skins. These were apparently Mexican bandits roaming the prairies, rustling cattle from ranches to skin them and sell the hides. I later learned that the ranchers called these bandits hiders.

. I still wrestled with how I might free Kate and Buck from the clutches of the Penateka Comanche. Wild Horse seemed less likely to be a help, though I found myself increasingly thinking on Blue Flower and her winsome smile. Perhaps she'd be more of an ally than I figured. I was still trying to figure out that look she gave me before leaving. I was pondering the mixed signals from Blue Flower while unconsciously stroking the beaded necklace when Wild Horse brought us to an abrupt halt.

My Comanche companion pointed off toward smoke rising far off in the distance. He chuckled. "Bluecoat fire," he stated emphatically. "Big fire."

I expected he knew what he was talking about. Whites, especially the military, weren't known for being especially subtle. "Shall we see?"

He shook his head. "Go to fort."

That got me thinking he'd likely been given specific instructions to talk to someone in charge, not some mere field officer on patrol.

As we altered our direction to give the Bluecoats a wider berth, I got to thinking that our friend George was probably with them. Having an ally in the Bluecoat camp would surely be an asset.

———

OTHER THAN SIGHTING the Bluecoat camp from a distance, our first day was uneventful. Verbal communication was kept to a minimum, as we might hear a threat before seeing it. As dusk approached, Wild Horse found us an overhanging rock formation that offered shelter on two sides.

I set about gathering wood for a fire.

"No *kohto*," he cautioned. He looked about suspiciously. His senses were on high alert as he grabbed jerky and berries from our supply sack.

"Wild Horse feel danger," I said in a near whisper.

He sniffed the wind and listened intently. There was a wolf howl that didn't seem quite right to his ears.

We sat and ate. Wild Horse had his bow beside him with an arrow already nocked. The Springfield rifle was at my side, along with the Colt revolver. If there was trouble, it appeared as though we'd be ready.

All of a sudden, Wild Horse grabbed his bow and stood facing the eastern boundary of our campsite.

I saw them before Wild Horse. At least five warriors were silhouetted against the rising full moon. Five against two, not great odds. As I stood, I cocked the hammer of the Springfield and stuffed the Colt in my waistband.

"White medicine man," came a voice in a strange dialect from what was shaping up to be a raiding party.

"Kiowa," hissed Wild Horse as he prepared to shoot.

"Peace," came the voice, again in a different tribal language.

Wild Horse understood enough to give me a glance of amazement. Nevertheless, he pulled back his bowstring.

"Peace," the Kiowa repeated and raised a hand with palm facing us. His gaze riveted in on Wild Horse's mountain lion claw necklace, and his eyes went wide. It apparently had considerable impact in tribal cultures. The warrior's eyes shifted to me. He repeated, "Peace."

I said a little prayer and reached my hand over to keep Wild Horse from releasing his arrow. I had no idea what these Indians were saying, but my intuition was in overdrive. I sensed that this small band wasn't a threat. "Come," I said, motioning them to advance.

They were indeed Kiowa warriors, and the leader looked vaguely familiar. As they drew near, I recognized him as the warrior from whose neck I'd pulled the arrow. I could now see a bandage covering the wound. "*Unha haksi nahniaka*," I said, asking his name using the Comanche tongue.

Wild Horse gave me a look as though I were crazy.

"*Kwihnai*," the Kiowa responded, also in Comanche.

I looked to Wild Horse to translate.

"Eagle," he said hesitantly. My Comanche friend's consternation over what I was up to spoke loud and clear.

I looked at Eagle, pointed to myself, and said, "Jack." I pointed to Wild Horse, "*Kobe*." It occurred to me that I was fully forgetting my manners. "*Ana o'a hi'it*," I asked while motioning toward our campsite. It made perfect sense to ask whether they were hungry and wanted to eat. It seemed the polite thing to do, savages or not.

Eagle nodded and dismounted. He motioned his companions to join him. They left their weapons with the ponies and walked toward us. Well, they didn't just walk. It was more strutting and preening to show off for two travelers whom they surely viewed as children.

I must admit to being impressed with their feather and bead-decorated buckskin leggings and breechcloths, ornate pipestone breastplates, heavily-beaded moccasins, and atop their heads feather-embellished roaches. Their hair was cut short over the right ear. They were quite a sight to behold, especially for a pair of teens like us. It appeared clear that they didn't see us as a threat. Besides, counting coup on a couple of young boys would not make for an impressive story for their people.

I cautiously placed my rifle on the ground, smiled, and made a sign for building a fire. "*Kohto*," I said, sticking with what little Comanche I knew. I could see Wild Horse smiling beside me. I wasn't sure whether he was impressed or not.

We spent the time after eating signing, scribbling in

the dirt, and speaking in halting Indian tongues about hunting, the best places to find drinkable water, sightings of buffalo, longhorn meat versus buffalo, and more. Wild Horse translated as needed. He was suspicious and reluctant at first but warmed to the task. Eagle even brought out a pipe. Several times in our conversation, Eagle mentioned my strong spirit. He was exceedingly appreciative of my not having permitted Wild Horse to scalp him. I began to realize that whatever we were smoking in that pipe had the effect of raising our spirits.

We'd talked and eaten for a couple of hours when Eagle stood and quite graciously told us they must leave. He assured us that we would travel safely, as there would be no trouble from the Kiowa.

As the Kiowa warriors mounted up and departed, Wild Horse turned to me and stared with an expression of wonder. "Jack, you strong medicine," he said with a tone of incredulity in his voice. He shook his head resignedly as he laid out his blanket for the night. "Jack watch first," he said, laughing. "Make Wild Horse safe," he said, chuckling at his own humor and drawing his blanket up around him. I had a feeling that he knew something I didn't.

I sat for a while, stirring the coals of the fire with a stick and pondering my adventures thus far in the Comancheria. I did feel just a tad light-headed. What path was God taking me on? There was little else to do but trust in Him. He hadn't failed me since the attack on my home. It seemed as though He was teaching me something I would never have learned at the old schoolhouse back in Pennsylvania.

I stared over at Wild Horse, both of him. Two? I shook it off as an aberration. I felt sleepy. All our wounds from the mountain lion had healed. The scars that remained served as reminders of a bond created between us. What lay ahead? I had no idea, save that I trusted in God's protection. I repeated a prayer my mother used to say when she'd tuck us in at night, "Now I lay me down to sleep, I pray dear Lord my soul to keep..." I was asleep before I finished.

———————

"JACK NO STAY AWAKE," Wild Horse scolded as he began making our breakfast. Then he smiled. "Smoke make sleep."

I recalled the pipe the Kiowa warrior shared with us.

"Peyote," announced Wild Horse.

I'd never heard of it, but apparently the Indians used peyote in their religion as it had the very sort of effect we'd experienced with the Kiowa. It was made from a cactus. The good news was that everyone had smoked just enough to stay happy.

"Jack eat." Wild Horse pushed food toward me.

"Jack no smoke peyote again," I told him. I wanted to have full control of my faculties. With that, I ate ravenously. I guess peyote stirs up an appetite.

Gray clouds were gathering to the south, indicating a possibility of some stormy weather. Of course, I'd learned that the weather in Texas was changeable on a moment's notice. Many were the days when we'd close everything up on our homestead only to have a storm pass by with nary a drop of rain.

Wild Horse shrugged as we began to break camp. "No rain," he assured me. "We go."

Soon enough, we were mounted and resuming our journey to Fort Inge. I was grateful that we were communicating better. I was picking up bits and pieces of Comanche while Wild Horse continued to learn English.

The terrain on our path grew rougher. The rain had an impact somewhere, because we came to a river that was swollen enough to represent a serious challenge for our ponies. We weren't sure that Paint would even be up to it. We had crossed the Guadalupe River easily, but that was before the rain storm.

"*Umaru*...rain make deep," counseled Wild Horse, pointing toward the river and using his hands for emphasis.

We dismounted and eased to the bank of the river. It was plenty deep, just as Wild Horse described, and running fast. We'd crossed the Sabinal River the day before, but this water seemed much colder. I'd later learn they called it the Frio River. The name fit. For now, we needed to find a reasonably safe crossing. We still had a ways to go to reach Fort Inge, and this river crossing was turning out to be an unanticipated inconvenience. We sure didn't want to lose horses or precious supplies.

Wild Horse pointed to the southeast, signing that there might be shallows where the current wasn't so strong. He wasn't up to risking his life either, especially with this life debt hanging over his head.

After what seemed like forever, we finally came upon a spot where the river broadened. The river bottom was rocky and slippery and there was a narrow channel along the northern bank where the water would be to our chests and our horses stressed. At least we wouldn't have to swim, and our weapons and supplies would stay dry.

Wild Horse waded in, leading the way with his hand securely holding Tuhibitu's halter and trailing our pack pony on a long tether.

I entered the river about twenty feet behind. I hung on to Paint's halter with my right hand while lofting the heavy Springfield rifle and Colt revolver over my head with my left. That of itself was quite a feat.

Wild Horse had reached the other side when the pack pony lost its footing. Down he came. For a moment, I feared he might be injured as he thrashed about to right himself with the awkward pack still securely fastened to his back.

I struggled to help the foundering beast, but it was hard to move swiftly in now waist-deep water. Wild Horse and I reached the pony at the same time and managed to avoid flailing hooves and get him on solid footing. Blessedly, Paint simply waded ahead and joined Tuhibitu on the south bank as though she hadn't needed my guidance at all. The big downside was that our supplies were now soaking wet.

We finally got everything on dry land. Wild Horse sighed resignedly as he began removing our supplies from the shaken but now steady pony. Fortunately, the food in the buffalo-hide sack stayed dry.

I hobbled our ponies and helped lay our other supplies out to dry in the midday sun. It wouldn't take all that long, but any time spent was wasted time. We made the best of it and ate some jerky.

"Bluecoat fort tomorrow," said Wild Horse. "Talk with White father about Jack sister and brother."

I still found it hard to believe that Wild Horse was going along with this ransom business. There was a certain ungodliness to the whole scheme. I had saved his life, but he was knuckling under to his tribal leaders. I understood that he felt obligated to obey the wishes of his father and appreciated that he'd been entrusted with going with me to talk to the White father at Fort Inge.

"Don't understand ransom," I finally said.

Wild Horse sighed. "You not like *tosa*, Jack. You have strong medicine."

There was that strong medicine business again. What on earth did that have to do with the present circumstances. "My God powerful," I responded. "Strong medicine. God of all *numunuu*...White...Black...Brown... Red..." I felt led to come on stronger about my faith. There was no more dancing around the fact that the Comanche *Taa Narumi* was no more than a bit player in God's scheme.

Wild Horse stopped loading the supplies on the pony and turned to me. "What is cross?" Holy smoke, but he was actually asking about what he apparently figured was a symbol of my power. Now I had a clue about one thing going through his mind during the long hours of silence on the trail.

I wondered how long this had been weighing in Wild Horse's thoughts. I motioned him to come sit by the river bank. "God see evil. Send his son in human form to teach man. Some men not learn. They kill God's son on cross."

"Kill God?" Wild Horse asked.

"God's son is named Christ. He lives after death and is seen by many. Now, he is what we call the Trinity. He is God, son of God, and spirit joined as one power. He is God of love and peace and forgiving. Trust in Him is freedom."

Wild Horse shook his head with wonderment at my story. "He die...then live?" he said incredulously.

"God use son to save his people," I said, trying to keep it simple.

There were no stories of this sort among the Comanche with *Taa Narumi* and all their other gods. This was totally new ground for him. "Why Whites kill?" he asked earnestly.

Reflexively, I wanted to say that the Red man kills, too. I hung my head sadly. "We still sin. Not all people trust Christ."

"Does George trust?" asked Wild Horse.

Wow, he remembered George insisting on praying at our meal. "George trusts," I assured Wild Horse. I could only imagine what was roiling around in my Comanche companion's mind. The shaman, White Knife, would likely not be pleased. I had the impression that Buffalo Hump already recognized his son as some sort of special thinker and potential leader of his people. Now, my hope was to guide Wild Horse along the road to trusting God. The door had been opened. My mother used to say, "Live the journey, for every destination is but the doorway to the next journey." So, it went with faith. The proverbial seeds of faith had been sown.

It was also occurring to me that my deep-seated anger and desire for vengeance were being displaced by forgiveness. Perhaps that is partly why the ransom struck in my craw. The Comanche should be punished for their deeds, not rewarded with trade bounty. I felt no urge to forgive so long as they continued their evil ways. Nevertheless, my pa's words from Matthew about vengeance hung heavily within me like some lingering shadow.

Wild Horse responded to my silence. "What Jack think?"

"God say ransom evil."

"We go to Bluecoats," he replied. He was not ready to judge his people.

———

LATE AFTERNOON of the third day of our travels from our campsite near the Penateka Comanche encampment and my beloved sister and brother, we were greeted by the sound of creaking leather and jangling weapons as George appeared riding but a few yards in front of a company of Bluecoats.

There was no time for us to hide. Drawing nearer to the fort, we'd been careless in not checking our backtrail.

"Hold up, Jack…Wild Horse," George said in a near whisper. He drew his rifle and pointed it at us. "Play along with me here. Captain Granger is right behind me."

"Who goes, Mr. Freeman?" Granger called out.

"Two young'uns headin' our way, Captain," he responded.

Captain Granger spurred his mount and pulled up alongside George. "Hmmm. An Injun and White boy," he observed. "They got names? What are they doing together? The Red one's a Comanche, isn't he?"

George quietly listened to the battery of questions. "What are your names?" He didn't dare let on to the captain that he knew us.

I looked at George quizzically.

He winked and nodded for me to play along.

"My name is Jack O'Toole, and my friend here is Wild Horse. He is a Comanche." I tried to not look overly confident. We'd already had some adventures of the sort that tended to make young boys grow up right fast, but it didn't seem to be the right situation to reveal us to the Bluecoats as anything but a pair of boys who'd lost their way.

"Where do they think they're going, Mr. Freeman?" the captain persisted. He refused to speak directly with us.

"Where you boys headed?" asked George.

"Fort Inge, sir. I think," I replied to George with a respectful eye on the captain.

Captain Granger chewed on that for a couple of seconds. "Something here troubles me, Mr. Freeman. Have them fall in with our column. We'll take them to Colonel Loring." The officer laid a long judgmental gaze upon us, then abruptly pivoted and rejoined the column.

I had a sense that Captain Granger was tired after a couple of weeks patrolling the southern reaches of the Comancheria with nothing to show for his efforts. We were either boys in need of help or captives, depending on what he cared to make of it. Examining the condition of the Bluecoats' horses, I reckoned they'd be just as glad as the captain to get back to the fort. I did feel blessed that it was George who had found us.

"You boys heard the captain," said George loud enough for the captain to hear and directed us to a spot in the mounted column. Our saddleless ponies and disheveled appearance were quite a marked contrast to the dust-covered blue uniforms of the mounted rifles unit.

We skirted around a little town called Encina and, within a couple of miles, found ourselves looking at Fort Inge. Dang, but there was a goodly lot of soldiers around. Must have been a couple of hundred at least.

I can't say that Fort Inge was especially impressive, even as my own image of frontier forts went. There were no walls. It was comprised of a pair of wooden barracks with thatched roofs and a large stone building that was a commissary. There was a smattering of tents that apparently supplemented the barracks. It lacked any sense of permanence. Nearby was a hill they called Mount Inge. From a strategic military perspective, it seemed a logical location with plenty of firewood, water, and game.

As we approached, a sentry saluted our column. I saw George say something to Captain Granger, who nodded. In any case, George rode with us while the rest of the Bluecoats fell out to take care of their horses. There really wasn't a gate, so Captain Granger led the three of us directly to the headquarters of Colonel Loring.

Granger lazily saluted the guard. "Captain in, Corporal?"

"Yes sir, Captain," replied the guard. He turned and knocked on the commandant's door.

"What is it?" came a muffled voice from within.

"Captain Granger reporting, Colonel."

There was a long silence and the sound of footsteps, then, "Send him in, Corporal."

Captain Granger entered, followed by me and Wild Horse, with George last through the door. Granger came to attention and saluted far more smartly than when he entered the fort. "Captain Granger reporting, sir."

Colonel Loring remained seated behind an old, beat-up, sorry excuse for a desk. The stench of alcohol hung in the air. His eyes fell upon George. "What's the n..." He caught himself upon realizing that a teen White boy was present. "What sort of rabble are you bringing me, Captain?"

"My apologies, sir. We made no contact with hostiles during our patrol but happened on these young boys— the White boy and the Comanche—a bit north of Encina. The Black here is our scout and speaks the Injun' tongue. He can translate."

"Got nothing to say to the Red boy, Captain." He rebuffed any courtesy to Wild Horse. "Boy." He looked at me through eyes that seemed to have trouble focusing. "What's your name?"

I looked at George for approval. That likely annoyed the two Bluecoat officers, but I was too nervous to care. I was intent on whether they might free Kate and Buck. "Jack O'Toole, sir," I finally responded.

"Your family homestead that place up north of here got attacked?"

"Yes, sir, my—" I tried to explain but was cut short.

"Sorry for your loss. Heard about the Comanche." He actually looked sympathetic for a moment. "What are you doing traveling with this savage?"

Wild Horse's expression gave way to an angry scowl.

"My friend Wild Horse speaks some English, Colonel, sir," I cautioned. "And he has a message from the Comanche," I worked in before the colonel could respond.

Colonel Loring looked up patronizingly at Captain Granger, as if resenting his bringing any problem before him. He looked at me and sighed. "What might that message be?" he asked, looking directly at me.

"Trade Whites for horses and guns," said Wild Horse boldly.

Loring glared at Wild Horse. "You speak when I say," he ordered derisively.

I was getting fed up with the colonel's overbearing attitude. He was clearly prejudiced against Black men and Red men. It was also obvious that the colonel would never understand why I might be traveling with a Comanche.

Loring turned to Captain Granger. "You say this here…er…Black man is a scout?"

"George is in our employ as a scout, sir."

A downright mean smile creased the colonel's lips.

"Good. He can lead you to the Comanche encampment and rescue the White boy's kin. Kill all the savages if you must."

"Sir?"

"You heard me! Dismissed, Captain Granger," he said in no uncertain terms.

Wild Horse and I grudgingly followed George out the door, but the captain was called back by the colonel.

"Granger, put those boys under guard. I don't want them warning those savages. Move out on the double quick." Loring expressed no sympathy for the captain having just returned from two weeks in the field. "Take fresh horses, Gordon," he said as an afterthought topped off by a dismissive salute.

As the captain emerged from Colonel Loring's office, it was clear that he was distraught and very unhappy. He was mumbling something barely intelligible under his breath about some standing order for soldiers not to be engaging Indians. "Corporal, take these boys to the brig," he snarled angrily. He gave us a sneer as he walked past us. "Come on, Mr. Freeman. We have work to do."

"Yessir, Captain," responded George. He dutifully fell in behind the captain, giving us a shrug followed by a wink.

I was not at all impressed by our encounter with the soldiers. Call them what you will...Bluecoats...Long Knives...they deserved no respect from me. It reinforced my decision to have not gone to them for help immediately after the attack on my family.

Wild Horse had a sullen expression spread across his face. "Bluecoats follow your God, Jack?" he half whispered and half hissed as we trudged along behind a sergeant and two privates on the way to what they called a brig.

What could I say? "Not all our people good," was the best I could come up with. I was thinking that his people were not exactly angels.

We arrived at a tent enclosed on all four sides with guards posted at the front and back. We were ordered to go inside and wait until told we could leave. The sergeant indicated that they would bring us some food and that our ponies and belongings would be taken care of. We sat on canvas cots and faced each other.

I wondered about what had become of my precious Springfield rifle and Colt revolver, not to mention poor old Paint. I couldn't imagine what was going through Wild Horse's head. I didn't have to wait long to find out.

"How we go free, Jack?" queried my Comanche friend.

"Sorry," I responded with a shrug. I wanted to say I told you so, but there was no point in adding that to our predicament. "Let me think," was my lame response. There was a porthole in the side of the tent. I stood, and from it, I could see troops assembling in the gathering dusk to march toward the Comanche encampment. It appeared that they were going to begin their march at night. As I found myself reflexively saying a prayer, I heard a thud and groan behind the rear entrance of our canvas jail.

The rear flaps of the tent parted to reveal George's glistening white teeth in a broad smile. George motioned us out of the tent. "Your horses and weapons are about a hundred yards north, hidden behind a live oak motte. Make haste. I must hurry and rejoin the captain." He smiled again. "I'll keep them moving but slowly." He paused and glanced back. "And God bless."

Wild Horse and I wasted no time silently sneaking out the back of the tent. The guard at the front was unaware of our escape, and we were intent on keeping it that way. We kept a low profile as we ran as low to the ground as possible. Far as I could tell, the fort garrison was fully focused on supporting the troops leaving on their new mission, as we encountered no soldiers on our little jaunt to our ponies.

Tuhibitu and Paint seemed none the worse for wear. Thanks to the Bluecoats, they'd been fed and rested. In fact, they were just a tad excited as though sensing that they were being called to something special. Our weapons and a sack of victuals were at the base of one of the trees. As we mounted, I glanced back at our supposed brig. The guard had come to, and he and the other guard were trying to figure out where we'd gone. Likely as not, they didn't want to face up to the sergeant. Had it not been so deadly serious, I might have laughed.

The surrounding landscape was rough as we carefully and cautiously picked our way around cacti and shrubs. Thanks to George, we'd have a pretty good head start. Plus, two can travel faster than forty or so heavily-armed mounted rifles.

We'd traveled for about an hour riding our ponies at an easy loping pace when Wild Horse signaled to stop.

"We rest here," he said.

I dismounted and broke out some of those victuals for us that George had thoughtfully provided.

"Bluecoats no ears," Wild Horse said between bites of biscuit and jerky. He was trying to tell me they wouldn't listen.

I wanted to tell him that their response was exactly what I expected. "Ransom bad. Make White father angry." It was as close as I could come to *I told you so.*

Wild Horse shook his head. But for the life debt, he'd likely have lit out on his own.

I pressed my argument. "Whites owned George. He escaped. Slavery is a sin...bad...evil. We not buy or sell people." I hoped I was getting through.

Wild Horse shook his head. "Comanche have slaves," he mumbled unconvincingly.

"Comanche trade White people for horses. Is no respect." I tried to get him to understand that it was an insult and a sin to have a price on a human. "Slavery is evil, a sin. My God tells us that if you sin, you are a slave to it." I vaguely recalled my pa quoting this to us, I think from the book of John. Whether this was sinking in with Wild Horse, I wasn't certain. The fact that he was still considering what I shared was encouraging.

He nodded and stood. "Wild Horse think." He walked over to his pony. "Must hurry." He was mounted and had nudged Tuhibitu into a walk before I could climb aboard old Paint. She was holding up well for her age, but the rest stops would be important.

I began to ponder how the Comanche would respond to their trade terms being refused. I held out hope that Kate and Buck would remain safe. Meanwhile, I tried to focus on how to head off any confrontation between the Bluecoats and the Comanche. We had at least three days ahead of us before we reached the encampment. And this time, I reckoned to talk directly with Buffalo Hump.

Knowing that the Bluecoats were not far behind, we were determined to get as far ahead as possible. My body ached for rest and sleep, but we had to keep moving.

TWELVE
BANDITOS

HEADING NORTHEASTWARD, we trod over some of the same rough landscape, including recrossing the Frio and Sabinal Rivers, that we'd traveled over in our journey to Fort Inge. Per Wild Horse's warning, I kept a keen eye out for trouble. I was grateful for the morning light. Given the many hills, dense foliage, arroyos, and streams, it was likely we'd happen upon trouble with little or no warning. The upper reaches of the Sabinal River took us into the very heart of the hills.

With the hilly landscape, we found ourselves negotiating dry creek beds, deep valleys, and steep inclines. Around midday, we pulled up near a stand of oak to rest our ponies. We'd been pushing hard to get well ahead of the soldiers. I dismounted and walked over to sit and rest against the trunk of a tree. I began to sit. I heard a buzz.

Wild Horse shouted, "Jack!"

I froze and looked up to see him with a nocked arrow on his bowstring.

He shot the arrow before I could move a muscle.

Danged if he hadn't shot that arrow through the head of a rattlesnake. The viper had been just about ready to strike. Dealing with snake venom in the middle of the wilds of Texas would not have been especially desirable.

Wild Horse sprang toward me with knife in hand and cut off the rattler's head.

"Thanks," was all I could say.

He smiled. Wild Horse had saved my life. If there was any life debt, it surely must have been satisfied now. Why then was he still with me and saving my life?

I sat beneath the tree and watched him as he cut the rattles from the snake's tail. He gave them to me with a solemn look as though telling me that they would serve as a reminder of the danger of the frontier, of the Comancheria.

I'm not certain whether I rested or recovered. The incident with the rattlesnake shook me. We'd endured dangerous human, mammal, and reptile encounters in our brief time together, yet I felt as though we were developing a friendship. It seemed clear that we were trying to understand each other and the cultures that had formed our lives thus far. Despite his Comanche upbringing, which was quite a contrast to mine, he was dispelling the prejudices I held against the Red man. I think we were developing mutual trust and respect.

We stopped once more just before sunset and ate the last of the food George had supplied us with. We'd been resting the horses by walking them whenever possible. Every now and then, we'd find a creek bed with enough water to satisfy their thirst.

We rode on under the stars, pulling up at a creek just before sunrise. We didn't figure to sleep, but the horses needed water and rest. We were emotionally and physically tired. Naturally, we dozed off.

"DANG, WILD HORSE. THAT HURT!" I awoke in response to the muzzle of a rifle being shoved in my side.

"Ah...*inglés!*"

I looked up at the gnarliest-looking human, featuring a big hat, broad mustache, and toothless grin. "Wh... Who are you?" I mumbled.

A deep belly laugh filled the broad brown face hovering above me. Broken teeth showed through a thick mustache that apparently hid part of a nasty scar running up his cheek.

"*Vamos a matarlos!*" came a threatening voice setting on horseback behind the laughing man standing over me. He looked like pure evil from head to toe, highlighted by a black patch covering one eye. A big black sombrero shaded his face and added to casting a dark wickedness over him. His chest was crossed with bandoliers packed with ammunition. He raised the rifle to his shoulder and began to sight down the barrel with his good eye. I was pretty much convinced that he was saying that he wanted to kill me.

By this time, I was fully awake. I looked about desperately. There were these three heavily-armed strangers in our camp. Wild Horse was nowhere to be seen. I glanced down, but my Springfield rifle and Colt revolver rested in the hands of one of the scary-looking strangers. They spoke Spanish, so I figured them for Mexicans. I recalled that my pa had told me that they were still unhappy about giving up Texas to the United States. These men clearly bore a serious grudge against what they called Anglos. "What do you want?" I asked, hoping they'd understand English.

"*Cómo te llamos?*"

I think he was asking my name, as though that mattered. This didn't seem like a friendly visit. I noted a cart drawn by mules sitting several yards behind the strangers' horses. It was stacked high with cattle hides. As my senses came around, I began to realize that they were in fact hiders. They had come upon me accidentally and were apparently disinclined to have witnesses to their crimes. Can't say that I blamed them, but I wasn't hankering to become a victim to cover up their lawbreaking.

The one-eyed man still had the rifle aimed toward me. About the time he thumbed back the hammer, I heard a whoosh and saw an arrow sink deep into his chest. His eyes widened in surprise as he slumped in his saddle, coughed once, looked back up with a pained expression, and slowly slid from his horse and into the Texas dust.

The man who had asked my name turned toward the threat, but before he could speak, an arrow found its way into his throat. He fell on his face, gave an involuntary shudder, and passed away.

The third hider turned and galloped away as fast as his horse could carry him. He rode a big dun with a dark rump that I figured to not forget in case I ever ran into him. As it was, my heart was pounding as with a thousand drumbeats.

A grim-faced Wild Horse stepped from a nearby stand of mesquite and cacti. His knife was in hand as he moved to the first body. The hider that had been shot from his saddle was barely breathing as Wild Horse grabbed a handful of his hair and placed the knife along the hairline. As he was about to slice away the hider's scalp, Wild Horse must have felt my eyes upon him. He sighed, dropped the man's head, and shoved the body to the ground. He reluctantly put his knife away.

I smiled. "Thank you, friend," I said. He was learning. By now, I had recovered my rifle and gun. My first actual encounter with death had been with my own family, and I was too caught up with grief and anger to be revolted by it. Even the near-death of the Kiowa warrior hadn't bothered me so much. My heartbeat eased. I stopped to more fully scrutinize and contemplate the two dead men, then found myself overcome with nausea. I nearly threw up.

We had no shovel to dig graves, nor did we have time. Our snooze had set us back. I swallowed hard. Despite the evil intentions of these men, did they deserve a prayer? One of them had been about to kill me. I closed my eyes, but words of prayer wouldn't come to my lips. No matter what had driven these men to pursue a life of lawbreaking, they had become pure evil. "We go?" I asked, regretting leaving the bodies exposed to scavengers. I mounted up.

Wild Horse nodded grimly and mounted his pony. "We go," he repeated.

He rode up alongside me.

I realized that he had taken one of the hider rifles along with its ammunition.

Wild Horse lifted the rifle and pretended to shoot. "Jack teach." He seemed overjoyed as he urged Tuhibitu forward at a brisk walk.

As we rode past the wagonload of cattle hides, I couldn't help but think on what a waste they were destined to become. Maybe the escaped hider would come back for them. Maybe not. On the lawless prairie, there wasn't a whole lot my Comanche friend and I could do about it. We definitely didn't want to be bogged down hauling a wagonload of hides. It occurred to me that the Bluecoats might come upon the wagon. That was unlikely, but it would slow them down if they did.

As we rode on a mile or so from our encounter with the Mexican hiders, a terrible odor wafted its way to us. We passed the first of several skinned beef carcasses. I couldn't help but wretch, though I managed to not vomit. Wild Horse reacted about the same.

"Brown men bad," he finally said to me.

What could I say? Every race seemed to have its sinful players.

Now, I got to thinking whether Wild Horse shooting the hiders relieved him of the life debt. He had saved my life twice now. Were we even? He wasn't acting like it, but I'd know for certain when we arrived at the Penateka Comanche encampment.

———

ON THE THIRD DAY, we crossed another river. The nights had been getting chillier, but we dared not build a fire and risk having it alert the Bluecoats. Even a mesquite fire with its minimal smoke could tip them off. I felt confident that we could count on George to do his very best to slow them.

"We close," Wild Horse informed me.

Visions of facing White Knife and Buffalo Hump turned over in my mind. What might it be like? How might they react to the Bluecoats turning down the trade? Would I see Kate and Buck? How would Blue Flower act? Such uncertainty. So many questions. I prayed silently but fervently.

Wild Horse must have sensed my uncertainty. He motioned me to ride beside him, as though that would offer protection. The trail wasn't getting any easier, which led me to believe that we were drawing closer to his encampment. There had been no sign of the Bluecoats. With George guiding them, it was a fair assumption they could be a full day or more behind us.

"When we reach Penateka people, my father send scouts to find Bluecoats," Wild Horse assured me.

In our naivete, we assumed that Captain Granger would attempt to negotiate for the Comanche to free Kate and Buck. In any case, there was no way more than three dozen mounted soldiers with their pack mules of supplies could approach undiscovered. The fact that they were well-armed with the most modern military weapons available would do them little good against an attack by experienced, well-prepared warriors on their home ground.

THIRTEEN
BUFFALO HUMP

THE TRAIL BECAME NARROWER and a tad rougher, so I dropped back and fell in behind Wild Horse. We rode silently. The ponies were tired, but this was not the time to travel afoot. Wild Horse was acting extra cautious, as though sensing that we were now being watched. The fact that he was the son of a chief likely accounted for us not being confronted. I wasn't sure what was going through his mind, but it seemed likely that he was trying to figure out what might be the best approach for telling the chiefs that the Bluecoats would not trade for the White captives.

The sun cast an orange glow as it sank toward the western horizon behind us. Billowy clouds were tinged with hues of purple and gold. It was surely a majestic sight, but I dared not look back and dwell on it. I said a prayer to myself for our safety.

We rounded a bend in the river, the trail widened, and dozens of teepees came into view.

Wild Horse raised his hand for us to stop.

I moved up beside him and looked over at him questioningly.

I almost fell off my pony as he extended his hand to me.

"Jack and Wild Horse brothers," he stated in no uncertain terms.

I took his hand as we locked eyes for a seemingly interminable time.

"Stay close," he advised and urged his pony forward at a slow walk.

In but a few feet, we had drawn the attention of several women and children. Briefly glancing over my shoulder, my peripheral vision caught several sentries falling in behind us. They had likely been following us for a while.

Wild Horse sat his pony erect and held his head high.

I followed suit. It was clearly important that neither of us show the least bit of weakness. By now, we were both much older and wiser than our fifteen years. We had much to be proud of. Wild Horse and I were not sniveling sorrowful boys crawling into the encampment.

Blue Flower was standing before her father's teepee as we approached. She gave us a look of curiosity crossed with admiration and respect.

Kate slipped in slightly behind her with Buck at her side. His young eyes were big as saucers as he beheld me in the company of a Comanche. He had a white-knuckle grip on Kate's hand.

About ten yards from Buffalo Hump's teepee, Wild Horse halted, slid from his pony, and motioned me to do the same. So far as I could tell, the teepee was larger than most in the camp and decorated with all manner of symbols that I reckoned signified his status as a chief.

Wild Horse and I approached Blue Flower. "Where *ap?*" asked my new brother.

She said nary a word but motioned for us to enter the teepee.

I winked at Buck as we eased past him and Kate. I ducked extra low to keep from embarrassing myself by hitting my head on the entrance flap.

Wild Horse and I found ourselves standing in front of a fire. On its opposite side sat Buffalo Hump, White Knife, and two other warriors I had not yet met. There was a momentary awkward silence.

It was obvious that they were prepared for our arrival. My senses that we had been watched along the trail were validated.

Buffalo Hump motioned for us to be seated. He even gave me just a hint of a smile, while White Knife scowled. The shaman was clearly not happy. A pipe was lit.

"Welcome home, *Kobe*," said Buffalo Hump.

That was apparently a cue for Wild Horse to speak. "*Ap*, this *Isa*," he said, motioning to me. I suddenly realized he'd referred to me as *isa*, the wolf. Apparently, he sought to invoke big medicine.

Buffalo Hump nodded and passed the pipe to me.

I reckoned this was a recognition of my place in the circle. I felt honored. I took a pull on the pipe and slowly let out the smoke. I thanked God that I didn't cough as I silently passed the pipe to Wild Horse.

Blue Flower appeared as if from thin air and passed gourds filled with something other than water but not peyote to each of us.

Buffalo Hump turned to White Knife as if signaling him to speak.

The shaman's scowl became more of a tight-lipped

countenance as he seemed to measure his words. He wore a heavily-beaded white buckskin shirt and a full-feathered headdress. "Bluecoats trade?" he asked, as though he already knew the answer.

Wild Horse glanced at me and then locked his eyes on the shaman's, as though testing White Knife's resolve. "No," he said firmly.

White Knife turned to Buffalo Hump, flashing a condescending I-told-you-so smile.

The chief was not to be so easily affected. This was his son and his son's friend. "What answer?" he asked Wild Horse in the Comanche tongue.

"Bluecoats no trade *numunuu*," answered Wild Horse. "Many come to free *tosas*."

Buffalo Hump nodded. He turned to the two other warriors whom I had yet to meet and said something in a near whisper too low for Wild Horse and me to hear. The chief looked directly at me. "Jack strong medicine. Wild Horse say you speak with straight tongue." He weighed his words. "*Tosa* girl and boy your people."

I nodded respectfully.

The chief passed the pipe again.

The air was thick with the thoughts swirling among the guests, as not a word was uttered. The pipe made another round.

Blue Flower reappeared with Kate and Buck in tow. My sister wore the necklace I had Wild Horse pass along to her. She and Buck stood nervously, as though awaiting some terrible fate. It wasn't as though they hadn't already endured a scary but blessedly brief time with the Comanche.

White Knife stirred the fire. "Jack strong medicine," he said, as though reminding us of what we already knew. "Jack stop Bluecoats."

Now, there was a huge challenge. The shaman was saying that my strong medicine could stop the Bluecoats. I figured that even with George on our side, we weren't likely to dissuade the captain from carrying out his orders.

Wild Horse gave me a helpless look, as though clueless as to how to counter the shaman's provocation.

I looked over at Kate and Buck standing off to the side. They were innocent. They'd done no wrong to deserve this fate. I hadn't a clue as to what led me to say it, but I blurted, "Jack talk to Bluecoats."

Wild Horse's eyes grew wide as saucers.

Blue Flower gasped.

Buffalo Hump's jaw nearly dropped, but he held his chin high.

White Knife simply smiled. There was a devious, almost evil feel to his smug smile. He nodded. "You go. *Tosas* stay."

It was obvious to me that Kate and Buck were now officially hostages.

Buffalo Hump stood to signal the end of the meeting. He appeared deep in thought. "*Kobe,* go with Jack."

White Knife made a motion to protest, but the chief waved him off. "I have spoken," he said in Comanche.

––––––––

ONCE WILD HORSE and I were outside of the teepee, he turned to me. "Jack, pray to God for help."

The very idea that he was recognizing God caught me fully off guard. "We both pray, my brother." I expect that I was making some sort of progress in bringing Wild Horse to faith in the God I had worshipped since I was knee-high to a grasshopper. What was second nature to me was new ground for him. Well, I'll be doggoned, but my young Comanche brother joined me in praying. It wasn't much of a prayer. Something like, "Dear God, help us persuade the Bluecoats to come in peace. Amen."

"We need good ponies," Wild Horse noted.

I figured he must be referring to Paint. Our travels were tough on the old girl. "We must find George," I reminded him.

He smiled knowingly. "Comanche follow George and Bluecoats."

I had forgotten that the Bluecoats were treading on Comancheria, and Wild Horse's people knew the land like the backs of their hands. They likely could have swept down on the mounted rifles had they been so inclined and inflicted quite a bit of damage. The warriors of the Penateka Comanche in the encampment likely had a three-to-one numerical advantage, but the Bluecoat weapons tended to even the odds. In any case, we didn't want any attack on the encampment, as women and children would be placed at grave risk. As I was about to ask Wild Horse when we would leave, White Knife walked by.

The shaman gave me a derisive look, as if to say he'd eventually have his way. It was clear that there was no love lost between us. As he walked on, he said something to Wild Horse. I don't know what it was, but my Comanche friend gave White Knife an angry—even defiant—look. Before this, Wild Horse had been respectful of the shaman, but that deference seemed to be wearing thin.

It was crystal clear that White Knife was stuck in the old ways of his people and committed to protecting them at any cost. He showed no interest in understanding the *tosa*. I was part of the invading horde of Whites that were overrunning the time-honored lands of his *numunuu*.

I sensed far more acceptance and wisdom in Buffalo Hump. I think he had a pretty-fair vision of what was coming, that the sheer numbers of Whites would overcome the Comanche. It wasn't difficult to see that he saw Wild Horse as the future leader of the Penateka Comanche who would teach his people the ways of the *tosa* and learn to live peacefully with them.

————

I HAD the luxury of spending the night in Buffalo Hump's teepee. He and Wild Horse made sure that they slept between Blue Flower and me. The chief had seen the way his daughter looked at me and wasn't taking any chances on me being of honorable intent.

The morning broke to reveal slate-gray skies. The air was dry, so we didn't expect rain. At breakfast, Buffalo Hump had indicated that the Bluecoats were a half day to the south. "We not take horses," he said with an ironic laugh. He saw no point in aggravating the soldiers but wanted to make his point that he could have harassed him had he so chosen.

I looked to Wild Horse who was laughing and chuckled in turn. I didn't figure it appropriate to overdo the humor.

As we finished eating and prepared to leave, Buffalo Hump took his son aside and spoke in whispered tones. Wild Horse nodded his head vigorously in understanding. From his facial expression, there was no question as to the serious nature of the chief's words.

Buffalo Hump pulled me aside, as well. Rather than speak, he gave me a buckskin shirt. It was plain but had none of the stains that my tattered shirt had garnered over the past few weeks. I felt honored at his thoughtfulness.

We emerged from the teepee to find Blue Flower holding the tethers of two ponies. The black was Wild Horse's pony, Tuhibitu, while the other was a chestnut pony, a stallion with a slightly lighter-colored mane and tail. He was spirited as evidenced by his snorting, whinnying, and just a bit of prancing with his forelegs.

I caught a cunning look from Blue Flower that said ride this pony if you dare. Not to be deterred, I walked over to him and got acquainted by offering a piece of fruit and gentle strokes to his forehead and neck. Amazingly, he calmed down right quick, much to Blue Flower's disappointment. I swung myself onto the pony's back, and he stood still as a rock.

Wild Horse handed me my rifle and revolver before mounting Tuhibitu. He was decked out in as much regalia as was permitted a youth who had not yet passed the tests to be a warrior.

Blue Flower handed us each a small sack containing venison jerky and pemmican for our travels. The look in her eyes spoke volumes as she handed a sack to me.

I gripped the sack, but she didn't release it until her eyes had taken a full measure of mine. *Uh-oh*, I thought. She was becoming a woman, and her intentions with me were becoming ever clearer. I figured to deal with the situation later. I had a budding friendship going with Wild Horse, the respect of her father, and what appeared to be a critically important mission ahead. I dared not mess that up.

As Wild Horse and I urged our ponies forward, two Comanche warriors joined us. Apparently, Stone

Thrower and Buffalo Horn would be accompanying us. I shot a questioning look at Wild Horse.

"My father take no chance, Jack," he advised me.

With my guns and plenty of arrows, we were a fearsome lot. With only four of us, we could travel far more efficiently than the Bluecoats. Importantly, we knew exactly where they were. We wouldn't be wasting precious time trying to track them.

———

THE SUN WAS JUST ABOUT OVERHEAD when we happened on two Comanche scouts. As I understood them with my barely adequate understanding of the Comanche tongue, the Bluecoats were about a mile ahead of us. They even described precisely where we would rendezvous. The plan was for us to appear on a hilltop in plain view of the soldiers. It afforded a good defensive position while enabling us to communicate that we wished to parley. Sure enough, it wasn't ten minutes later that we found ourselves atop a hill looking at a column of Bluecoats in the draw below.

I saw George stop the column and point up in our direction. I could have sworn that I saw his broad white-toothed smile, as he conferred with Captain Granger. A mere moment later, George, the captain, and another officer broke from the column and headed our way. A white cloth was tied to the muzzle of a rifle that George held high.

Wild Horse told our escort to hold fast as he cautiously headed down the slope with me alongside. We stopped at about halfway down and waited for the captain.

The captain halted roughly a half dozen yards in front

of us. "We meet again, Jack O'Toole." The way he said it was almost humorous, as though it was an ironic twist of fate. Maybe some grudging respect was brewing.

I glanced at Wild Horse and then back at the captain. "Greetings, Captain Granger."

"Do you understand our mission, Jack?" the captain queried.

I looked at George, who was clearly dying to give the captain worthy advice. I tried to look as grown-up as I could muster. "Captain, I am hopeful that bloodshed can be avoided. I am working to free my sister and brother, but your soldiers can only bring death and destruction. The Comanche wronged my family, and God will surely punish them. My pa taught me that, while the good Lord says in Exodus, 'an eye for an eye, tooth for a tooth,' He does not mean it as vengeance for past wrongs. Jesus was clear about that in His Sermon on the Mount." I paused to see whether my words were having any positive impact.

George couldn't hold back. "Don't stop, Jack," he blurted.

I continued, "The Comanche wish to live in peace. I am confident that I can free my sister and brother without shedding blood. You are outnumbered by the Comanche three to one. There is no reason for soldiers and Comanche to needlessly die. Does this make sense, Captain Granger?"

The captain was in a serious quandary. He knew my argument made sense, but he had a commanding officer who apparently didn't even consider folks of other races as human.

"Sir, may I have leave to speak?" George rode up beside the captain.

Captain Granger was desperate for a way to solve this

dilemma. He had no desire to place his troops at unnecessary risk but neither did he want to be branded a
coward or be court-martialed for disobeying orders. "Mr.
Freeman?"

"Er...privately, sir." George glanced at me and Wild
Horse as he urged the captain to back away.

George and the captain conferred for perhaps three
minutes, with the captain nodding and even smiling.
Finally, they finished their discussion and rode back to
Wild Horse and me.

Captain Granger smiled. "Mr. Freeman here has come
up with a plan that may answer our prayers, Jack...Wild
Horse." It was the first time he had actually recognized
my Comanche brother as being part of the discussion.
Perhaps we were making progress.

"What do you have in mind, sir?" I ventured.

"Mr. Freeman here, having spent time living with the
Pawnee, professes to understand that saving face is
important. If you and your friend Wild Horse were to
steal away your sister and brother from the Comanche,
we could chase you but never catch you. I could report
back to my colonel that we didn't engage the Comanche,
but your kin are free."

Wild Horse looked incredulously at me and then at
the captain. He shook his head. "Not easy, Jack. Not easy,
Captain."

I looked questioningly at him.

"White Knife angry. Get Comanche to hunt you and
your sister and brother...and me." He was essentially
telling us that it has a hair-brained idea.

I looked across at George and the Bluecoats. The
captain wasn't happy about attacking the Comanche
encampment, but orders were orders. George's wild idea
seemed the best solution. However, it would take Wild

Horse's cooperation to pull off the kidnapping that would be key to our success. "Wild Horse, my brother, we have no choice. You know my medicine is strong. We can do this."

Wild Horse could see the strong determination in my eyes. He looked at me, then at the column of Bluecoats nestled in the draw below, and then back at me. He sighed resignedly. "Big medicine, Jack. We do." He nodded to Captain Granger and boldly moved his pony forward beside the captain. He extended his hand.

The captain hesitated before overcoming his aversion to the Red man by grasping Wild Horse's hand. The deal was official.

"If I may, Captain?"

"Yes, Mr. Freeman," said the captain, fearing another crazy scheme.

"Perhaps I should trail after Jack and Wild Horse to be certain his kinfolk escape. I'll know what direction they head and can lead you on the chase."

Captain Granger thought on George's proposal. The entire plan was totally insane by any measure. If the Comanche decided to give chase, a battle could yet ensue. Did he have a choice? He could mass his men and head for the Comanche encampment. There would be bloodshed, maybe even his own. None of this was in any military manuals. "Yes, Mr. Freeman, you have my permission."

George looked over at me and Wild Horse. "There you have it. As my *vaquero* friends might say, *vaya con Dios*." He turned and followed the captain and lieutenant back to the waiting column of Bluecoats.

Wild Horse and I headed back up the hill. Upon reaching the crest, I looked about. Close to a hundred well-armed warriors were spread just behind the ridgeline. They were ready to attack had they been called to do so by Stone Thrower and Buffalo Horn.

———

AS WE HEADED to the encampment, Wild Horse rode beside me. Speaking in his halting English so our escorts would not understand, he shook his head and began with, "My father not be happy. White Knife be angry!"

He was stating the obvious. "You have better idea?" I responded.

He shook his head.

"This will test us, my brother." Test indeed.

We both knew that the shaman would gather warriors to pursue us. If they caught us, we would all die. The best Wild Horse might hope for would be his banishment from the tribe.

The warriors that had been at the hill had disappeared ahead of us. It was a reminder of the sort of force the Comanche could muster on but a moment's notice.

———

WE MADE our way along the river bank only to encounter a total surprise. Buffalo Hump had pulled up stakes. Not a teepee or Comanche was to be seen other than my companions.

Wild Horse smiled knowingly. He apparently had known all along.

"Where are they? Where did they go?" This didn't make sense, and it was going to make it more difficult to free Kate and Buck. I looked back to see whether George had followed us. I didn't see him, but I figured he was watching.

Wild Horse said nary a word but urged his pony around a motte of oak trees close to the river. Behind the trees awaited another surprise.

Blue Flower stood with two ponies and my sister and brother.

I was incredulous. I was about to leap from my pony to hug my kin when Wild Horse stopped me.

"Listen," he warned. "We must run." He waved to his sister to mount up, and he led us away at a gallop.

We had run hard for a couple of miles with Wild Horse leading the way when he finally pulled up beneath the sheer wall of a cliff. Blue Flower on one pony, holding Buck, and Kate on the second pony, had been barely able to keep up. Stone Thrower and Buffalo Horn had ridden with us. Apparently, they were loyal to Buffalo Hump and had been charged with protecting us.

Wild Horse turned to me. "This Buffalo Hump plan. Father wise. Not agree with White Knife."

"Why did we run?" I asked.

He smiled. "You did not hear Comanche in trees. White Knife set trap."

White Knife had apparently gone rogue.

"He will chase us," I opined.

Wild Horse shook his head. "Yes. We must run. He hunt us," corrected my Red brother. It would be a hunt, not a chase. He looked at his sister and smiled approvingly.

"Where?"

"My father say big water," he answered.

I gave him an incredulous look. The big water he spoke of was the Gulf of Mexico. His father had led hundreds of Comanche warriors to the big water fifteen years earlier. The chief had looted, burned, and killed. But, it seemed a good plan. "Buffalo Hump wise man," I observed. It remained to be seen as to whether the shaman would throw caution to the winds and follow us. When it was just Wild Horse and me, we could move along right quickly. With a five-year-old boy and two young girls having joined us, our risk of being caught by White Knife had increased substantially. The place where we were resting was well hidden but was only temporary.

Buffalo Hump had raised a wise son, and I had the good fortune to have saved his son's life. Whatever God had in mind, I was more than ready to follow.

FOURTEEN
ESCAPE

WILD HORSE CHECKED the boundaries of our temporary shelter. "We no rest long," he advised. He tended to our horses. The galloping pace had given them a good blow, but they seemed to be recovering quickly. The ponies couldn't sustain such a hard push without frequent rest and plenty of water. We would need to follow the Guadalupe River as much as possible.

I could see that my Comanche brother's brain was churning as he crafted our next move.

Finally, he turned to Stone Thrower and Buffalo Horn. "Must know how many hunt us. You stay. Guard *wa'ipu*. Jack and Wild Horse scout." Buffalo Hump's loyal warriors were turning out to be right handy.

I followed Wild Horse as he ran up our back trail to an overlook where we could see for about a mile. I was actually feeling rather appreciative of his having chosen me to come with him. I had hunted with my pa but was no scout.

"No like *aruka*. Wild Horse *pia wa'óo*," he whispered.

I understood immediately. We must be the hunters

and not the prey. "*Isa* ready," I responded, invoking my wolf spirit. Like the mountain lion, the wolf was a hunter. Wild Horse sought to turn White Knife into prey, *aruka* the deer.

We parted the tall grasses at the top of the overlook. We were downwind, so less likely to be detected. The skies remained overcast, but there wasn't even a hint of rain.

I pointed to movement in a ravine off in the distance to our left. There rode the shaman *Tosahwi*, leading perhaps a dozen warriors. He was resplendent in full regalia. The warriors were fully decked out in feathered headdresses, buckskin shirts, breechcloths, and moccasins. The black war paint covering the upper part of their faces gave them a sinister appearance. They would strike fear into the very souls of their enemies.

They carried plenty of weapons, including bows and arrows, lances, and war clubs. Those war clubs were especially nasty, and it sent a chill up my spine and a rush of anger upon recalling what they did to Samuel and Mary. The Comanche were focused on following the tracks left by our ponies. However, they moved very cautiously. I couldn't help but feel that White Knife feared my strong medicine. If he knew that it wasn't my medicine but that of my God, he'd be doubly fearful.

Wild Horse looked over at me and smiled. "*Tosahwi* fear Jack." Even my Comanche brother recognized the irony that lodged in the spirit of a powerful medicine man of the mighty Comanche being afraid of a fifteen-year-old boy...and a *tosa*, at that!

As we were about to leave, dust further off, nearer the horizon, caught my eye. "George and Bluecoats follow," I said, pointing.

Wild Horse smiled and held up two fingers to indicate

that Comanche and Bluecoats were hunting us. "We big prey," he said with a touch of irony. He motioned for us to go back to the cliff shelter. "Must move fast." He was anxious to put some distance between us and our pursuers.

As we ran down the trail, Wild Horse suddenly stopped. "We be *pia wa'óo* and *isa*." He clearly had something in mind.

"We hunt?" I asked as much as stated. He'd invoked the spirits of the mountain lion and wolf.

He nodded vigorously. "We hunt," he confirmed.

———

UPON RETURNING to the cliff shelter, we hustled to get everyone ready to hit the trail. I briefly but warmly hugged Kate and Buck. Oh my, but it felt good to have family in my arms again. "We will be safe," I assured them. It occurred to me that Buck hadn't said a word. I looked questioningly at Kate.

She shrugged. "He hasn't talked since home," she shared with sadness in her voice. Apparently, fear had captured his tongue.

I was resolved to iron that out once we reached a situation where we'd have a chance to deal with it. Meanwhile, we had to get moving.

Wild Horse had shared his plans with Stone Thrower and Buffalo Horn and decided to start out following the south bank of the river. Soon enough our party was strung out single file. The river was broad but shallow enough for us to wade across. We crossed several times in hopes of delaying White Knife, though we intuitively knew he was too wise for that tactic. Nevertheless, he'd be forced to follow us on the chance that we didn't recross the river. At any point, we could choose to head north or south.

I found the shaman not simply quickening his pace and catching up with us fascinating. We would have put up a good fight, but he had superior numbers. I think he sought to capture us, bring us back to Buffalo Hump, and make an example of us while showing off his power. Killing us would have been easy, but it would have proven nothing as to his spiritual power and his prestige as shaman among the Comanche.

As the sun's glow lit the breaking clouds on the horizon behind us into a fiery orange and purple glow, we sought shelter among a stand of pecan trees at the river's edge. Wild Horse built a small fire as though to taunt White Knife. He and I seemed to share a love of tormenting, even provoking our enemies. The chill in the air was caused by more than the cunning mission White Knife was undertaking as autumn lingered close at hand. Stone Thrower and Buffalo Horn took turns standing sentry duty while we ate and conversed in low voices, ever mindful of the threat to the west of us.

Kate held back from asking about how Ma and Pa and our sister and brother met their fates. She seemed comforted to know that I had given them a proper burial. She told little of her life in captivity, as much out of shame as fear. She had learned enough of the Comanche tongue to figure out that they were going to give her to one of the warriors as a third wife. The memory sent a revulsive chill through her body. Her story would eventually be told in her time.

The cloud cover had fully cleared, and a half-moon combined with the stars to cast enough light to navigate the rough countryside around us. If *Tosahwi* were to launch an attack, we'd escape across the Guadalupe River.

———

IT MUST HAVE BEEN midnight when Wild Horse shook me gently. He was wide awake and clearly had something in mind. "Jack, come," he urged. "Bring knife."

I stood up and shook off the sleep cobwebs. My Comanche brother was decked out in war paint and carried his full arsenal of weapons.

"*Isa* and *pia wa'óo* hunt," said Wild Horse grimly. This would be serious business. "We hunt White Knife sentries." Now, he smiled and rubbed his hands as though about to hatch a devious plan.

I followed Wild Horse as he headed us south and then westward.

It was slow going as we were upwind of our prey. Sounds and smells carried all too well in the moist night air. We ducked in and out of oak and cypress trees, cacti, Mexican buckeye, and clumps of tall Indian grass for at least two miles.

All of a sudden, Wild Horse stopped. Roughly twenty feet in front of us was a Comanche sentry standing alert to his surroundings. White Knife was not being so careless as to not guard his camp. Perhaps a couple of hundred yards off, we could see a campfire.

Wild Horse motioned for me to stay where I was. He used his lance in the moonlit dirt to illustrate his plan to circle around behind the sentry. At his signal, I would make the sound of *isa*. That would distract the sentry, as Wild Horse acted as *pia wa'óo* and attacked the warrior. I'd then close in to help. Wild Horse gave me a piece of rawhide that I was to give him once the sentry was subdued. The sentry was not physically large, but he was surely a seasoned fighter.

I waited patiently, watching the sentry as Wild Horse silently circled behind the Comanche. It seemed like hours but was likely no more than fifteen minutes. At last, I saw Wild Horse crouched no more than ten feet from the unwary sentry. I saw his hand wave. With that, I did my very best imitation of a growling wolf.

That got the sentry's full attention. He took a guarded step in my direction just as *pia wa'óo* jumped him and brought him down hard. The Comanche tried to make a sound, but Wild Horse reached around and stuffed Comancheria dirt into the warrior's mouth.

I ran over, but Wild Horse had the situation well in hand.

He rolled the Comanche onto his back and seated himself on the sentry's chest with arms pinned under Wild Horse's knees. He looked down at his prey. He knew this warrior. "You dishonor my father," said Wild Horse. The sentry's eyes were wide with fear and he was choking on the mouthful of dirt that Wild Horse wouldn't let him cough up or swallow. I placed the rawhide strip in my brother's hand, and he proceeded to bind the sentry's wrists.

I now realized that Wild Horse had no intention of killing a fellow Comanche. He was going to disable and embarrass the proud Comanche warrior as a warning to White Knife.

Wild Horse got up and pulled the warrior to a sitting position. He allowed the sentry to spit out the dirt. "No sound," he warned. The threat was clear.

The captive warrior finally realized that I was standing with Wild Horse. He'd seen me in the Penateka Comanche encampment with Buffalo Hump and knew of my strong medicine and all-powerful God. Word traveled fast among the *numunuu*, the people. There was total fear in his eyes as he looked from me to Wild Horse and back.

"Jack, take weapons." I dutifully gathered the sentry's weapons.

Wild Horse glared at his Comanche captive. "Go back to Buffalo Hump. No follow White Knife," he told him in no uncertain terms.

The Comanche nodded his head vigorously. He was already totally embarrassed at having been taken captive by a pair of teen boys. He much preferred facing Buffalo Hump and receiving some level of mercy.

Wild Horse gave the warrior a carved wooden totem of some sort. "Give to my father. He no kill." This was assurance that his life would be spared, though he faced punishment for allying with the shaman.

As to White Knife, he now had one less warrior in his band. I was impressed that my Comanche brother had come up with a strategy of attrition. We would wear down the shaman. Importantly, we were a team. *Isa* and *pia wa'óo* were brothers of the hunt.

We sent the sentry packing. With his weapons taken, there was no way he'd face White Knife. He would find his way west and rejoin Buffalo Hump.

We headed back to our camp.

Stone Thrower nodded as we reentered, smiling at our obvious indication of success.

MORNING BROKE WITH CLEAR SKIES. We quickly prepared to continue our escape from White Knife's evil intentions.

I was preparing to mount the sorrel stallion when I felt a hand on my arm.

"Where go at night?" asked Blue Flower.

I caught Wild Horse's warning look as I turned to Blue Flower.

"Where?" she repeated.

Wild Horse called over in the Comanche tongue. "*Tosahwi* have one less warrior." It was all that needed to be said.

Blue Flower looked back at me and smiled that winsome way she had with the corners of her lips turned up. "Strong medicine," she said and mounted her own pony.

Wild Horse rolled his eyes. "We must go...fast." He knew White Knife would be beside himself with anger.

Kate rode up beside me. She was becoming ever more comfortable with the likelihood of escape from her Comanche captors. "What was that about, Jack?"

"Wild Horse and I eliminated one of White Knife's warriors."

"You didn't kill him, did you?"

I shook my head in the negative. "He will fight us no more. Now come, we must ride hard."

We no longer crossed and recrossed the Guadalupe as we continued our escape. It did concern me that as we headed eastward, we would run into more *tosa* and even Bluecoats. My brother and others of my new Comanche family would be in ever-increasing danger.

There were many folks out there who figured the only good Indian was a dead one. The prejudices against Red men, Blacks, and Browns ran deep among a certain element of Whites. I racked my brain, trying to think on where we might find sanctuary. Meanwhile, we had to escape White Knife. God had led us down this path, and we'd have to trust in Him.

FIFTEEN
BLUE FLOWER

BRIGHT SUNSHINE GREETED us on the third day of our flight across Texas. During the night, Wild Horse and I had eliminated one more of White Knife's band. It would become more challenging, as the shaman would surely respond by putting out two sentries instead of one.

Having awakened early and despite the chill air, I headed to the river to wash away the accumulated trail dust. I had begun to strip off my clothes when I heard soft voices upriver. I considered my next move. Tempting as it might have seemed, there was no way I wanted to view my sister or Wild Horse's sister bathing. My Ma told me that discretion was the better part of valor—or something like that. My bathing would simply have to wait.

I had just pulled my pants back up when I found Blue Flower and Kate blocking my path back to the campsite. I can't say that I necessarily had a well-muscled physique, but God had endowed me with a muscle or two.

The girls' hair was wet, but they were both fully

clothed. Kate lowered her eyes with a sisterly blush, while Blue Flower seemed unable to take her eyes from me. For the first time, her feisty demeanor turned to a blush.

I thought as fast as my pea brain was able. "Shall we eat breakfast?" was the best I could come up with.

Blue Flower graced me with a smile that was provocative beyond her years, or at least beyond the years of any Christian girl of good moral character.

I picked up my shirt and hat and began to move back toward our campsite. God sure was testing me. As I walked past the girls, I felt Blue Flower's eyes more than follow me. It was as though they had tentacles reaching out to pull me in. I was relieved to encounter Wild Horse as I neared the campsite. I gave him a look that screamed for help.

Wild Horse just smiled. I think he was getting a perverse enjoyment from watching me deal with his sister.

Blessedly, we were soon back to the task of escaping. We dared not linger.

———

AS WE MOUNTED our ponies and had taken the first few steps along the river bank, we found our path blocked.

White Knife sat on his horse tall. He was formidable by any measure. The shaman was resplendent in his medicine man regalia. Five Comanche warriors loyal to him were behind him. It appeared that the mysterious disappearance of a couple of his trusted band had caused others to desert. They apparently decided that *Tosahwi's* medicine might not be so powerful after all. He'd apparently decided to end the hunt on his terms while he still had warriors loyal to him.

I stared him down. It was strong medicine versus strong medicine. My Springfield rifle lay across my lap, and it didn't take me but a split second to ease back its hammer. The Colt remained fully loaded in my waistband. All was silent. It was as though we were frozen in time. In the back of my mind, I wondered how close George and the Bluecoats were.

Kate had ridden up beside me. I passed the Colt to her. I knew she could shoot, and she might have to.

White Knife was sizing us up. How strong was our medicine? How tough was our resolve?

Wild Horse joined in the stare-down. Had it not been so serious, it might have been comical.

Finally, I decided that enough was enough. I looked up to the sky, folded my hands, and said a prayer, "Lord, I ask for protection for us. Please give me strength in what I am about to do. Amen." I could tell that Wild Horse understood most of my prayer.

White Knife looked perplexed.

"What are you doing, brother?" whispered Kate.

I ignored her. Wild Horse, Blue Flower, and our two loyal Comanche warriors looked on in wonder at what I might be up to. Buck sat in front of Blue Flower with a vacant look in his eyes, as though the moment was beyond the prison of his fear-damaged mind.

"*Tosahwi,* go!" I commanded. Imagine a teenager telling a battle-toughened warrior to leave. After weeks with Wild Horse and dealing with all manner of challenges, I guess I had grown up right quick. I took the Springfield rifle in both hands and raised it menacingly above my head. "Go or fight!" These were bold words tumbling from my lips. I laid the rifle back across my lap.

Staring down at White Knife a mere twenty feet away, I watched his facial expression. Beneath the war paint was a man with a serious dilemma. Who would blink first?

Finally, the shaman spoke, "*Tosa* all free. Wild Horse and Blue Flower come with me."

How about that? The man who held my sister and brother for ransom was offering a last-gasp deal. He figured he still had power over his own people. White Knife pointed to Wild Horse and motioned him to join his band. I expect he figured if he got my Comanche brother to cross over, that Blue Flower and the others would follow.

"Wild Horse stay with *Isa*," responded Wild Horse, invoking the wolf spirit. He had been taught respect for his elders, but the shaman had pushed beyond the bounds of respect.

White Knife's face grew hard from the combination of anger and frustration that swept through him. He could feel power slipping from his grasp.

"What y'all got goin' on here?" The familiar deep voice of George Freeman resonated across the clearing. Behind him were Captain Granger and his mounted rifles. Forty rifles were pointed the shaman's way.

White Knife's jaw just about dropped to the Comancheria dust. "Hee-yahhh!" he yelled and urged his pony to a full gallop westward. He shot past us like his pony's tail was on fire. His band followed.

George motioned with his head for us to take off so as to resume the faux chase by the Bluecoats.

We obliged.

———

WE QUICKLY PUT a few hundred yards between us and the Bluecoats, finally coming to a halt only to rest our ponies.

"Is anyone following us?" asked Kate.

Wild Horse laughed. She had no idea that the chase by the soldiers was a ruse to save face.

"What does your Comanche friend find so funny, Jack? What is going on?" she persisted.

I did my best to explain the situation to her, concluding with, "The only real danger was White Knife, the Comanche shaman. He has been embarrassed, so he is still a threat to us. We'll have to remain watchful."

"What is *isa*, Jack? And *pia wa'óo*?"

"I'll tell you tonight, when we camp," I responded. We needed to continue our escape, and there was no time for long stories.

Blue Flower walked over to Kate and me. "*Tosa* girl carry little *tenahpu*." Wild Horse's sister had decided she'd had enough of carrying Buck's extra weight on her pony and that Kate was certainly capable of tending to her brother.

Kate looked at me questioningly.

"Blue Flower says Buck will ride with you," I explained. "We won't be moving so fast, Kate. You can do it."

Blue Flower offered one of her increasingly alluring smiles at me for supporting her request. "Jack strong medicine, strong warrior," she said in her Comanche tongue. "Jack *isa*," she added.

I had a vague idea as to most of what she said. Normally, I'd be bust-a-button proud, but I didn't want to further encourage her attraction to me.

I was relieved when Wild Horse walked over.

"We must go, Jack."

"Are Stone Thrower and Buffalo Horn staying with us?" I asked, seeking reassurance.

"Loyal to my father. They stay."

With that, we all mounted up and continued our escape. I reckoned that at some point, George would catch up with us and the chase by the Bluecoats would end.

_____

WE CAMPED CLOSE ENOUGH to the Guadalupe River to hear its swirling currents. I recalled that a fellow named Colonel Kinney had built a ferry crossing near a place called Corpus Christi. I figured that we were as yet a good way from the ferry. Importantly, it would signal that we were very close to what we White folks called civilization.

Stone Thrower was standing first sentry duty.

The night was especially clear. There seemed to be a million stars twinkling above us. Needing some private time to think about what my future might hold, I strolled over to the river bank and sat near a pecan tree. It wasn't but weeks earlier that I'd been fishing not so far from here. I longed for my fishing pole and my family homestead. In fact, we were so near that I gave a fleeting thought to visiting what had been our home for nigh unto two years. Likely, I could have dealt with it, but I didn't figure the others were ready. I began to think on the future. I was totally absorbed in these reflections. The rushing waters of the Guadalupe had a soothing effect.

"Jack?"

I started at the sound of my name whispered. The

voice was all too familiar. Blue Flower was determined to catch me alone.

She magically moved beside where I sat and gazed out at the river. "River good. Stars good," she said in halting English.

I didn't look up. "Yes...good. What are you doing here?" It occurred to me that she had applied some sort of fragrance as a sweet aroma wafted over me. Dare I stand? Where was Wild Horse when I needed him? I stood up but still didn't look at her.

Blue Flower moved closer to me, then paused as she faced me. All of a sudden, her eyes grew wide. Her hand grasped the grip of my Colt revolver, yanked it out, and, before I could stop her, she'd aimed it past me and pulled the trigger. The blast was like that of a cannon echoing through the night air. I had no idea she even knew how to use the gun.

I grabbed it from her hand.

She stood aghast. Her hand covered her mouth, and she began to sob great trembling sobs. A moan and then a low wail emerged from deep within her.

I pivoted to see a lifeless form lying alongside the riverbank. There was no doubt as to whom it was. "*Tosahwi!*" I exclaimed. The shaman had doubled back with the intention of ending the grip my strong medicine had over him.

By now, everyone was wide awake. An unexpected gunshot on a still night will tend to do that.

Wild Horse was first to run to the shaman's side. He looked up at me and nodded his head, confirming White Knife's death. "Bad medicine," he said hoarsely.

By now, Blue Flower, in her anguish, had buried her face in my chest.

Blessedly, Kate came over, embraced her, and eased her away from me.

"Thanks, sister," I mumbled as I joined Wild Horse. "How did he get so close?" I asked.

Sadly, it didn't take long to find Stone Thrower's body. White Knife had not only killed the brave warrior, but mutilated him. The deed had been done likely out of anger over the warrior's loyalty to Buffalo Hump.

I hardly had time to think on all that had happened when I realized that Buck was crying. It was the first emotion he'd shown since the attack on our homestead. I ran over and kneeled before him, holding his little shoulders in my hands. Tears were streaming down his cheeks.

"J-J-J-Jack," he blurted as he pressed himself to me.

"You're safe now, Buck. You're safe." My, but I prayed those words rang true.

Blue Flower was still grief-stricken at what she'd done but had mostly stopped crying. She walked over to me with Kate's reassuring arm around her. "*Tosa* talk?" she said. It caught me off guard, given the horror of just minutes before.

I hugged Buck for but another minute and motioned to Kate to take him. I had to help Wild Horse and Buffalo Horn to prepare to honor the dead Comanche. The tribe had its burial rituals. White Knife would be so honored despite his recent deeds.

We began to gather long pieces of wood to build the traditional burial scaffolds. White Knife had no wife, but Stone Thrower's wives were with Buffalo Hump. They would grieve when they eventually learned of his death. For now, there would be no women grieving over the dead Comanche.

About the time we finished the scaffolds, George appeared. Upon the gunshot echoing through the night, he'd been given permission by the captain to investigate. He'd ridden up quiet-like on that big horse of his. "Y'all alright?" he asked.

"George, all is just fine," I responded.

"Well, what was the gunshot about?" he said, looking from me to Wild Horse.

"Shaman bad. He die," responded Wild Horse.

"But there's two..."

"Stone Thrower with Big Father," added Wild Horse.

"White Knife was going to kill me. He killed our sentry, Stone Thrower. Blue Flower saw the shaman and shot him with my gun before he could get close," I explained.

George nodded. He looked at the long faces gathered around our campsite. Finally, he smiled. "It looks as though God was lookin' out for you again, Jack."

As I thought on it, if Blue Flower had not sought me out at the riverbank, I very well could have been killed and my scalp decorating White Knife's lance. I looked at her with her tear-reddened eyes. Yes, she'd been at the right place at the right time and acted from her heart to save me. I so wanted to embrace her in thanks, but I still dared not. I surely didn't want to jeopardize my ever-strengthening bond with Wild Horse. Still, the fragrance of her perfume hung on my senses.

"Y'all have any eats?" George broke the melancholy silence.

Kate took up the task while Wild Horse and I built a fire.

We were soon chowing down on the last of our food supply. Naturally, we blessed our meal. With George there, we couldn't overlook that. We'd have to do some hunting the next day if we were to avoid starving.

"Where do we head now?" I asked Wild Horse.

He looked thoughtfully into the flickering flames of our campfire. "We make peace with Penateka."

I guess it made perfect sense. I would want peace with my earthly father.

We actually made conversation, as we sat around the fire. Kate talked about replacing her buckskin dress with a new cotton one. Buck hadn't yet asked about the fate of our family, but I figured that would eventually happen. George got on fine with Buffalo Horn, chatting in some combination of Pawnee and Comanche.

"We head west, my brother?" I asked Wild Horse.

He nodded. "You come?"

"We brothers," I replied. Was there any doubt after all we'd endured together? "Wild Horse need Jack's strong medicine."

I was just about knocked clean over with his response.

He pointed to the stars and responded, "God protect us." Wild Horse clearly wasn't referring to his *Taa Narumi*.

"Wild Horse wise," was all I could say.

Blue Flower had sat mostly in silence during our meal. Much weighed heavily on her young mind. Finally, she looked my way. Her facial expression was worth a thousand words. It was disarming.

Wild Horse looked from his sister to me and could only smile. He laughed and held up ten fingers. "*Suumaru puuka.*" He chortled. Her dowry was ten horses. Finally, he grew serious. "We sleep. Ride in morning."

I suppressed an urge to take Blue Flower in my arms. There would be another time, another place. Perhaps I was wiser then I thought, but this seemed not the time or place. As I headed for my blanket, George interrupted.

"I better head back and report to the captain. He'll be

pleased," he said for all to hear. He then wrapped one arm over my shoulder and pulled me along on the way to his horse. "You're doing the right thing, Jack. Get to know these people. God has you on a path. Stay with Him," he counseled. As he placed his foot in the stirrup, he whispered, "That Comanche girl has a thing for you, Jack. Don't you be doin' anything dumb."

I smiled knowingly. "Not to worry, George. Safe travels, *via con Dios*."

I waved to him as his image faded off into the starlit night. Returning to my blanket, I found that Wild Horse had moved his blanket between mine and Blue Flower. He wasn't taking any chances.

THE TRAIL WEST was now a lot easier, knowing that rogue Comanche and Bluecoats weren't tailing us. Over the next two days, I managed to keep Blue Flower at bay while reveling in my little brother Buck coming out of the dark cloud that had held him. The slow pace gave me time to ponder the future, though events of the past few days hung heavy.

Along with the joy of freeing Kate and Buck, an ever-closer friendship with Wild Horse, and ending the threats from the shaman and the Bluecoats, it had begun to more fully hit me that gaining Kate's and Buck's freedom came at the price of lost lives, deceitful ruses, and displaced loyalties. To top it off, I now had the added weight of responsibility for my brother and sister.

Would my dream of breeding horses ever come to reality? Was this all God's plan? Would he use evil means to achieve worthy ends? It seemed a contradiction. I was deep into this thinking when Wild Horse slowed and fell in beside me.

He placed his finger to his lips to indicate silence and

pointed to the ground. There were dozens of hoofprints. They were unshod. Wild Horse dipped low from his pony's side, reached into a clump of Indian grass, and picked up what appeared to be a piece of red cloth.

I tried to read Wild Horse's thoughts. Who did the cloth belong to? Were the riders of the ponies a threat? They couldn't be our Kiowa friends, and the Penateka Comanche were much further west.

"Apache," he finally whispered knowingly.

I had heard little of the Apache during my brief days in Texas or of their reputation. To my limited knowledge, they roamed far to the southwest of the Penateka Comanche lands. They barely encroached upon the Comancheria. From the size of the Apache band, they outnumbered us by nearly two to one. If they were of a mind to attack, we'd be at a distinct disadvantage. We motioned Buffalo Horn to join us as we took stock of our situation.

By this time Kate and Blue Flower had grown curious as to what we were huddling about. Naturally, they rode up to join our circle.

"We stop?" asked Blue Flower.

"We saw Apache sign," I advised. "They may be watching us." Actually, they were likely sizing us up for an attack.

Wild Horse pointed to a motte of live oak atop a slight rise that afforded a good view of the surrounding area. If the Apache had ill intentions, it would serve as a good defensive position.

I thought on that. My gut told me that was what the Apache would expect. But what was the alternative? Only four of us were armed. Buffalo Horn and Wild Horse had their bows and arrows, lances, and war clubs. Kate had my revolver, and I had the trusty Springfield rifle.

Formidable would not describe our armament. My mind raced to come up with an alternative to Wild Horse's plan.

My Comanche brother had already begun to lead us toward the motte.

I pulled up. "No," I called out decisively. I pointed to a stand of trees a hundred yards in the opposite direction from the live oak motte. "Follow me." I dug my heels into the sorrel's sides and headed for the trees at a gallop.

Blue Flower didn't hesitate to follow me. She must have figured my strong medicine was at work. Kate followed with Buck holding on for dear life.

Wild Horse and Buffalo Horn nearly waited too long. A half dozen Apache appeared at the very motte we'd been heading toward.

Thankfully, the raiding party hesitated. This allowed us to establish a true defensive perimeter among the trees.

I dismounted and grabbed the Springfield. I got down on one knee and took a bead on the Apache that I thought might be their leader. I squeezed off a shot and watched as a piece of the savage's headdress went flying. I hadn't killed him, but I sure got his attention.

Wild Horse and Buffalo Horn did the best they could with a couple of arrows, but the range was a tad long.

I fired off another round and hit one of the Apache horses. I guess I was getting too close for their comfort as they moved away from the motte.

Finally, the Apache who had felt my first shot rode to the crest of the knoll with his hand raised. I could see blood on the side of his face. I'd nearly sent him to meet his maker and apparently knocked some sense into him. It simply wasn't going to be a good day for the Apache warrior. He pointed his lance down, then turned and led his band away.

"They no fight," observed Wild Horse.

We all breathed guarded sighs of relief.

"We camp here," I announced.

Wild Horse left his defensive position and walked over to me. "How you know?" he asked.

I shrugged. I wanted to invoke *isa* and strong medicine, but I knew my strong medicine was my faith. I had simply sensed danger. Had God spoken through me? Finally, I simply pointed to the sky.

Wild Horse nodded. "God save *tosa* and Comanche." He was learning, and our bond was growing.

Kate came over with Buck in tow and hugged me.

Blue Flower simply stared incredulously at me. She sat cross-legged behind the tree where she'd jumped from her pony to hide from the Apache.

"Are you folks going to stand around?" Even little Buck started picking up sticks for a fire. Moments later, we were blessed when a deer strolled within Wild Horse's shooting range. A single arrow provided us dinner and more. As I helped field dress and butcher the deer, I thought on the dangers we'd yet be facing. A wild-haired idea crept into my mind. I looked to the heavens, "Are you sure?" I mumbled just loud enough for Wild Horse to hear.

"What?" he responded.

"I have an idea...a plan," I said, gazing off momentarily.

Wild Horse was major curious now.

"There is danger for Blue Flower, Kate, and Buck."

Wild Horse nodded in agreement.

"I propose that we take Kate and Buck to Fort Inge.

They will be safe there. Then, we can go to your people." It seemed like a perfect plan.

Wild Horse had seen enough of my supposedly strong medicine and, most recently, avoiding the Apache ambush to trust my instincts. "My brother wise. Plan good," he affirmed.

It seemed so simple.

"Send Buffalo Horn to Penateka. Tell my father," suggested Wild Horse.

I liked having the extra protection that Buffalo Horn afforded us, but I really couldn't argue with my Comanche brother's thinking. Buffalo Hump needed to know that we were alright and that the threat from White Knife had been ended.

We'd finished butchering the deer. *"Ana o'a hi'it,"* I pleaded. I was ready to eat.

Wild Horse laughed at my broken Comanche. "You good *tosa* brother, Jack."

The girls had a good cooking fire going. Before long, we had venison sizzling along with some late-season berries Blue Flower had gathered. We would bed down with full bellies this night.

Once again, Wild Horse bedded himself down between his sister and me. He was taking no chances, and I was pleased to avoid the temptation. If God was testing me with this girl, he was sure giving me a tough exam.

UPON AWAKENING, I realized that Buffalo Horn had already headed out on his journey to the Penateka Comanche encampment. With what appeared to be another sunny day ahead, the rest of us took our sweet time preparing to head south to Fort Inge. Unsaid was the aim of letting that Apache band get some distance on us. We sure didn't fancy encountering them again.

Ahead of us lay the hilly landscape of central Texas in the belly of the Comancheria. Wild Horse and I had trod this territory before on our way to deliver the Comanche ransom message, so we had a pretty good idea of what we faced. Allowing for walking the ponies and occasional rest stops, we had about three days of travel ahead of us.

While a straight line would have been more efficient, the hills, valleys, and streams of the landscape led us along a path that seemed to meander all over. We regularly checked the position of the sun to ensure our course southward. From what we could recall of the trail ahead, there'd be sheltered places for camping and access to plenty of water. What could possibly go wrong?

Ever since the terrible tragedy at the homestead, God seemed to be protecting me. I felt his presence more than once, and it was clear that Wild Horse was coming into the fold. Maybe, just maybe, that was what I was being led to do. A new dimension had been added with Blue Flower. I wondered whether she was in God's plan for me. Actually, I was startled that I had begun to think about that possibility.

By my estimate, we had journeyed a little better than twenty miles when the perfect camping shelter came into view. There was a rocky overhang that afforded shelter on three sides, a panoramic view of the surrounding landscape, and a reasonably lush grassy place to hobble our ponies. We brought along some of the venison from the previous night, and it had held up well. Had we time, we'd have made some venison jerky, but that was a tall order during our travel.

As we sat around the campfire, Kate finally asked a

question that had been lingering in her mind ever since she and Buck had left the Comanche encampment. "Jack, what are we to do? What of the future?"

I glanced at Wild Horse and Blue Flower before answering. My ever-tighter bond with them was coloring my thinking. "Far as I know, the homestead is still ours," I ventured, now aware that it had been taken from the Comanche. "Pa wanted to breed horses, and I'm inclined to do that. I love the beasts. They're right beautiful, and good stock fetches plenty at the market. We could make a living."

Kate chewed on that a moment. "What of our Comanche friends?"

I had never discussed my plan with Wild Horse. With Blue Flower now in the picture, she hadn't been in my consideration either. In a way, I almost felt as though I needed their permission, even though the powers that be had granted the property to my pa. "What Wild Horse think?" I asked.

Blue Flower spoke before he could open his mouth. "Love ponies," she offered hopefully, as she smiled all-too-warmly at me.

Wild Horse nodded. His beloved sister had her own mind. "Whites own land. Comanche not own land." He paused in deep thought. "White father offer treaty to Comanche. Want to give us Comanche land," he said with an ironic sort of grin.

"How can our people sell the Comanche the land they've lived on for many years, Jack?" Kate quickly grasped the failure of the government to truly under-stand the way the Comanche and other tribes saw the land.

Wild Horse was quick to respond, for he had a strong inkling as to the future. "*Tosa* have their way. Many *tosa*, few Comanche." He recognized the unending stream of Whites that would soon fully overrun lands that had been hunted by his people for centuries. He had accepted that reality. "Many fight ahead," he added, knowing that there would be resistance.

Kate turned to Blue Flower. "Do you agree?"

Wild Horse translated for her.

"Love ponies," said Blue Flower with a glance at Jack. She quite clearly had other things on her mind than the clashes of competing cultures.

"Jack breed plenty pony," said Wild Horse, attempting to change the direction of the discussion. "Jack breed pony on land Comanche give."

I can't say I was displeased with the outcome, but there was still the question of what was to become of Kate and Buck. "We'll build a bigger cabin, Kate. There'll be plenty of room for you and Buck."

"What if?" My ten-year-old-going-on-eighteen sister was already thinking on a family future.

I laughed. "We have time, sister. Don't you be worrying just yet." I was secretly thankful we'd put Kate's concern to rest...for now.

Wild Horse took a walk around the vicinity of our campsite. Upon his return, he took me aside. "See more Apache sign," he advised. "Same Apache."

I cogitated on that for a moment. "We know trail. Travel at night," I suggested.

He nodded in agreement.

Now, it remained to figure out how to spend the day without alarming the girls and little Buck.

I had the answer. "We will tell Blue Flower and Kate that we need to rest the ponies for the tough trail ahead. One of us can bag another deer, and the girls can make jerky and pemmican."

Wild Horse nodded. "Plenty deer." With that, he picked up his bow and arrow and was off before I could say another word.

"Where did Wild Horse go?" asked Kate upon my return to camp from talking with him.

"We will rest here. The trail ahead is very rough. Very tough on ponies. Wild Horse will hunt deer. You and Blue Flower can make jerky and pemmican for our travels." I figured that I'd explained our plan plenty thoroughly.

"Then what?" she asked.

I sighed. "We travel at night."

That put a chill on further questions as Kate figured out what I was alluding to.

———

I WAS mighty grateful that game was plentiful. The rutting season was close at hand, and deer were beginning to fatten up for the winter. Wild Horse returned with a big-antlered buck right soon after he'd departed. He avoided the does, as he feared the rut might come early and he looked forward to plenty of hunting in the spring.

We set to work helping Blue Flower and Kate by cutting venison strips for jerky and grinding meat for the pemmican while they gathered berries. We'd be eating well on the trail, the horses would be well-fed and rested, and the travel by stars and moon would be a bit safer.

We had one undesirable visitor. As Buck was chattering away and helping where he could, a rattler had the boldness to coil itself in the youngster's path. The scene unfolded as though in slow motion as I threw my knife from about six feet away and it found its way through the snake's head. Buck was startled but safe. Of course, Blue Flower was impressed. To be honest, I never gave the knife throw that much thought. I'd been carving pieces of wood during our rest stops and throwing it at unsuspecting trees. I guess I was getting fairly accurate with it.

Wild Horse skinned the snake. I recalled that he'd given me the tail of a rattler he'd killed, so I did the same for him. I hadn't a clue as to what that meant, but he seemed pleased. He stroked the mountain lion claws of his necklace. It seemed that we collected these animal parts to evoke memories of our time together.

Oh, naturally, we cooked and ate the snake. The critters do make good eating. Even Buck liked the delicacy.

We kept busy pretty much all day, even taking turns going down to a water hole below our campsite and washing away the trail dust. I much appreciated no further uncomfortable bathing encounters with Blue Flower.

As the sun began to settle on the western horizon, sending out its majestic tapestry of gold and purple hues, we packed for the ride ahead. We'd travel more slowly and do less walking, so it was good that the ponies were well-rested.

We headed out single file. Wild Horse led the way while I brought up the rear. My job was to be sure that Blue Flower and Kate kept up. Buck now rode quite comfortably with his sister, and the pony handled the load well.

The hills at night were an adventure unto themselves, as moonlight cast shadows we might not see during the day. It was quiet, save for the occasional muffled sound of unshod hoof on rock or the distant sounds of coyotes howling or owls hooting.

We seemed to make a fair pace, stopping once at a creek to water the ponies and ourselves and another time simply to rest. At the first sign of daylight, we began to look for a sheltered place to spend the day. By sheer luck, we happened upon the Frio River. We'd made very good time in our journey to Fort Inge.

It finally occurred to me that we needed a plan for temporarily housing Kate and Buck at the fort. I wondered whether we might find a better place in Encina, the little cluster of a town just north of the fort. If I could keep Colonel Loring out of our plan, I reckoned to feel better.

SEVENTEEN
BLUECOATS AGAIN

WE EASED into Encina on the third day of our southward journey. I had shared my idea with Wild Horse of finding some nice folks in the little town but had not told Kate just yet. Also, there was the question of whether Blue Flower would return with us or stay with Kate and Buck.

Encina was small, very small. Apparently, some fellow named Reading Black had laid out the town. It featured a store, a couple of nearby rock quarries, a lime kiln, and an orchard.

We could see sheep grazing on the grasslands beyond Encina. It's hard to imagine how we must have looked meandering into the town. A couple of Comanches and three Whites plodding single file up the narrow main street. I noted that Mr. Black had some sort of plan because areas for plazas had been laid out. He sounded like someone I should get acquainted with.

We pulled up at a stone building. I dismounted and knocked on the door.

"Hang on a gosh-darned minute!" came the cry from within.

I looked back at my entourage. "Somebody's home," I observed with a hopeful smile.

The door opened with a black-clad gentlemen giving me the once-over. He scanned my companions. "Who ya be, where ya headed, an' what ya lookin' for?" he asked directly.

I cleared my throat. "My name is Jack O'Toole. My sister and brother are over yonder. Our homestead up on the Guadalupe was attacked by Comanche but we survived. The Comanche with us are our friends." It was about as short an introduction as I could come up with. "We are headed to Fort Inge, but..."

Black gave me a look that combined suspicion with curiosity. "You Christian folk?"

"Yes," I responded.

He stared at Wild Horse and Blue Flower. "All of ya?"

"Yes, sir."

He drew out a bandanna and blew his nose. "Dang chill nights," he apologized. "My name is Reading Black." He shook my hand. "Y'all look tired. Come on in. Bring yer friends."

I signaled everyone to follow me inside.

Black motioned us to be seated at a large oak table. "Y'all be lucky. I was just fixin' to tend my sheep. Expect they can wait a bit. Dang wolves have been at 'em."

Wild Horse and I exchanged a knowing glance.

"Now, what did y'all say yer purpose was to travel to the fort. Trouble?" he inquired as he served up some coffee and laid a plateful of buttered biscuits on the table. He nodded to help ourselves.

Kate was about to reach out when I stopped her. "Gotta bless it, sister."

I offered a short blessing. Even Blue Flower bowed her head, though she had no idea why.

"Git ya some bacon shortly," enjoined Black.

I reckoned it was up to me to explain ourselves. "We've dealt with Kiowas and Apaches, chased off hiders, and fought off mountain lions. I saved Wild Horse here's life from mountain lions, and we became friends. He helped rescue my sister and brother from his people." I left out the ransom part of the story. "Wild Horse has an obligation to his people, but I don't want to put my brother and sister through what might be difficulties ahead. In wanting to keep them safe, I thought to leave them in the care of the soldiers at Fort Inge. However, the colonel has ill feelings toward the Red man. He even sent troops with orders to attack Wild Horse's people."

"Hmmm," said Black. "I'm friends with the local Tonkawas but have had a tough time with the Comanche. I sympathize some with the colonel, though I'm a Quaker and do try to avoid violence."

I raised my eyebrows a tad but continued, "After helping my Comanche friends, I figure to head back to my homestead and breed horses with my sister and brother. Wild Horse and his sister will help."

"That's quite a tale, Mr. O'Toole," observed Black. He pondered my story. "I could use a woman's touch 'round here."

I prayed that I was making the right decision for Kate's and Buck's sakes. Black seemed to be a solid enough citizen. I looked at Kate and Buck. Kate was surprised, and Buck looked as though clueless in trying to wrap his five-year-old mind around the situation. I regretted not sharing my plan with them, but what was done was done. "What do you think, Kate? I'll return in a couple of weeks, and we'll head home."

Tears welled up in the corners of her eyes. We'd

already been through so much together, and now it seemed as though I was abandoning them.

I put my arm around her, but she shrugged it off. I felt helpless. I looked to Wild Horse and Blue Flower for help.

Blue Flower shook her head before looking up. "Kate strong. Jack strong medicine. Come back for Kate." She was actually trying to help me.

"God has been protecting us so far, Kate. I promise I won't be long."

"Blue Flower stay with *tosa*," suggested Blue Flower.

Wild Horse raised his eyebrows. "Father not be happy."

She smiled defiantly at her brother. "Me Comanche woman," she stated proudly and quite emphatically.

Wild Horse could do naught but shrug. She wasn't going back short of being hog-tied and thrown over the back of a pony.

I turned to Black. "Would this be okay with you, sir?"

Black was weighing the obligation with its benefits and shortcomings. He'd have plenty of help around his home but risked the ire of folks carrying anti-Indian sentiments. His faith in God won out. "I figger it'll be alright," he finally replied. "Y'all better git back here afore the snow."

I was overjoyed but tried not to show it. "Wild Horse here and me still need to visit the fort. We'll stop by on our way north to be sure all is well."

By now, it appeared that Kate was warming to the situation. Having Blue Flower with her would surely help, but spending more days in the rough, hilly landscape of central Texas was daunting. I'm sure she longed for the days not so long ago, when she was helping Mary and my ma with chores around our homestead. The prospect of doing decidedly normal chores around Black's home was a vast improvement over camping and certainly her days doing the dirty work in the Penateka Comanche encampment. In fact, she had no desire whatsoever to revisit the Comanche village, even as a guest.

Black turned to the girls. "There's a spare room thataway," he said, pointing up a dimly lit hallway. "I 'spect the young'un can stay with ya."

"Thanks kindly, Mr. Black. We'd best be getting on with our business at Fort Inge," I said. Wild Horse and I hugged our sisters, and I kneeled low for Buck. "You take good care of these ladies while we're gone, Buck. We'll be back in no time." We bided no further time but bade farewell to Mr. Black and headed out on our ponies.

———

WITH JUST THE two of us, we made it to Fort Inge right quick. The guard was the same one on duty at our supposed imprisonment on our previous visit. He seemed to bear no grudge, as he called for an escort to take us to the colonel.

I sure hoped that the corporal who escorted us was not typical of the garrison. He looked down his decidedly long nose at us, as though we were the dregs of the earth. "You boys say you been here before?" He halfsneered. "He don't take kindly to Injuns or them's friendly with them."

"Colonel Loring knows us, Corporal," I replied with a respect he hadn't earned.

He gave a derisive laugh. "Colonel Loring got hisself replaced, Injun lover. Yuh gotta deal with Colonel Steele," he snickered. "You scalped anybody lately?" he added, not letting up with his disrespect.

I'd had enough. I arose as tall as I could muster on my pony. "You looking for a haircut, Corporal?"

Guess he figured me to be physically big enough and likely tough enough for a young man not to take me on. He suddenly grew tight-lipped and escorted us in silence the rest of the way to the colonel's headquarters.

"These er...travelers say they must talk with Colonel Steele," the corporal told the guard on duty.

The guard was hardly any better than the corporal so far as attitude. "The colonel don't see just anybody without an appointment. Y'all going to have to wait."

"Would you please tell him that Jack O'Toole is here about Comanches?"

Just then, who should happen by? Yep. George Freeman. "Jack...Wild Horse. Thought I heard your voice, Jack. What brings you here?"

"We felt it right to assure the colonel that my sister and brother are safe, and he need not pursue the Comanche."

George gave us one of his broad, toothy white grins. Out-of-earshot of the guard, he advised, "I don't think the colonel cares, gentlemen. Given half a chance, Colonel Steele would march the entire garrison on the Comanche camp. Here tell he's an Injun hater through and through."

"Does he know that Apache raiding parties are in the hills? Is he aware of the hiders rustling cattle and selling hides? It's not just about the Comanche, George." I expect I was feeling more confident in expressing myself to adults, as even George was taken aback.

"You do make some good points, son. Guess it wouldn't hurt for Colonel Steele to hear firsthand." George turned to the guard. "I'll vouch for these young men. They must talk with the colonel immediately."

The guard gave a nod. "I'll ask," he said reluctantly as he proceeded to knock on the colonel's door.

There was a scuffling from within the office, followed by footsteps. The door opened to reveal Colonel Steele, upright, unshaven, and with just a hint of the aroma of alcohol. He was no young sprout and clearly not happy to be assigned to Fort Inge. "Don't just stand there gaping. Come in!" he commanded us. He tottered over to his desk and sat as we stood before him.

"Get that translator fellow in here," he snarled, motioning to the guard to escort George into the office.

"My friend speaks English, Colonel," I ventured.

The glare he threw back at me could have cut me in two. "You talk when you're told, boy!" He proceeded to shuffle some papers before looking up at me through rheumy eyes. He sure didn't seem to be enjoying his Texas command.

I glanced around the office. Nothing special stood out save for a couple of official-looking framed certificates on one wall. There was a bookcase with a couple of well-worn books.

The colonel struck a match and lit the oil lamp on his desk. "What are you boys doing here? I understand you're the boys that nearly cost Captain Granger a court martial but for the ni...um, I mean scout, here."

"My sister and brother are safe, sir. My friend Wild Horse's father freed them. We're going to go back to our homestead and breed horses. I felt it important to let you know, sir. The Comanche did the right thing."

The colonel looked dead-on at Wild Horse. "I'm awaiting orders to corral those Injuns and put them on a reservation. If they resist, I'll kill them all."

I stood stunned. I could see anger welling up in Wild Horse's face. We needed to leave Fort Inge quickly. "Sir, I

just wanted to let you know"—I swallowed hard—
"there's more, sir." I struggled to be respectful. "We
faced Kiowa and Apache on our way here. Apache are
getting especially active." I didn't figure to offer details.
"We'll be leaving now, Colonel."

"You'll leave when I say so," commanded the colonel.
"I've a mind to punish you for your disrespect of Captain
Granger."

I glanced at Wild Horse and then at George.

"By your leave, sir?" George spoke up.

"You have no voice here, Sergeant," he said,
expressing his dislike of the Black man in no uncertain
terms.

It was the first time I'd seen George get angry. "I ain't
your sergeant no more, Colonel." He tore off his stripes,
gathered us up, and stalked out.

"Lieutenant! Lieutenant! Stop them! Arrest them!"
shouted Colonel Steele as he drew his sword and began
waving it about.

The guard nearly shut the door in the colonel's face
as he waved at us to leave. "Go before he gets the whole
garrison after you!" The guard held no love for the
colonel and must have figured it worth earning the
colonel's ire by helping us escape.

Wild Horse and I dashed to our ponies, grabbed our
weapons, mounted up, and headed out on a dead run.
The corporal at the gate had no time to react.

George ran off to gather his things before following
us. Turns out he did much more. Not one to miss an
opportunity, he opened the corral gate and stampeded
most of the horses the Bluecoats relied upon.

We could hear Colonel Steele's shouts behind us as
we headed north toward Encina. We galloped about a
mile before stopping to wait for George.

"*Eekasahpana paraiboo* bad," spat out Wild Horse in angry Comanche. The colonel was indeed bad. Wild Horse was still seething about the officer's disrespect. He made the motion of the bow and arrow, followed by mimicking scalping.

"After Jack," I responded, pointing my thumb at myself. I wanted to pound some respect into the old officer, though, in reality, my inbred respect for elders made that unlikely. I could think it, but not do it.

For Wild Horse, it was another matter. I—and a garrison of Bluecoats—was all that stood between him and the colonel. As we waited, he began to cool down. "What we do, Jack?"

"I don't think it wise to leave Blue Flower, Kate, and Buck anywhere near Fort Inge. If the colonel hears they are connected with us, it could spell trouble."

Wild Horse nodded. "We must still go to my people," he reminded me.

"I think George will help us," I said confidently.

Just about that moment, George rode up to us. "It's chaos back there. The colonel will be chasing us. We'd better ride!"

"Wait, George."

He pulled up.

"We're going to get the girls and Buck up in Encina and head to Wild Horse's Comanche encampment."

He stared thoughtfully at me for a few seconds, then smiled. "Of course." He headed his horse north toward Encina, and we scampered to catch up.

———

READING Black's house was dark when we pulled up. But for the moon and stars, we'd have ridden past it.

I swung down from my pony and ran to the door, banging on it furiously to rouse the girls. I soon heard footsteps, and the door opened to reveal a disgruntled Mr. Black, who didn't especially care for being awakened.

Black looked at us through squinty eyes, then fumbled for his spectacles. "Who the...oh...what in God's name do you want at this hour?"

"Mr. Black, there was a problem back at the fort. Colonel Steele is none too happy." I hoped I was getting through to him. "We need to take Blue Flower, my sister, and Buck and head home." I thought it best not to mention the Comanche encampment.

"Slow down," said Black. "What'd y'all do to get the colonel riled?"

I was brought up short by his challenging me. "He doesn't take advice from folk my age, and he doesn't like Comanche and Black men. He wanted to hold us at Fort Inge."

Black scratched his chin as he searched for an answer.

As if by divine providence, George and Wild Horse strode up behind just as Blue Flower and Kate, with Buck in tow, appeared behind Mr. Black.

"What's going on?" asked Kate.

Black looked around bewildered. He was outnumbered and being out-thought.

"The colonel is coming after us. We need to leave," was all I could say for the moment.

George was more definitive. "Gather your things, ladies. We're leaving pronto."

Faced with a large black man, Mr. Black decided discretion was the better part of valor. "Er, do as you must," he said resignedly. "Colonel don't like my sheep, no how." He might have had mixed feelings about races and cultures but seemed sorry to see us go. Guess he'd accommodated having Kate and Blue Flower around to help with his house.

Wild Horse and I helped the girls gather their belongings and Buck while George fetched their ponies from the corral.

We were ready to go in seemingly no time at all. We were traveling light for sure.

As we mounted up and prepared to ride out, Mr. Black walked up to me. "Y'all are welcome to visit any time." With that, he handed me a sack. From the aroma wafting from it, we wouldn't be going hungry.

"Much obliged, Mr. Black. We're grateful for your hospitality."

"I'll tell the colonel that y'all headed east," he said with a devilish grin.

In a heartbeat, we were headed northward.

EIGHTEEN
APACHE REDUX

THE TRAILS WERE GETTING EVER MORE familiar for me. We traveled as silently as possible, though Wild Horse and I continued to learn each other's languages at rest stops. Even Blue Flower and Kate joined in. A school-marm might have been proud.

Wild Horse always took the lead, as his ability to sniff out danger was far better than any of us. I continued to ride in the rear, ever keeping my eyes and ears alert to our backtrail. George would alternate between riding alongside Wild Horse or me as the landscape permitted. I was concerned that Colonel Steele might be chasing us.

Buck was holding up pretty well, considering all he'd been through. I expect it all seemed like some grand adventure to him. I'm not sure he fully understood what had happened to our family. After he came out of the trance-like state he'd been in with the Comanche, he began acting like a five-year-old might be expected to. I think our present journey was like a game to him. In fact, he seemed to be at his happiest when we were walking the ponies and he got to sit on the pony's back by himself. I did have a gnawing feeling that, at some point he'd wake up from this odyssey to realize that Ma and Pa were gone. Kate shared that same anxiety with me. I also feared how Buck might react at the Comanche encampment.

As we made our way northward, I had plenty of time to think. In a way, I missed the adventure Wild Horse and I had before the girls, Buck, and George joined us. There seemed ever less time for us to connect and bond our friendship.

Bugles or war whoops? I had a feeling we'd encounter one or the other. All I could do was trust in God to protect us. We'd come a long way and had already experienced far too many flirtations with danger for my liking.

———

WE WERE CROSSING the Sabinal River on the morning of the second day following our run-in with Colonel Steele at Fort Inge. The food Mr. Black had so graciously provided was already getting low. We'd have to hunt for food sooner rather than later.

As I rode past a tree along the bank of the river and prepared to cross, I heard a whiz followed by the thump of an arrow that stuck in an overhanging branch. It was too close to my head. An Apache war whoop followed along with more arrows and a couple of gunshots. Why the savages had waited to attack me at the rear of our party was beyond my immediate understanding.

Wild Horse, Blue Flower, and Kate, with Buck aboard, had already crossed. George was midstream but turned back to me as he realized we were under attack.

I slid from my pony and took cover with my Springfield rifle at the ready.

George had cleared leather and launched several shots in the general direction of where he figured the attack was coming from. He headed for my position, dismounted, and slipped in alongside me.

Silence.

Where were they?

Wild Horse and the girls were hunkered down on the opposite river bank. Kate had the Colt revolver at the ready.

Still silence.

"I think they messed up their ambush, George," I whispered.

He nodded. "They're out there figurin' what to do," he responded.

"Wish to tarnation they'd show themselves," I added. I strained to look over to the other side of the river. Wild Horse signed that he had no clue as to where our attackers were.

All of a sudden, there was all sorts of war whoops, gunfire, and at least a dozen Apache frantically escaping past us through the shallows of the Sabinal River.

We didn't have long to wait as to who or what had flushed them out. A band of a couple of dozen horsemen galloped past with guns blazing. It was a sight to behold!

At least two Apache fell before our eyes. One got up, only to be shot again. The pursued and pursuers soon disappeared from our sight. Only the occasional sound of distant gunfire reached our ears.

"That was Captain Nate Benton leading those men, Jack. He's a Texas Ranger. I met him back at Fort Inge just a couple of weeks ago."

"Texas Rangers?" I asked.

"Tell you later. Let's cross over and get on up the trail."

I was curious but had no choice but to save my questions for later.

"What happen?" asked Wild Horse after we crossed over.

"George says those were Texas Rangers. Expect he'll tell us more later."

"We need to get going," insisted George.

We resumed our travels, though it took a while to shake off the ambush. It seemed we couldn't be too vigilant, and even that was no guarantee.

George fell back alongside me as we walked the ponies. "From what I understand, the Texas Rangers were started up about thirty years ago by Stephen Austin to protect settlers. They were more like militia than lawmen. They travel in companies like we saw today and are heavily armed. They are tough men and fight tougher. I've never known one to back down from a fight.

"About ten years ago, fourteen Rangers under Captain Jack Hays routed eighty some Comanche up on the Pedernales River. They called it the Battle of Walkers Creek. With Colt revolvers blazing, I hear tell they wiped out half the hostiles."

"Do they work with the Bluecoats?"

George laughed. "Not if they can help it. They don't like to fight by the Bluecoat's rules," he added in his deep voice that resonated up the valley we'd meandered into.

"What do you mean?" I asked as we all stopped to water the horses.

"I heard at Fort Inge that a Texas Ranger captain named Callahan pursued Apache into Mexico, fighting and kicking the Injuns all the way. The Bluecoats can't do that...or won't," George explained.

"How come?"

"They call it diplomacy. The United States doesn't want to upset the Mexicans."

"Sort of ironic, George," I suggested. "We fought off Mexican hiders. They didn't belong here."

"Yep, that's the irony of it, Jack. And those thieving Apache go back and forth across the Rio Grande any time they please." George chuckled. "And those Mexicans resent it, our folks chasing the savages. They call the Texas Rangers *rinches*."

"*Rinches?*" I asked.

"It's sort of like a nasty word they call us Black folk."

I nodded. *Rinches*. I cogitated on that. I reckoned I just might come to appreciate having those Texas Rangers handy.

"What call Blacks?" interjected Wild Horse out of curiosity.

"Nothing you need to hear, my Comanche friend," responded George.

I whispered what I thought the word was in Wild Horse's ear.

He shrugged his shoulders.

Kate looked at me curiously.

"Let's get going. If we keep stopping, it'll be winter before we know it," I said with a nervous laugh at having changed the subject.

"Go ride up front with Wild Horse, Jack," suggested George.

I rightly obliged. As I rode past Blue Flower, she gave me one of her ever-warmer smiles. She sure was pretty, and I sure was smart to resist. I was relieved to pull up beside Wild Horse.

———

THE TERRAIN WASN'T GETTING any easier, but we were making reasonably good progress.

"Apache bad medicine, Jack," observed Wild Horse.

I figured my Comanche brother was looking to open a larger conversation. "They sure are," I responded.

Wild Horse's face spoke volumes as to his line of thought. "Texas Rangers strong medicine." He was seeing God's work in this.

"They came at right time," I said, reinforcing his perspective.

"We thank God?"

"Yes, my brother," I responded. There really was no accounting for the Texas Rangers having arrived at precisely the right moment except that it must have been God's timing. Was it God's work or simply chance? It was all about trust and faith. What if the Texas Rangers hadn't arrived when they did?

"Apache on Comanche land," said Wild Horse out of the blue.

I hadn't figured the Comanche, Kiowa, or Apache owned land, though they were territorial. The Apache seemed more interested in raiding White settlers and testing the strength of the Comanche than in grabbing territory. We were in the midst of a culture war between the two tribes.

"You must tell Buffalo Hump," I suggested.

Wild Horse grinned. "My father know."

I was confused.

"Texas Rangers kill Apache. No Comanche die."

Wild Horse was telling me that his people had recognized how to take advantage of the *tosa* guns. The Comanche would let the Whites take the risks.

I shook my head ruefully. "Texas Rangers fight

Comanche," I opined. Wild Horse's people weren't getting off the hook.

"God let that happen?" Wild Horse asked.

"Comanche kill *tosa*, Texas Rangers kill Comanche." It was actually quite simple.

"But God good," he insisted. There seemed a sudden resolve in my Comanche brother to warn his father.

"But evil punished. Killing is evil," I warned. Forgiveness didn't wash away punishment. Much to our distress, the clash of cultures was beyond Apache, Kiowa, and Comanche. If Wild Horse were to embrace God, he'd need to understand this and trust in God's attributes. Shucks, even I struggled with embracing God's attributes. The world around us made it tough at times. Nevertheless, trust was the focus.

We dismounted. It was time to give our ponies a rest.

George strode forward. "Couldn't help but hear y'all."

That drew Kate's and Blue Flower's attention. They seemed to be waiting for a contribution from the mostly silent Black man.

"What about punishment, George?" I asked.

He tossed that around in his head for another moment. "Y'all set a spell," he said, motioning us to sit. "There's punishment, and there's punishment," he said, then smiled at the confusion in our faces. "There's punishment as a penalty for wrongdoing, and there's undeserved punishment for the sake of control. If I steal a loaf of bread, the honest work of another, I must be punished for my deed. Who delivers that punishment is another matter. We live under a system of laws, God's and man's. God's law says, 'Thou shall not steal.' Man's law says that if you steal, you will be judged by a jury, and if found guilty, you'll be punished. Whites have these laws. Pawnees have them. Comanche have them.

Mostly, the punishment suits the crime. Man's law mostly lines up with God's law."

"You said punishment for control, George. What's that?" I asked.

George's face grew serious. "When I was owned by another, I was whipped to remind me that I was a slave. The overseer showed his power and control that way. It wasn't right, but that's the way it was."

Wild Horse got up and stroked his pony's neck. All that George and I had talked about was new to him, and it had made a deep impression. "Why evil?" he challenged.

"Why good?" I responded. "Because good wins, evil loses."

"Why evil?" he repeated.

I shrugged.

"God sent his Son to deliver us from evil, but He didn't destroy evil. I'm afraid we must deal with it as best we can," added George.

Blue Flower's thoughtful expression showed that she was grasping the conversation despite her limited understanding of English. "*Numunuu* evil?" she asked.

"There's some evil in all of us. We place our trust in God to give us the strength to conquer it."

Wild Horse translated my words for her.

"We'd best be gettin' on," George urged. "I'll take rear point."

––––––––––

IT HAD BEEN my hopes and prayers that we were done with the Apache. Fate would deem otherwise.

We reached the banks of the Guadalupe River on the afternoon of the third day. We were ever wary of dangers that might be lurking. Wild Horse was in his usual position leading our little band. The first clue that something was wrong was the buzzards circling. Wild Horse dug his heels into his pony's ribs and sprinted ahead.

I followed.

Wild Horse came to an abrupt halt. He looked at what lay ahead, turned, and signaled everyone to give the area a wide berth.

I caught a glimpse of what he'd seen, and it was as ugly as anyone could imagine.

As Wild Horse rode past me to lead the others around the scene, he said in a low voice, "Apache. Comanche kill."

A half dozen Apache lay in the Texas sun. They were buzzard bait, having been tortured to death. I wasted no time returning to our band.

"What was that?" asked Kate as I rode by.

My face had become suddenly pale despite weeks in the Texas sun. "Nothing for your eyes, sister," I blurted. What more was there to say?

Wild Horse must have said something to Blue Flower, because she looked terribly unsettled. She put her heels to her pony and caught up to me. "Was bad medicine, Jack?"

I nodded. My addled brain was at a loss for any verbal response. Despite her fourteen years among her people, she'd never seen the horrors they could inflict upon their victims. I had seen what the Comanche did to my mother, but the Apache were another matter. Their ends spoke volumes of hatred and a clear warning to stay clear of Comanche territory.

As George caught up to me, Blue Flower gave me a strange look and fell back.

"Did you see, George?"

"Nope. I figured the reaction of you and Wild Horse spoke volumes. Weren't no point."

I decided to put the scene behind us by changing the subject. "What are you figuring to do after we meet with Buffalo Hump?"

"Let's see how that turns out, Jack. I sure can't head back to Fort Inge. The folks down there won't be offering a friendly welcome," he said sarcastically. "Been thinkin' on ranching up toward Wyoming and the North Platte country."

One question had been lingering in my mind, and I finally asked it. "You ever think of settling down? I mean, a family?"

If George could have squirmed in his saddle, he surely would have. "Interesting question, Jack," he responded. "Maybe...with the right woman...maybe."

I smiled. It was an honest answer.

NINETEEN
THE NUMUNUU

AS WE TRAVELED EVER CLOSER to Wild Horse's people, I found myself praying ever more fervently. What awaited us? Would we be welcomed? Knowing that White Knife had met his fate was little comfort.

Having George and his hardware with us gave me a greater sense of security, though we'd be easy pickings for a couple of hundred experienced Comanche warriors. I hoped and prayed that Wild Horse's ever-deeper acceptance of my faith, in combination with the life debt he still held to, would serve as a protective bulwark against any aggression.

The rolling hills soon gave way to the meandering waters of the Pedernales River. A recent drought in the region had slowed the flow considerably. Rain would have been welcomed. I could see that Wild Horse and Blue Flower couldn't suppress their excitement at returning to the *numunuu*, the people.

We rounded a bend in the river, and Wild Horse pulled up. He scanned the trees and grasses, then smiled. "We camp here." We were drawing close to his people, and he figured to enter the encampment well-rested.

It was clear that we were being watched. We all sensed it. Shucks, the Comanche could have been standing in plain sight and it would have been nearly impossible to see them.

"I'm going to keep an eye out," said George. He wasn't taking any chances. While the girls busied themselves with the fire and digging out the last of the pemmican and jerky, George would keep watch.

Kate pulled me aside as she and Blue Flower built a campfire to take the chill from the early evening air. "Must we go?"

"You and Buck will be safe," I assured her. In my mind, I was crossing my fingers and toes. Could we fully trust the heathen Comanche?

Wild Horse walked over and motioned me to join him. We walked off along the river bank. We stopped under a large cypress that spread its wings out over the riverbed. He seemed to be carrying a heavy load on his mind.

"Jack go home...Wild Horse go home," he said, opening the conversation.

It looked as though we were going to be splitting up, going our separate ways. "Wild Horse is brother," I reminded him.

He nodded. "Jack strong medicine. Strong God. Wild Horse bow to God."

I was blown away. He was quite literally telling me that he was following God. The question that yet lingered for me was the nature of his belief. It wouldn't do for the God I shared with him simply being more powerful than his *Taa Narumi*. I had to trust in God. I recalled my pa telling me that whatever a man sows, so shall he reap. I expect I'd sown quite a few seeds with my Comanche brother, and I'd have to trust in that. Plus, it struck me that my anger and desire for vengeance had transformed into forgiveness and redemption. "Wild Horse wise brother," was all I could come up with.

"We brothers as sun rise and set."

That pretty much seemed to be forever.

Wild Horse then took me totally off guard by embracing me. Yes, it was a man hug, but it symbolized our bond as men of God. He pulled away. "Jack, pray," he said.

"Lord, please watch over my brother Wild Horse and keep us all safe under your ever-watchful eyes. May we live in peace and meet again in your holy name. Amen"

"Amen," Wild Horse added.

We returned arm-in-arm to the campsite.

Upon seeing our smiles, everyone seemed to be uplifted. All would be well.

We ate the last of our food, told stories, and laughed as the fire died down to flickering embers.

As I pulled the blanket up over me, I realized that Wild Horse no longer bedded down between me and his sister. Blessedly for me, she kept a decidedly respectful distance, though she smiled at me just as I was closing my eyes. I must admit she was getting inside my head. She'd been mostly quiet during our journey, though I suspect that may have been Wild Horse's doing. The image of her beauty gave me peace as I drifted off to sleep.

––––––––

I AWAKENED to a decided chill in the air. Autumn had arrived, and winter wouldn't be far behind. I looked about while drawing the blanket up around my head. Both Wild Horse and Blue Flower were gathering their few belongings for the final leg of our journey. They stirred the coals and added just enough wood to begin to take the edge off the crispness of the morning. I stood and shook myself a bit to warm up.

As we silently pitched in to prepare for travel, a voice announced the presence of Buffalo Horn. Draped across his pony was a freshly killed *aruka*, a deer. *"Ana o'a hi'it,"* he proudly announced that we should join in breakfast. He dismounted along with a sack containing corn and berries. It appeared that Buffalo Hump wanted us to visit with full bellies.

Blue Flower promptly went to stoking the campfire. We'd be feasting on venison steak. Buffalo Horn shared stories of what had transpired since the Penateka Comanche had relocated the encampment. He included an encounter with the Apache, but we were already aware of how that turned out.

The venison was about ready to eat, and I was leaning forward to avail myself of a piece when Blue Flower gently pushed me back. She promptly served me a prime cut, smiling and bowing as I took it.

Wild Horse rolled his eyes and laughed. "You have trouble now, Jack," he advised, nearly spilling his food.

Of course, Blue Flower didn't yet know enough English to figure out what her brother had said. But she sat with her eyes riveted on me.

Kate, only ten years old but growing up faster than most girls on the frontier, giggled.

Buck simply looked from me to Blue Flower. He hadn't a clue.

"Jack, I'm going to see you and your kin safely back to your home then be headed to Wyoming. The North

Platte country beckons, and I'm not getting any younger. Y'all can come visit any time, though I figure you might have your hands full raising horses."

It had become a sort of farewell meal, and we hadn't even arrived at the encampment yet. It was mid-morning when we doused the fire and headed up the Pedernales with Buffalo Horn in the lead.

―――――

IT DIDN'T SURPRISE me that we had but a short distance to travel. The view of the Comanche encampment was impressive, though it wasn't easy to see the beautifully-decorated teepees with all the *numunuu* who had turned out to welcome us. Buffalo Horn turned off and let Wild Horse lead us to his father's teepee. Buffalo Hump was dressed in full regalia as he stood tall in front of his teepee. He'd taken a new wife in our absence, and she stood dutifully behind him.

We rode to within perhaps twenty feet, then pulled up and dismounted. Buck clung to Kate, but we otherwise looked relaxed.

As Wild Horse moved forward to greet his father, I was struck by how old Buffalo Hump seemed in contrast to Wild Horse's tall, strong physique. He still bore the nasty scars of the mountain lion attack, but they added a fierce sort of character to his presence. The two hugged, and then Wild Horse backed off and deferred to me.

I reached out my hand to the chief and was taken by complete surprise when he grasped it and pulled me in to embrace.

Eardrum-busting whooping and hollering by the *numunuu* followed. If there had been even a hint of tension, it was now gone.

Buffalo Hump raised both arms. "Comanche welcome return of Wild Horse and Jack," he announced proudly in the Comanche tongue. With that, he dispersed the crowd. The look in his eyes spoke volumes as to his joy at our return. There would surely be celebration this night. Meanwhile, the chief ushered us into his teepee. We'd sit and smoke and tell of our travels.

I missed the icy stare that Buffalo Hump's new wife laid upon Blue Flower. But she dealt it right back. Blue Flower's recent experiences had matured her and raised her confidence. She held to the feat of having shot and killed White Knife. Only our small circle knew it was she who had ended the shaman's threat.

———

SMOKE FROM FIRE and pipe spiraled its way up toward the vent at the top of the teepee. Wild Horse, George, and I sat in silence, smoking the pipe and waiting for Buffalo Hump to open our talk. As was custom, the women were not included. Blue Flower and Kate lingered outside the circle with little Buck seated behind them. It was actually a tad warm in the confines of the teepee, and I could feel beads of perspiration on my brow.

Buffalo Hump finally looked dead on at his son. "Wild Horse stay with *numunuu*." By implication, that included Blue Flower.

In my peripheral vision, I saw her look of disappointment. It was as though someone had stabbed a dagger into her heart. I had no idea how much she apparently had set her sights on journeying to the homestead with me. I mean, there had been nothing romantic between us. It had been what I viewed as a young girl's fantasy.

Wild Horse took a long pull on the pipe and sent smoke skyward. "Yes, *ap*." He nodded in agreement.

Buffalo Hump turned his attention to me. The wrinkles in his face seemed deeper now in the flickering light of the fire. He took a thoughtful drag on the pipe. "Jack strong medicine," he said in surprisingly good English. Perhaps he'd been holding out on me so far as his understanding of the White man's tongue. "Jack friend of Comanche." There was a step I hadn't expected. He handed the pipe to me.

I dutifully smoked the pipe. "Jack friend to Comanche, brother to Wild Horse."

"Jack go home," he said, as though having already figured out where we'd be headed. "Make ponies." It appeared it was his way of saying that I would breed horses.

I nodded in the affirmative.

Buffalo Hump turned his attention to George. He took another pull on the pipe. "George strong. Help Wild Horse and Jack. Keep Bluecoats away. George friend of Comanche." The chief apparently understood how George had slowed the march of the mounted rifles to enable the Penateka to move and to protect his son and son's friend.

George smiled that broad, glowing smile that had become his trademark. George wasn't used to being recognized for what he figured to simply be his duty. He took his turn with the pipe. "Comanche good people," was about all he could muster for the moment.

With that, and much to my total surprise, Buffalo Hump turned back to me and motioned Blue Flower forward. He smiled broadly. "Jack make ponies." He raised his hand toward Blue Flower. "Fifteen ponies," he said.

Blue Flower turned about as red as anyone of her race could. Her blush contrasted starkly with her white buckskin dress adorned with strips of fox and intricate beadwork. She looked radiant.

Wild Horse's jaw just about hit the floor of the teepee as his father's offer took him by total surprise. He had jokingly said she was worth ten ponies. However, this was real. His father must have observed how his daughter looked at me. It didn't take a mental giant to understand her desires. He also understood that his new wife had trouble accepting Blue Flower. I suspect these sorts of observations contributed to why he was chief. Breed them or steal them, fifteen ponies was the price.

In a way, Buffalo Hump had just relieved a huge amount of pressure from me. I did not have fifteen ponies, and he knew it. He'd made me an impossible offer while satisfying his daughter's desires. She looked at me like I was going to corral fifteen ponies tomorrow and take her to my homestead as wife. "Jack grateful to Buffalo Hump. Blue Flower fine woman," I said. To be honest, she was very much a woman among the Comanche, even at fourteen years. "Jack must make ponies."

Everyone, and I mean everyone, nodded affirmatively.

With all of this out of the way, we could enjoy a meal. The girls scrambled to serve it up. It was well worth the wait. Buffalo Hump went on to describe the coming evening festivities honoring the return of Wild Horse and me. He never mentioned White Knife, so I assumed that was already relegated to Comanche history.

————

UNLESS YOU'VE BEEN to a Comanche celebration, it's exceedingly difficult to understand much less describe. The entire village turned out in their finery. Chiefs were in full regalia. Warriors were outfitted so as to show off their hunting and fighting prowess through rhythmic dancing. The beat of drums and the melodic chanting would have been hypnotizing were there not so much wild dancing that accompanied them. Drink was aplenty, and I'm fairly certain that we were taking in our share of peyote.

I was all too aware that Blue Flower couldn't take her eyes off me. I'm sure she was working to convince herself that I'd come up with fifteen horses. To be perfectly honest, I had begun to figure how long that might take. She was a beauty, and there were a few worthy rivals. For better or worse, she'd set her sights on the *tosa* with the strong medicine. I wondered whether she would accept Christ. To be with me, she'd have to.

Kate sidled up to me. "What is with Blue Flower, brother?"

At only ten years old, I could understand her naivete. She wasn't yet thinking about boys beyond a companionship role. Playful and, at times, antagonistic. I chuckled a bit. "She likes me, Kate. She wants to live with me like Ma and Pa." I wasn't sure how best to frame my answer. It hadn't occurred to me that the comparison with Ma and Pa wasn't timed well as tears came to her eyes.

"I miss Mary and Sam and Ma and Pa, Jack."

I placed my arm around her shoulders. "They'll be with us always, Kate. They'll be watching over us from heaven. God is well pleased." It was the best offering of comfort I could muster. "Do you like Blue Flower?" I asked, hopeful of lightening the situation.

"She's nice. She must learn English," Kate observed.

"Enjoy the celebration, Kate. We leave for home in the morning," I added and turned my attention to the Comanche festivities.

I guess the peyote must have kicked in because I suddenly yielded to an urge that even took me by surprise. I grabbed George's and Wild Horse's hands in as ironlike a grip as I could, pulled them into the circle, and began to dance. It was one of those Irish step dances that I'm certain no Comanche or even George had ever seen before. My feet moved like they were on air. Several Comanche stopped to watch in amazement. I found myself so carried away that I grabbed Kate's hand and then Blue Flower's. They watched and were soon doing a right fine job of mimicking my dance.

The drums and chants suddenly stopped.

Absorbed in my dancing as I was, I managed a few more steps before coming to a halt.

Buffalo Hump raised both arms as a signal that the party was over. He was breathing heavily from the exertion of the festivities as well as the effect of the peyote. The chief looked at me and at Blue Flower and smiled.

It occurred to me that in the heat of the dancing with all its gyrations, I'd gotten closer to Blue Flower than she'd been on the night she shot White Knife. It seemed that God was telling me something, and I needed to listen.

We all slept well.

TWENTY
THE GUADALUPE BECKONS

OUR PONIES WERE READY, including a pack pony for our supplies and belongings. Kate and Buck were overjoyed that we'd be heading home. By comparison to our four-day journey from Encina, we reckoned our travel to our beloved home would take about two days. Excitement would tend to make it seem longer.

I had mixed feelings, as I'd be returning to where I'd buried part of my family. I had departed the homestead with feelings of anger, vengeance, and guilt, but had been shown a path to forgiveness and redemption. God had carved quite a trail for me.

I wondered whether the message I had scrawled inside the shed had endured. It could well have washed away in a goodly storm. My thoughts were interrupted by a send-off party of Buffalo Hump, Wild Horse, and Blue Flower. The chief's new wife was nowhere to be seen.

George was all smiles. Buffalo Hump had gifted him with an ornate pipestone breastplate. It wasn't likely to stop a bullet, but it looked right fine, and George wore it proudly. But for his black skin and bald head, he might have been mistaken for a Red man.

Wild Horse was intent on leading us out for the first couple of miles of our journey, so he was already mounted. The next time I would meet him, he would, in all likelihood, be a full-fledged warrior.

Blue Flower stood beside her father. She had a certain glow about her, the kind that got a man to thinking about fifteen ponies. She was decked out in her finest buckskin dress, and her hair hung in a pair of beautifully-decorated braids. She gave me a delicate goodbye wave, one that Buffalo Hump couldn't see.

The chief gave me a hug and thrust a carved bone totem into my hand. "This tell Comanche Jack is friend," he explained. With a wink of an eye, he reminded me, "Fifteen, Jack." Then he gave me a serious look and pointed to a mare being led over to us. He made a motion over his stomach to indicate that she was pregnant. It seemed that Buffalo Hump wanted to get my breeding operation started.

Well, there was a lot of work ahead. We had a cabin to build before winter set in.

"*Tosa* friend to Comanche," were my parting words to the chief. The Bluecoats might not have shared our points of view, but there were plenty among our people who wanted peace.

We followed Wild Horse from the Penateka Comanche encampment. There was a certain sorrow in that we'd become such good friends. It had all begun with the *pia wa'óo* and *isa*, the mountain lion and the wolf, and it had ultimately been overlaid with the Cross.

A couple of miles from the encampment, Wild Horse pulled up and slipped from his pony's back.

I did the same. I grasped his outreached hand, and we

hugged briefly. "I will miss you, my brother. May God bless you."

Wild Horse uncharacteristically had what appeared to be tears in the corners of his eyes. He took my hand again. This time, he deposited a gift. "Bless you, *isa*." I looked in my hand. He had given me a cross carved from mesquite.

I grasped his shoulder for a moment, gazed into his eyes, and remounted. "See you soon, *pia wa'óo*." The spirit totems had become a meaningful bond transcended only by our faith.

As we rode off and faded from Wild Horse's sight, I looked back a final time. We waved.

———

THE TRAVEL along the Pedernales was not especially difficult. We would yet face the tougher challenge of the hill country before reaching the Guadalupe River. That would mean we were nearing home.

I found myself missing the company of Wild Horse and Blue Flower. George's presence helped us feel more secure, but there still seemed to be a gaping hole in our little band. It even struck me that there was no longer a bow and arrow among us. If we were to bag any game, we'd be firing a shot or two that could be heard for quite a distance. Sound seemed to amplify in the rugged hills of Texas.

George brought up the rear while I led the way. It challenged my budding trailblazing skills, but I felt up to it. I reckoned I could count on George giving a holler, if I strayed off course.

Buck had now become quite content riding with Kate. Thankfully, she was diminutive enough that there was plenty of space on the pony's back.

We stopped to rest at a spot where the Pedernales took a decided shift to the south. A half day of walking and riding due south would take us to the headwaters of the Guadalupe. Everyone dismounted to water the horses and ourselves.

I kicked back under a cypress while George checked the packhorse and the mare. It was about as relaxed as we'd been since the peyote-induced stupor with the Kiowa a couple of weeks back. I closed my eyes for but a moment when Kate sidled over to me with Buck in tow.

"Buck wants to ride with his big brother," she announced.

I could see from the look in Buck's eyes that he sought a more adventurous diversion from riding in his sister's lap. He wasn't up to being babied out here on the frontier. Riding with his big brother would be an extra special treat. The only downside that I could see was readiness in the event of danger. It'd be tough to swing the Springfield into firing position with Buck sitting in front of me. Then, an idea struck me. "Do you think you can hang onto the mare, Buck?"

He scrunched up his face for a second before offering up a broad, triumphant smile. "Buck big man," he said, puffing out his chest.

I breathed a sigh of relief.

George walked over, leading the packhorse and mare. "We'd better ride. There's a creek between here and the Guadalupe where we can bed down tonight." There was an urgency in his voice that demanded response.

"Well, let's ride," I said, reinforcing George's sentiments. With that, I sprang to my feet and almost ran to my pony. The sorrel stallion reared up with surprise, but thankfully, his hooves missed me. I stopped, as I had nearly forgotten my offer to Buck. "George, we're going to let Buck ride the mare for a while." With that, I picked up my brother and placed him on the mare's back. She seemed to not be bothered. She'd already proven to be a surefooted cayuse, so I had no reason to worry.

I led the way through a gap in the Indian grass. The sun cast its brightness from high overhead and lit the way. We'd be dancing among the oaks and juniper for the next few miles with hills rising high above. George and I were on high alert, as the valleys and draws were perfect for ambushes. By sheer luck, I found an old trail. According to George, the trail was called the Pinta Trail years ago and was used by Apache, Comanche, and other tribes before the Whites moved in. No matter its name, it sure made for easier travel, though we had to be especially alert for Indians and bandits.

Blessedly, our travels were uneventful save for an occasional rattlesnake, deer moseying across the trail, wild longhorns, and the ubiquitous and always dangerous buffalo that we steered clear of.

WE AROSE on the second day to warming rays of sunshine that beckoned us eastward. As the nights grew chillier, the sun was always welcome. I approached homecoming with just a bit of trepidation. We'd have to set to work building a cabin of some sort for protection through the coming winter, as well as repairing the shed that would house our livestock. George would surely be a big help, but it was uncertain how Kate and Buck would handle seeing the graves of our family and facing the reality of what happened.

On the practical side, I wondered whether any of

Ma's garden plantings had survived in the weeks I had been absent in my mission to free Kate and Buck.

As we mounted to begin the final leg of our journey, I could sense the excitement in Kate and Buck. They were going to be growing up fast. I had the feeling that the next few days would be fraught with emotional peaks and valleys, highs and lows.

I dreaded viewing the burned-out remains of our cabin. When I'd headed out to find Kate and Buck, I was overwrought with emotions. Anger, grief, and guilt tended to blind me to reality. I would be seeing in the cold light of reality the devastating damage wrought by the Comanche. There would be the clothesline post where Ma had been tortured to death. The sacred places where I found the bodies of Pa, Mary, and Samuel and the makeshift family headstone. Was the message I wrote in charcoal still inside the shed?

There was no hurry, though I'd have galloped if the ponies could have endured it. As it was, we stayed disciplined. Ponies and humans needed rests, and hurriedness could lead to carelessness when we needed to stay alert for possible dangers.

Around mid-morning, we reached the Guadalupe River. I was in the lead and had just rounded a bend in the riverbank trail, when I looked up, felt my stomach seem to rise to my throat, and nearly swallowed it. I found myself looking dead-on at six Indians in full war paint.

Turns out they were Kiowa. They were about as shocked as we were.

I said a little prayer and raised my hand in a sign of peace. I stared hard. The lead warrior's face looked familiar despite the war paint. *"Kwihnai?"* I ventured.

Eagle's face broke into a broad smile. "Jack!" he

announced. He raised his hand and spoke rapidly to his companions. The atmosphere grew decidedly relaxed.

Kate and Buck rode up beside me, mouths agape. George simply rode up, smiled, and tipped his hat. Notably, he had slipped on the ornate bone breastplate that Buffalo Hump had given him. It added just a bit of what the Indians called strong medicine.

Eagle looked at George and nodded. He apparently recalled running into the big Black man a few weeks back when they raided the cattle drive and fell victim to his accurate shooting. He was held in deep respect for his battle prowess. The Kiowa warrior looked about. "*Kobe?*" he asked.

"*Kobe numunuu,*" I said in Comanche, trying to communicate that Wild Horse was with his people.

With that, Eagle produced a pipe. He figured to rest and have us join him.

I was on guard not to succumb to the peyote shared by the Kiowa weeks back. A brief rest smoking the pipe with our Red brothers seemed like a small price for ongoing peaceful relations.

Eagle asked where we were headed by signing and scribbling in the dirt.

I pointed eastward and said, "Jack *numunuu.*" Saying I was returning to my people was about as close as I could figure to saying we were heading home.

The Kiowa gave me a curious look. He signed that people were on my homestead.

On the one hand, I hoped that he was mistaken and simply didn't know the O'Toole homestead from any other White man's ranch. However, if what he said were true, we had a problem ahead of us.

We spent less than an hour by my estimation. Eagle shared some pemmican with us in between passing the pipe around. George still remembered some Pawnee language and told a couple of jokes that amused the Kiowa. I did share with Eagle that the Comanche encampment was less than two-days ride. He would be careful, as they were enemies. Kate and Buck mostly looked on the proceedings in utter bafflement.

Our friendly interlude with the Kiowa soon came to an end, and we were able to resume our journey. The Kiowa mounted their ponies and began their journey up the river. Before they departed, Eagle paused and took a long look at Buck. He rode over and drew an arrow from his quiver. He smiled at Buck and gave him the arrow.

Buck was thrilled. "Th-th-thanks," he stammered with a huge smile spread across his face.

Eagle raised his hand in a sign of peace, and Buck followed suit. The Kiowa warrior had just given my little brother a major thrill that would be the subject of ever-taller stories later.

Eagle waved as he rode off with his band.

"What do you think, George? We could be facing a problem at the homestead," I ventured.

George shrugged. "We'll just deal with it, Jack. No sense worrying just yet. Gotta trust in our Lord."

I appreciated his guarded optimism but couldn't lose the prospect of squatters out of my thinking. Homecoming would be tough enough without a challenge to our rights to the land.

———

WE'D BEEN MAKING PRETTY-FAIR time on the Pinta Trail. All had been quiet save for the sounds of wildlife.

As our band of weary travelers rounded a bend in the trail, George was brought to a halt by the jingle of spurs and squeaking of leather coming up behind us. He turned to find himself face-to-face with Captain Nate Benton, leading his company of Texas Rangers. These were the same Rangers that had chased off the Apache a few days back. They had picked up our trail.

Of course, the sudden noise behind us caught my attention. "What's the ruckus, George?" I hollered, as I couldn't yet see what the fuss was.

Kate and Buck simply sat bewildered on their ponies.

I turned and doubled back, quickly coming upon George engaging the Texas Rangers.

"Jack, this here's Captain Benton. He's got some news for us."

I rode up and tipped what remained of my hat to the captain. "Pleased to meet you, Captain. My name is Jack O'Toole."

"Our pleasure, Jack. We hear you've been quite a traveler," replied Benton. How he heard of anything of my travels was beyond my humble brain to figure out. "Sorry about your folks, but pleased that you found your sister and brother."

"Thank you, Captain. The good Lord has surely watched over us."

"Indeed, He has," said Benton. "You have good company here in Mr. Freeman, but I expect that you know that. We ran into a young Comanche the other day. He spoke darned fair English, so we parleyed a bit. We wanted to know where his people were camped. No plans for trouble, but sort of keeping track of the whereabouts of these Red men. Anyway, we learned about his travels with you. Said you were brothers and that you had strong medicine." Benton finished with a smile.

"Wild Horse is wise," I said.

"More than wise, Jack. Wish there were more like

him. It sure would make my job easier." An expression of earnestness took hold of Benton's face.

"What job is that, Captain?" As if I didn't know.

"Protect settlers from Indian predations. If it means killing, that goes with the territory."

I scanned the collection of men riding with Benton. It was an understatement to say they were heavily armed. They each sported a pair of Colt 1851 Navy revolvers, a Sharps rifle, a Bowie knife, and plenty of ammunition. A couple of the Rangers included a shotgun in their arsenal. They rode prime horseflesh well-suited to the rough landscape of the Comancheria.

"Do you know what we're facing up ahead, Captain?" I asked.

Benton sighed resignedly. "Afraid not, Jack."

"I heard that a couple of folks are squatting on my folks' homestead. About the only claim I have is my folks' graves and a message I wrote in charcoal on the back of the shed saying I'd return. Can you offer any advice?"

Benton rubbed his chin thoughtfully. "We aren't lawmen, Jack. Sounds like work for the local law. I suspect any land ownership papers were likely burned, though there may be a copy in Austin." He looked genuinely sorry that enforcing the law wasn't part of his mission.

The answer was disappointing. It wasn't what I wanted to hear, but had been somewhat helpful. If need be, we might be able to get papers from Austin. Meanwhile, I'd have to hope that the squatters would depart peacefully. The situation caused me a bit of anxiety. "Thanks, Captain," I said, resigned to what lay ahead.

"Tell you what, Jack," said Benton with a pleasant smile. "We'll stop by your place in a day or so and be sure there's no trouble." With that, Benton made ready to depart. "Good that Mr. Freeman here is with you. If there's trouble, your sister and brother likely won't be much help."

With that, Kate drew out the revolver she kept in her waistband.

Captain Benton smiled. "Enough said. Y'all travel safely. Keep your eyes and ears alert for Apache." He tipped his hat to us and led his company away.

As they rode off, George and I stared silently at each other.

"We'll deal with what we must deal with, Jack. We've come this far dealing with all sorts of challenges," George observed. "The Lord has protected us so far, and I expect He will continue to keep us safe."

I nodded. "Let's go." I turned back up the trail with Kate, Buck, and George falling in behind.

We ate a little dust from the departed Texas Rangers for a little while.

TWENTY-ONE
HOME

THE LATE AFTERNOON sun was laying long shadows from the cypress along the banks of the Guadalupe when we reached my favorite fishing spot. Two miles off would be the burned-out hulk of the family cabin.

Even at a distance, it was hard to miss the slim wisp of smoke spiraling from where the cabin used to be. Kate, Buck, and George had reined in beside me. We all looked off into the distance. I wasn't certain whether Kate and Buck understood the situation that lay ahead. They had a lot of growing up yet to do despite the horrors of the Comanche attack, the time spent with the Comanche, and the dangerous adventures encountered on the trail.

"Might as well head on in and see what lies ahead," I said to no one in particular.

"Lead the way, Jack. I've got your back," said George through those pearly-white teeth of his.

Off we rode with me in the lead.

AT ROUGHLY A HUNDRED yards from the burned-out cabin, I could make out a man and a woman. So far as I could tell, they were unarmed. The man wasn't especially tall, but he appeared physically rugged with a dark beard and well-muscled arms. He wore a black flat-brimmed hat, a dirty white shirt, and black trousers. The woman was petite compared to my sister Kate and looked to be pregnant. She smiled timidly beneath some sort of sunbonnet atop her head. They had a tent pitched beside where the cabin used to be. The man was doing some sort of work on the shed. This didn't look as though it would be easy.

"Hail the camp," I called out.

The couple froze. The man looked about in seeming desperation, likely for a firearm.

I nudged my pony forward. The four of us must have been quite a sight for these folks. I decided to be bold with a touch of friendliness. "Welcome to my homestead. I'm Jack O'Toole. I see you've already made yourselves at home."

The couple appeared flabbergasted. Obviously, they'd taken a chance that the property had been abandoned, and now they were caught. Guilt spread like melted butter across their faces. They were speechless, at least for the present.

"Glad to see y'all have made yourself at home while I was off rescuing my sister and brother here from the Comanche that burned us out. Oh, this here is Kate, and over there is Buck." I pointed to George. "This here is my friend George."

George sat extra tall in the saddle. He was a big man anyway. He managed a friendly smile, just to let the couple know that he wasn't going to blow their heads off with the rifle sitting across his lap.

"Er, I'm Isaac Fisher, and this is my wife Sarah."

It was fast becoming obvious that the couple was no threat. In fact, they might be an asset. I was glad to have not prejudged them too negatively. I recalled my pa's advice from the book of Luke, the sixth chapter I think, to the effect that we shouldn't judge and thus won't be judged.

George looked at me knowingly. He nodded in the direction of the tent. A flintlock leaned against the entrance flap. The gun was ancient, likely sixty or more years old. From the look of it, firing would be an iffy proposition.

"We've traveled a long way, and the sun will be setting in a couple of hours." I dismounted and walked toward Isaac with my hand extended. We shook.

"I see y'all have a tent. We'll get comfortable in the shed, if y'all don't mind."

Any hint of fear seemed to leave Isaac. He was obviously not inclined to challenge my ownership of the homestead. "Er...we appreciate your hospitality, Mr. O'Toole."

Given that Isaac was likely a half dozen years my senior, him calling me mister felt pretty respectful. I motioned to Kate and Buck to dismount. "Let's have some dinner, and we can get acquainted," I suggested.

Kate pitched in to help Sarah prepare the meal while George rode out to scrounge up some firewood.

I saw a wagon on the other side of the tent but no livestock to pull it. It was then that I realized the mules or horses had likely been served up as meals. "I grew up near Gettysburg. Where are y'all from?" I inquired curiously.

"Lancaster," answered Isaac sheepishly. "We were Amish."

"Were?" I asked.

"It was a falling out with Sarah's father," said Isaac. It was clear from his body language that he wasn't going to expand on the story.

"Where's the musket from?" I figured that wouldn't be too personal a question.

"We Amish can use guns for hunting." Isaac took a deep breath and glanced over at Sarah. "I made the mistake of threatening another man with it," he confessed. "We were asked to leave, and here we are."

George returned from his mission to find wood and added his contribution to the cooking fire. He went to work putting the horses on a string, since there was no corral. Once finished, he strode on over.

Isaac looked at George and then back at me. "What happened here?" he asked.

"Comanche," I responded. It was almost enough said, but I gave him the short story. "Over yonder are the graves of my ma and pa and a sister and brother. I was off fishing during the attack and came home to find them along with the burned-out cabin. Kate here and Buck were nowhere to be seen, so I figured they'd been taken captive." I was about to tell more when Kate walked over.

She had tears in her eyes. "Where, Jack? Where?" With the anxiety of dealing with the Fishers and emotions of coming home, she'd been distracted.

"Excuse me, Isaac." I took Kate's hand, gave her a hug, and led her over to the gravesite. It had held up right well during my brief absence.

Kate kneeled beside the grave and let her grief flow forth. Heaving sobs racked her shoulders.

I felt helpless.

Thankfully, Sarah pulled away from dinner preparation and quietly kneeled beside my sister. "They're in a joyful place, Kate. I can feel their love."

It seemed a blessing that Kate hadn't had to deal with the discovery of our loved one's bodies. She could remember them in life, despite the final chaotic moments when she and Buck had been taken captive.

———————

WE SPENT the next few days getting acquainted. I didn't know much about the Amish faith, but I reckoned Isaac and Sarah to be honest, God-fearing folks.

We went to work building a corral and expanding the shed. And yes, my prophetic words of return were still emblazoned on the back wall. With the weather turning cooler and winter not far off, building living quarters was a high priority. Plus, Sarah's belly was growing and she looked to be drawing ever closer to the blessed event. It seemed logical to establish some sort of arrangement with the Fishers.

One evening, as we sat around our makeshift table, I ventured an idea. I winked at George and turned to Isaac. "I need to concentrate on breeding horses and hunting. George has his dream of heading to the North Platte country of Wyoming and establishing a cattle ranch. I sure would be obliged if y'all would commit to staying here. I'd be pleased to carve out some land that you could call your own." In the inner recesses of my mind, I was thinking of how handy they'd be to offer a stable family situation for Kate and Buck.

"We were thinking the same, Mr. O'Toole," responded Isaac. He insisted on calling me that, even after better than two weeks of working side-by-side.

"Come spring, we'll go to Austin and make it official," I stated.

George smiled. He knew what I was up to. After dinner, he and I took a short walk out to the shed. He turned to me knowingly. "You have Blue Flower on your mind," he confided suspiciously.

I must have blushed at his accurate observation. "She's been on my mind, George."

"Fifteen ponies." He laughed. "You only have four."

"Gonna be five in another month," I retorted with a grin. "Truth be told, I saw a herd of wild ponies on the other side of the Guadalupe. I couldn't see any brands. Must have been two dozen, and they were bigger than most Indian ponies. Shucks, Buffalo Hump would likely be overwhelmed."

"Expect you want my help fetching them," added George.

"Tell you what, my friend. You can take three with you to Wyoming to start breeding your own."

George looked off, as though in deep thought. "Make it four, and we've got a deal." He about busted a gut laughing. "You've turned into quite the man, Jack. Your pa would have been proud of you."

I felt the warmth of a blush sweep over me. "Despite the tragedy, we've been blessed, George."

He nodded. "Let's wrangle those horses early tomorrow. Time's a wasting for me to head north afore the winter snows set in. I have a friend up in Wyoming who'll take me in."

The look in George's eyes said it was a lady friend. Enough said.

"Do you think you can herd fifteen ponies to Buffalo Hump?"

I nodded. "Likely not do it until spring, George. The horses will have to be broke a bit."

"From that look in Blue Flower's eyes, I'm sure she'll wait."

TWENTY-TWO
NEW BEGINNINGS

"HOW MANY TIMES have you fired that antique of late?" I asked Isaac.

"A couple," he responded sheepishly. "Shot a doe last week."

I was thinking about how long it took to load that relic of times long past. It didn't measure up to the more accurate rifled bore of my Springfield. New-fangled improvements seemed to be happening so fast it was hard to keep up with them. I hadn't had one in my hands, but I heard that Samuel Colt manufactured a repeating rifle with a cylinder similar to his famous revolvers. On the one hand, I admired Isaac's piece, but out here on the Comancheria, more firepower was a must. I was determined to get him a better rifle first chance. "Is it an old family piece?" I inquired.

"It belonged to my father. He fell in the Mexican American War, and I inherited it."

"Well, Isaac," I continued. "Setting out here in the open like we are, we're going to have to get hold of a couple of more rifles...likely a pistol or two, as well."

"We don't shoot at—"

I stopped him in mid-sentence. "You're going to have to overcome that, Isaac. I understand your faith teaches nonviolence, but when a savage Comanche or Apache is breathing down your neck, he's not going to pause for niceties. It's simply a fact."

Isaac half nodded, but it was clear that he wasn't convinced. It left me to wondering whether he could be relied upon to help defend us if we were under attack.

"When George heads to Wyoming, we'll be short three guns. I've made friends with some Kiowa and Comanche, but we dare not rely on that. We'll only have my Springfield, your musket, and my Colt that Kate carries. It won't be much against a war party of thirty or forty Indians. Do you catch my drift, Isaac?"

Isaac sighed.

"You'd protect Sarah, wouldn't you?" I made my appeal more personal.

Finally and reluctantly, he nodded in agreement. "It's a different world out here, isn't it, Jack?"

I couldn't help but grin. "You nailed it, my friend."

"How do you propose to obtain more guns?" All of a sudden, Isaac had grown practical, a characteristic I would eventually come to appreciate.

"I hear tell there's a new settlement south of here called Bandera. I figure to venture down there and see what I can rustle up. Maybe get us a saddle or two as well. Meanwhile, I spotted a herd of horses on the other side of the Guadalupe. George and I figure to go bring them in. They're wild, so it won't be easy. Getting them in the new corral will be tough, too."

"You need help?" Isaac asked.

"Your job is to protect our home. Can Sarah shoot that musket?"

He shook his head.

"Might do to give her a lesson or two, just in case."

George strolled over. "You ready to round up some hosses, Jack?" He looked at Isaac and me. It was easy to see that we'd been having a serious conversation. "The good Lord blesses us in wonderful ways, Isaac. How we respond to the opportunities he affords us is our choice. It's about trust, about faith in Him." George followed that advice with one of his big grins. "We've got work to do, Jack. Let's get started."

As we headed out, I double-checked the temporary fencing we'd installed in a huge vee pattern to funnel the horses into the corral. It would be a brilliant idea, if it worked.

———

WELL, there they were. Maybe thirty wild horses were nearly close enough to reach out and touch. I had read somewhere that what was called the Nueces Strip of southern Texas was also called the Wild Horse Desert. Horses imported with the Spanish conquistadores had multiplied and then some. Their numbers were rivaled only by longhorns and buffalo. No surprise that the Comanche and other tribes became excellent horsemen over the years.

I rightly reckoned that getting them over the Guadalupe River would be our biggest challenge. I was wrong.

As George and I scanned the herd to pick out the lead stallion, my Black friend pointed off into the distance.

"Do you see them?" he asked, his eyes wide open with downright fright.

They were hard to miss. Must have been a couple of

dozen Indians that could be barely seen on the horizon. They hadn't sighted us, and we were upwind. Given that we were a mere three miles from the homestead, this was all too close for comfort.

George handed me one of his Colt revolvers.

If we had to fight, I'd need to be firing more than my Springfield.

I pointed to a stand of live oak, and we eased on over. We did our best to blend in.

"We'll wait them out, George," I advised. It never occurred to me that I was speaking with a man twice my age with many times greater experience. I had grown up fast, but not that fast.

George simply smiled and nodded.

The Indians disappeared from our sight, but we figured we weren't out of danger just yet. There was no telling what they were up to or where they were going. From a distance, we were unable to even figure out what tribe they were. I vainly wished Captain Benton or even my Comanche or Kiowa friends were nearby. After what seemed forever, we ventured out from the shelter of the trees.

I looked over at George and shrugged. "Let's get those horses!"

We threw caution to the winds and began rounding up the herd. It wasn't likely to be easy, as the lead stallion had a mind of his own. His number one job was protecting his *manada*, the herd under his control.

What I knew about horses was what my pa taught me, as he reckoned that I'd be helping realize his dream of breeding the beautiful beasts. I knew that horses had great eyesight and hearing, as they had to be on guard against predators. As a prey animal, they also had to respond quickly, attaining gallop speed in a flash.

Watching Wild Horse with his pony and observing how the Comanche cared for their ponies was highly educational. The horse was their primary mode of transportation, so it was critically important to take good care of them. The Indians were highly regarded for their horsemanship.

Horses are social animals, and it takes practice to become familiar with how they respond to outside stimulation. For example, the position of a horse's tail can reveal whether they are stressed, irritated, playful, or exhausted. The same can be said for ears, eyes, legs, facial expressions, and even the sounds they make.

Reading horses becomes critical to taming them, breaking them, if you will. I'd seen more than one cowboy or Indian tossed by a bucking bronc that had simply been approached wrong. It's especially notable that a horse's coat is highly sensitive to touch, which I suppose is why they love to be curried or stroked.

Important to George and I today, was recognizing the social structure within the herd. Among the thirty or so cayuses we saw, there were three stallions, a slew of mares, and foals and yearlings. One of the mares was likely what the cowboys called a boss mare. She made a lot of the decisions as to where a herd headed. From what I'd learned of horses, this herd was about ready for a new herd to break off as led by a young stallion.

While it was tempting to start the herd to running by firing our guns, those Indians we'd seen were likely still in the vicinity. Nope, shooting off guns wouldn't be especially wise. In addition, it likely wasn't the greatest way to get acquainted with our equine friends. George and I would get a chance to exercise our voices. Our own horses were going to be hard-pressed as we'd be striving to steer the herd in the direction we wanted them to go. We only had three miles to cover, but we might ride ten or more to get them where we wanted them.

I had managed to find some rope in the old shed, so I had what could loosely be called a lasso to wave around as necessary. I murmured a little prayer for our success, and we put heels to our horses and headed for the lead stallion. We pulled up well before he could sense a threat and be panicked.

George's drover skills would be put to the test, though longhorn herds didn't behave like horse herds. Each breed had their own psychology and behaviors, including the cowboys. For one thing, we had to keep in mind that horses are social beasts.

The lead stallion was a sorrel, similar in color to my pony. His natural reaction was to look us over right carefully. Had we galloped in, we'd likely be chasing the herd to kingdom come. The idea was to engage him and bend him to our will. I'd seen the Comanche herd a hundred ponies. Though these horses were wild, the social behaviors were pretty similar.

I slowly nudged my pony toward the lead or herd stallion while George positioned off behind the herd to minimize any escape route. I decided to call the herd stallion Big Red hereafter. He was wary as all get out. I tried to mimic the nicker sound horses make to comfort each other.

I think Big Red was trying to make a decision between fight, flight, or be social. While the third option was highly unlikely, the fact was that Big Red wasn't moving. He stood there, eyeing us warily as if trying to figure us out.

I moved closer and maintained eye contact.

Big Red stood his ground.

I turned my pony toward the river and urged him into a fast walk.

Meanwhile, George gently waved his lasso and made those comforting nicker sounds while moving toward the herd.

Big Red was conflicted between my behavior and George's, yet he didn't seem inclined to escape. The big stallion was no dummy. He knew something unusual was happening and was trying to decide whether to go along with us.

I circled back a bit, then resumed heading toward the river.

George kept gently pushing in from the rear of the herd.

All of a sudden, Big Red's nostrils flared and he gave a big warning snort followed by a whinny. His ears pointed forward, and he took a couple of tentative steps in my direction.

Thankfully, my Comanche pony held steady. I held eye contact and threw in an occasional nicker to show that I wasn't a threat.

What on earth could be going through this big stallion's mind? Clearly, he'd been roaming the Texas plains and hills for quite a while. Had he never encountered anyone who wanted to domesticate him? Then again, maybe this was God's work.

Big Red whinnied and began to lope toward me as I picked up my own pace toward the Guadalupe River. His herd began to move with him.

George simply followed the herd, amazement writ large across his face.

As we drew ever closer to the river with a herd of thirty horses, I prayed fervently that there'd be no trouble getting my new-found followers across. The river was fairly shallow. The big question would be whether they'd stop for a drink and then follow me to the homestead?

Big Red pulled up on the river bank, and his harem joined him in a long drink. He eyed me with more interest than suspicion. Why he didn't see me as a threat was beyond the grasp of my tiny brain.

I waited patiently. When it appeared that the herd had sated its thirst, I headed across the river, all the while keeping eye contact with Big Red.

The big stallion looked at me, glanced back at his herd, and then turned and pranced across the Guadalupe. Big Red was soon following me right into the mouth of the fence funnel we'd built.

Soon, we had a good-sized herd with just about the right amount of space to feel comfortable. It was nigh time for me to get acquainted with Big Red. If we were going to make a go of the ranch, we needed to gentle these wild horses sooner than later. We also needed to build out the shelter. We needed a full stable and more pasture.

From what my pa had taught me, I caught on early in life that horses are a fascinating species so far as what drives their reaction to folks. They're observant. Yep, they observe your every move. It gives them a sort of presence in the moment. A cayuse can figure out a lot about you before they ever let you get close, peacefully close, that is. They can read you like a newspaper from across a corral or a wide piece of prairie. I suspect Big Red had me figured out from the time we first came upon him and his herd that day just north of the Guadalupe River. Once a horse trusts you, it'll pretty much do your bidding. I've heard of riders literally riding their mounts so hard as to ride them to death. Sad, but true.

———

GEORGE SIDLED up to me as I hung on one of the corral rails. "I've been mulling it over, Jack. I have an offer for you." He greeted me in that beautiful bass voice of his. He took a deep breath. "I saved up a bit of money from the droving and the scouting work. I figure to use most of it up in Wyoming." He gulped just a tad. "Happy to loan you some money for the barn plus the supplies you plan to get in Bandera."

My jaw dropped. George seemed to always be with me whether needed or not. His generosity was astounding. In my mind, he was a true servant of God, giving to others before himself. I prayed that I could be so selfless. "That's mighty generous, George. Are you certain?"

George wasn't finished. "You've grown quite a bit in the past few weeks, Jack. God has work laid out for you, Jack. You're on a journey. As my momma used to say, 'Live the journey, for each destination is but the doorway to the next journey.' You have big dreams you aim to fulfill, but I'm reckoning the biggest will be helping other folks. Your friendship with Wild Horse and generosity with the Amish folk are just the beginning." He paused.

"I really hadn't thought on it that way, George."

He laughed. "That's the beauty of it...that is the beauty of it." He looked over at Big Red and back at me. "So, are you two going to get acquainted or just stand here gawking at each other?"

I opened the corral gate and entered cautiously. My eyes never left Big Red's as I slowly approached. He whinnied just a bit, then nickered. I spoke gently to him and held out my open palm with a cube of sugar that Sarah had given me from her stash. The big stallion sniffed. If he could have smiled, he surely would have.

Big Red gently licked the sugar cube from my hand. It left me to wondering whether he'd always been wild. The look he gave me spoke volumes. I took a step closer and reached out to stroke his nose. His nostrils flared briefly, but he was soon nuzzling my hand. I stroked his neck. My, but he was a beautiful animal.

Over the next couple of days, we all got better acquainted with Big Red's herd. We fenced a greater area of the ranch to give the horses relatively free rein.

After two days of getting acquainted, Big Red finally let me slip up onto his back. I hugged his neck and spoke soothingly. He shook his head and whinnied a couple of times when I first climbed on. It wasn't long before we were riding around the corral. I began to work with him on turning, stopping, and other necessary commands. Big Red was the most intelligent horse I'd ever ridden, as he seemed to relish performing just as I led him. He hardly blinked when I put George's saddle on him.

I finally took Big Red for a ride beyond the confines of the corral. He wasn't too happy about leaving his mares, but he sought to please me. We were soon loping along on the prairie, even occasionally urging him into a gallop.

———

FIVE DAYS after the horse roundup, I prepared to head for Bandera. We had managed to repair the Fisher's wagon, lightened it as much as possible, and hitched up a couple of our ponies. I took both the Springfield rifle and Colt revolver, as there was no telling what I might run into. If all went as hoped, the entire excursion would take less than a week.

Arriving in Bandera, I found myself unimpressed. I'd heard that it was a new settlement, but didn't reckon it to be so sparse so far as structures. Few buildings were to be found. It was obvious from orderly rows of stakes that a town had been laid out. I did pass a lumber yard of sorts along a beautiful cypress-lined bend in the Medina River.

The operation was cutting cypress shingles with a horse-powered sawmill. Far as I could tell, there wasn't a general store of any sort just yet. The first couple of folks I met could barely speak English, and those that did had heavy accents. While inquiring about supplies, I learned that this strange language was Polish. Apparently, several Polish folks had decided to establish roots in Bandera.

In a way, it was reassuring that a town was springing up just beyond the recognized boundaries of the Comancheria. As I drove my wagon up what would be the main street, I couldn't miss a remuda of horses near its end. They looked vaguely familiar.

"Hey, Jack! Jack O'Toole!" rang out a voice I thought I'd heard before.

I squinted into the midday sun in the general direction of the voice, and my eyes came to rest on Texas Ranger Captain Nathan Benton. "Captain? Howdy, sir," I responded.

Benton walked on over to me. "What brings you to Bandera?" he asked.

I might have asked the same question, but held my tongue. "Supplies, sir."

Benton unobtrusively glanced into the back of my wagon where a couple of saddles, a Sharps carbine, three

Colt Navy revolvers, and some household supplies lay in the bed. "Did you settle back into your homestead?"

"Yes sir, Captain. Seems the Fishers had thought the place abandoned. We worked out a peaceful arrangement," I explained. There was no point in concealing anything. "We've been working hard. George and I rounded up about thirty horses last week, so we've begun breeding. I reckon the Rangers and the Army will be needing good horseflesh."

Benton nodded. "I'll be headed in the general direction of your place tomorrow morning, Jack. There has been a bit of trouble with some of those danged Apache sticking their tails up again. We'd be pleased to give you an escort."

What could I say to that? The trip south to Bandera had me constantly alert for lurking dangers. "I'd be much obliged, Captain." I did get his reference to the Apache sticking their tails up, as that's what horses do when excited. I didn't laugh.

"Meet me here at sunrise, or better yet, come join us for dinner this evening. You're welcome to bed down with my company."

I couldn't help but leap at the opportunity. I reckoned it would be exciting just to get to know some Texas Rangers. If the Apache were indeed roaming around looking for trouble, me being under the protection of the Rangers would be most welcome.

————

SITTING around a roaring campfire with actual Texas Rangers was educational. Some of them, including Benton, had ridden into Mexico chasing Lipan Apache with Captain James Callahan. Apparently, it had caused big diplomatic problems, and Callahan had his rear spanked by both Mexican dragoons and United States politicians. What did catch me was the degree to which most of the men sought to kill Indians, especially Comanche. The oft-used phrase, *the only good Injun is a dead Injun*, found frequent use in the Ranger camp.

I decided it was wise to not talk about my friendship with Wild Horse, my growing interest in Blue Flower, or my peaceful relationships with Buffalo Hump's Penateka Comanche and Eagle's Kiowa band. There simply wasn't any point in stirring up emotions, especially since they'd be escorting me through the Comancheria. I figured that I might encounter Benton at some future time, and we could talk about our views on the Indians. Like my spirit totem, *isa*, I'd have to be smart.

———

BANDERA DID SEEM to be capturing attention. As we headed north just after sunrise in a column of twos with my wagon in the middle position, we encountered a patrol of Bluecoats riding south. They were part of the mounted rifle regiment serving under Colonel Steele at Fort Inge. I might not have thought too much of their passing but for a couple of empty saddles and some of the men sporting bandages and looking roughed up.

The Texas Rangers remained silent as the Bluecoats rode by. It was clear that there was no love going on between the two forces. They seemed to barely tolerate each other.

I looked back from the wagon seat as the unit passed my section of the column. The Ranger riding in front of me spoke over his shoulder, "Don't pay 'em no never mind, son. They run into them Apache we was talkin' 'bout."

I couldn't help notice that the Rangers were far-better-armed than the Bluecoats. By my guess, Colonel Steele would be none too pleased at the whipping they'd taken. It appeared that the Army was testing the resolve of the Indians, though there was no hint of any serious campaign against them. I had a suspicion that the Indians were more a Texas matter.

———————

AS MY HOMESTEAD came into view off in the distance, Captain Benton brought the column to a halt and rode back to my wagon. "Not going to burden you with us bedding on your place tonight, Jack. We'll be pleased to ride on around and camp on the Guadalupe. I'll double back in the morning, as I'd like to see the progress y'all have made. Who knows, we might be buying your horses one day," he said with a broad smile.

"Thanks kindly, Captain. I appreciated the escort. Do come visit in the morning."

With that, the Texas Ranger column peeled off and left me to drive the rig the final half mile or so into the homestead proper. I was relieved, as a couple of pieces of the decrepit wagon had fallen off during the trip. I felt fortunate that it had held together enough to take me home.

Isaac was the first to see me approaching. He hustled toward me with arms waving. "Jack, welcome back." As he drew near, he caught his breath. "That mare you brought with you dropped her foal. He's a pretty little fellow."

I was disappointed at missing out but figured I'd be

seeing plenty more mares birthing young'uns. "That's great news, Isaac. Is everyone alright?"

He looked quite elated at my having asked. "Sarah is getting close to her time," he shared with me.

About this time, everyone else had run to the wagon.

Kate was the first to speak. "Did you get everything, Jack? What was Bandera like? Did you see any Indians? Are there any boys in Bandera?"

The rapid-fire questions caught me by surprise, especially the last one. She was nearing her eleventh birthday, and I suppose growing up faster than I figured. That seemed to be the way of the frontier.

There was no end of questions. I saw that good progress had been made on the cabin. Isaac and George had already begun installing a roof. It would be good to get relief from the new barn with the heady aroma of horses. With winter coming upon us in another month, a warm abode could be important to our very survival. Also, the horses would need the protection of the barn if a blizzard were to hit us.

I told about the Texas Ranger escort and described Bandera as best I could. I didn't mention what had happened to the Bluecoat patrol as I didn't want to frighten Kate or Buck.

George quickly fell to examining the two slightly-used saddles and the Sharps rifle. "Good choices, Jack," he assured me. "Big Red's been prancing around like he misses you. You better take him for a ride. Isaac and I will take care of the wagon."

That pleased me no end. I had already developed a fondness for Big Red. He surely wasn't going to be one of the fifteen headed for Buffalo Hump's encampment come spring. Besides, the big stallion had to earn his keep. We had a herd to build.

———

IT APPEARED as though my arrival with supplies contributed a note of normalcy to the homestead. It signaled new beginnings. Henceforth, I determined to call it the Rising Cross Ranch. I reckoned God might cotton to that. Rising Cross lent itself to a right smart-looking brand, too. The way I laid it out would make it tough for any rustlers to over-brand it.

Captain Benton stopped by briefly in the morning a little after sunrise. He seemed impressed with what we were doing and assured me that he'd mention our horse breeding operations to Captain Callahan. He intimated that he might even mention it to Colonel Steele if his travels took him back near Fort Inge.

It was tough to see Benton go, but it gave everyone a sense of reassurance in knowing that he was patrolling the region.

———

THE DAY after Captain Benton departed, I headed out early morning to hunt deer. I had a hankering for venison, especially since I hadn't had a square meal since before the Bandera trip. I wasn't especially impressed with the culinary fare that the Texas Rangers survived on, and the larder here at the Rising Cross was a bit lean. I decided that the Sharps would be overkill for shooting deer, so I took my trusty Springfield along with one of the Colt revolvers. I was getting tired of stuffing the pistol in my waistband so I resolved to acquire a holster one day soon.

To say game on the Comancheria was abundant would be an understatement. It took me less than an hour to bag a buck with an impressive fourteen-point rack. I field-dressed the buck, draped the carcass over behind the saddle, and headed Big Red home.

I was less than a mile out from the cabin, when I noticed some unusual goings on. I picked up Big Red's pace but ducked behind a rise in the landscape until I could figure out what was going on. As I peeked from behind an oak tree a couple of hundred yards from the cabin, I realized that everyone—George, Isaac, Sarah, Kate, even little Buck—had their hands raised and were facing the barrels of rifles held by three of what looked to be some sort of troublemakers. I reckoned that I needed to eliminate the threat sooner than later. Then I noticed the dark rump on the dun horse of one of the men. The rider wore the same black sombrero he'd worn when he beat leather from us weeks back. The hider had apparently recruited a couple of *amigos* and was out to make trouble.

I decided that the Springfield wasn't going to be enough. There were three of them, and there was no way I could fire it fast enough. I had to get close such that I could use my revolver. I'd have to shoot fast and shoot accurately. A tall order for someone as unpracticed as me at this sort of thing. Worst case, I'd stir up confusion.

I snuck up in the tall grasses, coming as close as I dared. I finally caught George's eye. He nodded imperceptibly. Blessedly, his rifle leaned on the cabin door jamb behind him. Knowing George as I did, it was sure to be loaded.

Upon further reflection, I decided that opening fire wasn't such a great idea. There could be what was called collateral damage with a passel of not-so-well-aimed bullets flying about. Then, it hit me. I recalled what one of the hiders had said by way of a threat. "*Vamos a matarlos!*" I said in the deepest, most-threatening voice I could muster. This was followed by the clicking sounds as I pulled back the hammers of the Springfield and the Colt. Each of my hands was so occupied.

The Mexican mounted on the dun visibly cringed. He immediately recognized whom he was dealing with. He surely feared the possibility of Comanche arrows every bit as much as my bullets. His hands went up, and his rifle dropped with a thud in the Rising Cross Ranch dust. His companions wasted no time in following suit.

George immediately grabbed his rifle and helped hold the Mexicans at bay.

Now, it was a question of what to do with the men? They'd threatened peaceful citizens and likely committed crimes we knew nothing of. An idea came creeping into my mind as I dismounted. I kept my guns on the trio as I ushered Kate, Sarah, and Buck into the cabin and told them not to look outside.

"What are you up to, Jack?" asked George curiously.

I motioned to the Mexicans to dismount. "Isaac, take the saddles from their cayuses."

He looked uncertain as to what I was up to but did as I asked.

The Mexicans could do naught but look on.

I proceeded to unbutton my shirt as part of demonstrating to the would-be bandits to take their clothes off.

The bandits were incredulous.

George began laughing heartily.

"*Por favor, no,*" pleaded the bandit leader.

Soon enough, the trio stood naked. I had to agree with George that it was laughable, as they were a sight to behold.

I directed them to mount their saddleless horses. We tied their wrists, then tied their ankles together on a rope beneath their horses' bellies. Upon placing the reins in their hands, we gave slaps to the horses and sent the three wide-eyed Mexicans on their way. With any luck, they just might avoid Comanche or Apache or Texas Rangers or Bluecoats.

George, Isaac, and I had good belly-laughs as they disappeared from sight.

We called Sarah, Kate, and Buck from the cabin. The piles of clothes, guns, and saddles gave them enough to join us in the laughter.

It had been a relief that the incident turned out so well. There was a touch of comfort in no harm having been done. As for me, I looked forward to sharing the event with Wild Horse. He'd appreciate the irony of one of us encountering one of the hiders again and likely laugh as heartily as we did.

WINTER SET IN HARD. There were no further threats to peace on the Rising Cross Ranch. Snow and ice seemed to be the order of the day. In the two years of my pa and ma working the homestead, we hadn't experienced any rough winters. It was clear that Texas weather was a strange phenomenon. We had a couple of blizzards, for which we felt blessed to have the barn to afford protection for most of the livestock. I even gave passing thought to bringing a couple of foals into the cabin. I think Kate figured I was cogitating on that, as she gave me a look that gave off an emphatic no. Enough said about that.

As the weather began to break toward the end of March, I worked ever harder toward raising the horses. I even started thinking about trying my hand at raising longhorn cattle. With Bandera nearby, there'd be a ready market for beef.

On April first, Sarah had her baby. Kate made a great midwife despite her youth. And Isaac? His pride belied his humble Amish roots. He named the boy Jack in my honor. Doggone, but that was humbling.

A couple of days after Isaac and Sarah brought their child into the world, George approached me after dinner. "I think it's time, Jack. By the time I reach the North Platte up in Wyoming, the snows will have begun to melt." It was clear that he yearned to have his own place and settle it with the mystery woman he intimated about but never identified.

I nodded. "I understand. You've been a terrific help, George. It would have been a far more difficult struggle here without you. I'll be ever grateful that God placed you in my life."

"You must come visit, Jack," he said, then grinned deviously. "Perhaps you could bring our friend Wild Horse and..." He let the words trail off. "Fifteen horses," he mumbled.

I felt a blush coming on, but Buck interrupted. "Can I ride a horse, Jack?"

He'd been spoiled a bit on the ride from the Comanche encampment and then watching George and me break them. "I've got to break some more first, Buck. We're going to need help with the colts, too." It hit me that our herd had grown by about a dozen head since we'd corralled them.

"Can I help?" he asked.

"We'll find a job for you, Buck. You can watch us handle the horses, so you can do it when you're big enough."

That seemed to satisfy his need to be involved with

man work. He obviously didn't especially like hanging around with Kate and Sarah doing household chores while we men did what looked like exciting work.

George grew just a tad serious. "I'll bet your Comanche friend becomes the next tribal shaman, Jack. He's got the mind for it and the spirit."

"I hope he doesn't forget what he learned of our Christian faith, George." I knew that Wild Horse's faith needed to be strengthened. Hanging with a few hundred heathen Comanche could work negatively. I hoped and prayed that the seeds I'd sown would take root.

"You've come a long way, Jack. Had you not lifted your own faith, you'd have been unable to forgive. Bitterness and vengeance might have overtaken your life, and you'd have never found peace," George counseled.

George was ever-wise, and I knew that we would all miss him. His kindness in taking us under his wing had likely led to our very survival. "I still haven't totally figured out why so many folks find it necessary to fight each other. Seems folks should need each other."

George stroked his chin. "Folks get wrapped up in themselves, Jack. They seek to preserve their own little piece of the world, to gratify only themselves. It's a selfish thing. They deceive themselves." He turned his most serious gaze on me. "You're the man of the house, Jack."

Such simple words, though heavy-laden with the very real burden of responsibility. I was nearing my sixteenth birthday, and, so far as the frontier world was concerned, I was an adult. I sighed deeply as the full realization hit me. It wasn't that long ago that I was fishing the Guadalupe with hardly a care in the world while my pa ran the homestead. It finally struck me that he'd given his life trying to protect us, his family.

George nickered at me as he would a horse.

It shook me from the silent depths of recollection and thought that had overtaken our dialog. "I think we'll make it here, my friend. Isaac and Sarah are good folks, and Kate and Buck will grow strong." I looked off into the distance. It rarely left my mind that but a couple of months back, we had rounded up a herd of wild horses.

Lingering even stronger in my thinking was the vision of the Indians we'd seen on the horizon that day. We could deal with coyotes, lynx, rattlers, and an occasional mountain lion, but the savages that peopled the Comancheria were an ever-present threat. They hadn't visited us, not that we were aware of.

I turned my attention back to George. "I expect we ought to give you a send-off dinner so you'll never forget us," I said, laughing.

Naturally, George's lips broke into that broad grin of his. It was a sort of trademark. Unforgettable. "I'm thinking you're going to be a fine rancher, Jack. I see plenty of beeves and hosses in your future. Maybe you can bring a few of those unruly longhorns on up to Wyoming. Droving cattle—especially longhorns—isn't easy, but you'd sure be the man for it. Keep in mind that those longhorns have been roaming free for many years, unhandled by man. It's turned them into truly wild animals. And in the wild? Nothing like coming on a bull or cow with a six-foot horn spread staring you down with those big glowering eyes. But...they can be broken, and you're a man that can do it. You might find help down Bandera way aside the Medina River."

I was quite taken with George's confidence in me. I hadn't really given serious thought to raising beeves and driving them to market, even as my curiosity had been aroused back when I first met George.

WE DID INDEED ENJOY a celebratory feast. Sarah and Kate went all out, whipping up roast venison, baked potatoes, and beans and carrots soaked in butter. It was all topped off with a berry pie that Kate baked. It was a fitting way to thank George and consecrate his departure.

We retold stories of the adventures we'd faced, since George came upon Wild Horse and me marveling at a dust cloud kicked up by a distant herd of longhorns. We'd packed a lot of life into a brief time.

———

AN UNDULATING VISTA of sparkling frost glistened as far as the eye could see as we gathered to see George off on his journey northward. It was an unusual chill for mid-April. George sat astride his trusty steed with three horses in tow. Two of them were packed with both the food and equipment he'd be using on his travels and the goods he'd need in settling up on the North Platte River. The third was a spare for riding. In a way, I found myself envying his determination and grit, and I hoped I would measure up.

"We're going to miss you, George," I offered in parting. "May the good Lord bless you and keep you safe." I knew the latter was especially important, as he'd be traveling through a lot of rough country. We'd heard of tribes to the north that were every bit the measure of the Comanche in the savagery they could wreak. My pa had shared stories of mountain men like Hugh Glass and Jim Bridger confronted by marauding Indians, and my history lessons had told of the dangers faced by Lewis and Clark.

"You be sure to come visit, Jack," responded George.

His forced smile couldn't hide a certain sadness in his eyes. I think he was a tad conflicted, worrying about our survival on the one hand and about his own future on the other.

"We'll make it here, friend. Don't be fearing for us," I said, forcing a reassuring smile. "I'll be sure to come visit. I'll bring Wild Horse, if he's willing."

The big Black man nodded to me, turned his horse slowly, and silently began his journey northward. Even his horse seemed reluctant to depart. He had soon ridden out of sight, and we turned to the myriad tasks at hand. There were livestock to tend to, building repairs after the harsh winter, and gardens to plant. And we stood constantly on guard against ever-lurking threats, be they animal or human.

———

I WAS AMAZED at how quickly the Rising Cross Ranch was growing. I sold some horses to the Texas Rangers and continued to breed longhorns and horses. Up to now, I hadn't experienced even a hint of threat from Indians. Perhaps the word had gone out to the Comanche and Kiowa to stay clear of Jack O'Toole's place. I could hope that was the case. As to the Apache, I think the presence of the Texas Rangers kept them at bay.

We'd constructed the cabin to double as a fortress in the event of an attack. The walls were fortified with natural limestone rock combined with cedar and oak timbers. At George's suggestion, we placed gun ports strategically around the structure. It was nothing like the fire-tinder cabin my folks had built. The roof was wooden, though we hoped to replace it with clay tiles in the future. We kept a goodly area clear around the perimeter to minimize the chance of an enemy sneaking up on us. Sounded pretty safe, didn't it?

I decided to give Big Red a bit of exercise one warm spring evening after dinner. It was around mid-May. I had begun to think about paying a visit to Wild Horse and his Penateka Comanche people.

Looking off into the distance, I could see dark thunderheads and an occasional bolt of lightning contrasted against the distant purplish-gray of the hills. The storm was happening much too far away to be concerned about. One of the phenomena about living out west was the sky seemed far bigger than back east. The horizon seemed to stretch forever across the grassy prairie.

I heard a wolf and found myself half tempted to respond. *Isa* didn't seem to be too far off. I wondered what happened to the one I'd encountered early in my adventure with Wild Horse? Why had it not attacked me? Why had it trusted me? Was God teaching me something? I suppose it was a lesson in trust.

I stared out into the distance, thinking on the future —mine, my remaining family, and the Rising Cross Ranch. What did God have in store? What was His plan?

All of a sudden, a chill swept over me. I looked about but was surrounded by utter stillness. I headed Big Red for the barn. A good session of currying and stroking would sooth any senses of foreboding.

Upon entering the cabin to bed down, it seemed notable that everyone had turned in early. I eyed my bed, such as it was. A wooden frame with a straw-filled mattress. A candle on the old oak table gave off a welcome glow. I reckoned it was nice of someone to have remembered that I was outside enjoying the night air and would appreciate enough light to navigate inside the cabin. There were a few embers in the fireplace that helped ease any evening chill. It was still blanket weather at night.

I looked about. All seemed at peace. As was my custom, I leaned the Sharps rifle alongside my bed and one of the Colt revolvers beside my pillow. Why I did this every night, I couldn't tell. It was a habit, sort of like when my pa had insisted that I carry a Colt when I went fishing.

I hung my hat, removed my boots, stripped down to my skivvies, and climbed into bed. I'm not sure how long I was sleeping when I was awakened by a thud from the front door. It was a familiar sound, and it just about stopped my heart. I expect I'm a light sleeper, as no one else was awakened. I tip-toed over and slid aside the cover to the peephole that we had the smarts to insert in the door. There was a second thud. I could make out an arrow, perhaps a foot below the peephole. I stepped back and closed the cover. I moved but a foot from the door when a third arrow pierced the peephole cover. A deadly arrowhead took up the space where my face had been but a second before. It was far too close for my comfort. "Isaac!" I called out. "Kate! Sarah!"

EPILOGUE

THE AMERICAN WESTERN frontier was mostly unforgiving, a meeting of savagery and civilization. *Perilous Trails: Jack's Adventure Begins* offers insights into the courage, faith, endurance, and pure grit entailed in the conquest of the west. It presages the decades it would take to reap the bounty the region would eventually deliver.

Life expectancy on the frontier was nothing like today. A male Indian did well to live beyond age thirty, and women could expect to live a tad less. Little wonder that older tribesmen were highly respected. Life expectancy for Whites wasn't much better. A White man on the frontier tended not to live beyond his late thirties. Notably, the brevity of life generally meant that folks had to mature sooner. By the time a man or woman reached age fifteen or sixteen, he or she was pretty much an adult in terms of others expecting him or her to carry an adult set of responsibilities.

Dangers? Anthropology-minded folks claim there were as many as thirteen tribes of Comanche, from the

Quahadi—or *antelope eaters*—in the north to the Penateka —or *honey eaters*—in the south. Mix in Kiowa, Apache, and Tonkawa, and settlers had their hands full. The very name Comanche loosely translates in the Ute tribal language as *enemy*. Capture by the Comanche invariably led to terrible outcomes. A fearsome lot these tribes were.

Notably, Penateka Comanche Chief Buffalo Hump led more than 600 warriors on a raid through the heart of Texas in August 1840, murdering Texans, looting the city of Victoria, and looting and burning Linnville on their march to the Gulf of Mexico. It was not until 1858 that Texas Ranger John Salmon *Rip* Ford led a force of 102 heavily-armed Texas Rangers into the Comancheria and brought the Comanche to their knees at the Battle of Little Robe Creek on the Canadian River.

Oh, I do refer to bison as buffalo. Just for the record, bison and buffalo are quite different. Visualize the water buffalo and then the shaggy, awkward bulk of the American bison. Seems that *buffalo* came into common usage in America to refer to the bison, so I've chosen to use it in my writings.

Jack had no modern creature comforts. Invention of cell phones and social media was a century and a half into the future. Transportation? Horses and mules were the vehicles of choice. Jack had no refrigerator to preserve sweet treats. There were no flush toilets or showers. Folks mostly ate what grazed upon or grew from the land. Learning was squeezed from the few books that might be found, especially The Holy Bible.

By way of example, my own great great-great-grandfather brought his collection of books from Ireland in 1851. As a serious and religious-minded pioneer, he had gathered quite an impressive library for his time. It included *The Holy Bible*, three volumes of *Lives of the Saints*, *Lives of Irish Saints and Martyrs*, Geoffrey Keating's *History of Ireland*, Edward Clarendon's *History of Ireland*, a *History of the Christian Church*, lectures and sermons by Father Burke titled *Instructions for Youth*, Hume's *History of England*, *Trials of a Mind*, Moore's *Life of Lord Edward Fitzgerald*, *Washington and His Generals*, a *Bible History*, and Cobbet's *History of the Reformation*. Sort of makes a head swim, doesn't it?

Can't say that the living of the era was luxurious unless you counted the sheer grandeur of majestic landscapes and of nights so quiet you could hear the stars twinkling. To fully appreciate the place, you simply had to love the beauty of the outdoors. Fishing the meandering Guadalupe River in Texas, hunting deer and antelope, raising cattle and horses, and reaping the bounteous yield of the rich soil was sheer joy for a courageous, visionary few. For a teen on the frontier, life could be pretty good...mostly. Otherwise, it was downright dangerous.

As Jack O'Toole traveled the paths to manhood, he had conquered fears and prejudices, fought Indians and bandits, defended against wild beasts, traveled the wild country, and found the love of his life. As you have seen, he especially draws upon his faith and what he was taught by his parents. He has to learn to trust in instincts forged from his biblical lessons. Yes, Jack is on a frontier adventure and more.

A LOOK AT BOOK TWO:
WYOMING CALLS: JACK'S RISKY QUEST

Wyoming Calls: Jack's Risky Quest, the second gripping installment of *The Frontier Chronicles*, plunges young Jack O'Toole into a daring adventure from Texas to Wyoming, testing his courage, faith, and endurance like never before.

Joined by his steadfast Comanche friend Spirit Talker, sixteen-year-old Jack faces perilous trails and uncharted territories dominated by Lakota, Crow, Cheyenne, Pawnee, Kiowa, Shoshone, and Comanche tribes. Each step northward into this rugged no-man's land pushes Jack to the limits of his grit and determination, embodying the essence of frontier resilience.

Thrown into Comancheria, the most dangerous part of the frontier, Jack's fate intertwines with divine guidance, steering his path through the wilds.

Will Jack survive the brutal challenges of the western frontier? Can his faith and friendship with Spirit Talker see him through the most treacherous journey of his life?

Discover the answers in *Wyoming Calls: Jack's Risky Quest* and join Jack on a quest where the stakes are higher and the risks greater.

AVAILABLE SEPTEMBER 2024

ACKNOWLEDGMENTS

Authoring books simply doesn't happen in a vacuum. The author provides the creative talent and crafts the stories, but there's so much more that demands acknowledgment. There are lots of folks and places that contribute to my authoring endeavors. So it is with *Perilous Trails: Jack's Adventure Begins.* The tale is set in 1855 and shares the trials and tribulations of a teen forced to meet the challenges inherent in the dangerous vastness of the Comancheria, but this novel stands apart. At its core, it is also about the taming of the frontier. Step in two teen boys becoming men. The protagonist epitomizes the freedom of America's western frontier and represents a final bastion of honor in America. Hopefully, readers will find *Perilous Trails: Jack's Adventure Begins* worthy of their time and emotional involvement.

I've been blessed with many friends and family who have supported my writings. My wife Carolyn's reviews and encouragement were a huge help, along with very important tech support from our sons Mike and Matt. Thanks to my nephew Shawn for his faith insights. Many more friends and family have contributed support at some level to the creation and publication of *Perilous Trails,* be it encouragement or advice.

Naturally, I am major grateful to the great folks at Wise Wolf Books. The team they bring to publishing is first-rate in editing, cover design, narration, and the myriad tasks that lead to successful book sales.

It's only right to acknowledge my ancestors who were actual settlers of the south Texas frontier. In addition to inspiring me, they provided a quite helpful true-to-life framework as to the life and times on the Texas Nueces Strip. It has been appropriate to weave them into the tapestry of my western novels. Matthew Dunn (1815-1855) immigrated to Corpus Christi from County Kildare in 1845, established a homestead on Upriver Road, and served as a sutler to General Zachary Taylor's Army in the Mexican-American War. Peter Dunn (1807-1890) immigrated from Ireland in 1850 and established a blacksmith shop in Corpus Christi. John Dunn (1803-1889), my great great great grandfather, raised cattle and grew thousands of acres of cotton. Lawrence Dunn (1837-1864) fought and died with Captain Ware's Confederate cavalry. My great great grandfather Nicholas Dunn (1835-1912) was a rancher, drover, livestock speculator, and Comanche fighter of some repute. My cousin John Beamond *Red John* Dunn (1851-1940) served as a Texas Ranger in the 1870s under Captain Bland Chamberlain (Company H), subsequently joined a *vigilance committee*, became a farmer and merchant, and curated a museum of military weapons displayed to this day in the Corpus Christi Museum of Science & History. Red John Dunn's brother Matthew Dunn also served as a Texas Ranger, and another cousin, Rut Evans, served as a Texas Ranger in the 1890s (Company E, Frontier Battalion, Alice, TX). My cousin Patrick Dunn was quite successful at raising longhorns on North Padre Island just east of Corpus Christi from 1883 to 1937. John Hillard Dunn (1883-1958), whose personal narrative about his family and his own adventures drove my pursuit of my Texas family legacy, inspired my own writings, and led me to write his yet-to-be-published biography *Tough Hombre—*

Recollections of a True Texan. Finally, my grandfather, Horace Charles Greathouse, served as a Texas Ranger in 1920 (Company C, Austin, TX). Such real-life characters, coupled with actual events, have served to reinforce the historical settings for my writings.

Most of my authoring has occurred in my office as decorated to channel my inner Texan, but my creative juices have often been inspired and my imagination stoked in cafés and coffee houses across America. My favorites were Hester's Café & Coffee Bar in Corpus Christi, TX, Nueces Café in Robstown, TX, Java Ranch Espresso Bar & Café in Fredericksburg, TX, PAX Coffee & Goods in Kerrville, TX, Ragged Edge Coffee House and Bantam Coffee Roasters in Gettysburg, PA, 1889 Coffee House in Helena, MT, Dunn Brothers Coffee in Rapid City, SD, Postmasters Coffee & Bakery and Brio Coffee-house in Waynesboro, PA, Birdie's Café and American Ice Co Café in Westminster, MD, Deja Brew Coffee House, Carroll Valley and New Oxford, PA, and Balti-more Coffee & Tea Co., Frederick Coffee Company & Café, and Dublin Roasters in Frederick, MD. I must admit to also frequenting a few Dunkin Donuts and Star-bucks around our fine nation. The décors and easy-listening music in these fine establishments combined with savory cups of coffee tended to set me in the right creative frame of mind.

Last but not least, I'm especially thankful for the many folks who have read and enjoyed my books.

I do believe it's important to acknowledge how the old west represents the brave pioneering spirit of settlers who met the challenges and transcended mere survival to enable America to achieve exceptional growth. The settling of the American frontier west is replete with tales of leveraging freedom for individual achievement. I hope you'll agree that reliving our past—even through history-based fiction—often has the effect of pointing the way to an ever-brighter future. Might we be up to it? I hope that the inspiration I've drawn from my having walked the very earth my characters have trodden, coupled with my extensive historical research, will enable readers to fully experience the grit, adventure, and passion of my characters while sensing aromas of gunsmoke, trail dust, leather, and bluebonnets.

Thanks kindly to all of you, and please do enjoy *Perilous Trails: Jack's Adventure Begins.*

ABOUT THE AUTHOR

Award-winning author Mark Greathouse's love for the western genre draws upon his deep family roots and love of the outdoors honed from teen years hiking the Appalachian Trail and family travels across America's frontier. Greathouse began writing full time after a successful career as a business executive and later as an entrepreneurial investor and advisor. His service as president of several business and community nonprofits led to their extraordinary growth. He holds a BA in English and MBA in marketing. Greathouse donates time and books annually to support wounded military warriors. He was a Boy Scout leader (Eagle Scout) and served on a local school board.

A member of Western Writers of America and the Wild West History Association, he also contributes articles on the history of America's west to western-themed magazines. Greathouse was recognized as a 2024 Finalist in western genre by the American Literary Book Awards for his sixth Tumbleweed Saga, *Nueces Truth: Texans Face War's Realities*.

His *Frontier Chronicles*, a series of western novels aimed at adventure-minded teens and young adults while weaving a Christian message within their fabric, are aimed at lighting fires of truth, faith, hope, and life purpose in the bellies of today's teen boys and girls. Just as seeds must be sown to reap the harvest, so the seeds of faith must be planted to raise tomorrow's men and women.

GLOSSARY

DEFINITIONS

Big Father—All-powerful Comanche deity.

Bota bag—A canteen fashioned from leather and popular among Indians, mountain men, and many travelers of the western frontier.

Life debt—A cultural phenomenon in which someone whose life is saved or spared by another becomes indebted or in some way connected to their savior.

Pemmican—Lean dried strips of meat pounded into a paste, mixed with fat and berries, and then pressed into small cakes.

Possibles bag—A leather or canvas sack carried by cowboys and containing essentials like soap, matches, bandages, extra spur, smoke makings, and playing cards

Remuda—A herd of horses frequently used on trail drives and by Plains Indians.

Shaman—Comanche medicine man.

Teepee—An enclosed conical transportable shelter constructed of long poles and buffalo hides with a vent at the top to permit smoke to escape.

COMANCHE TRANSLATIONS

Aitu—Not good

Ana o'a hi'it—Phrase for *desire to eat*

Ap—Father

Aruka—Deer

Eetu—Bow

Ekakwitsʉbaitʉ—Lightning

Ekapitu—Red

Eekạsahpana paraiboo—Army officer (soldier chief)

Hawokatu—Hollow, loose

Hoikwa—Hunt, look for prey

Isa—Wolf

Isa wasu—Poison

Kaahaniitu—deceive, cheat

Kahni—Life

Kamakuna—Loved one

Kee—No

Kobe—Wild Horse

Kohto—Build a fire

Kooitu—Die

Kutseena—Coyote

Kwakuru—Defeat someone

Nahuu—Knife

Natsuitu—Strong

Numu—Teepee

Numunuu—Referring to the members of the Comanche tribes. Literally: people.

Ohapitu—Yellow

Paa—Water

Paaka—Arrow

Peeka—Kill

Pia—Mother

Pia huutsuu—Bald eagle

Pia wa'óo—Comanche words for mountain lion, puma, or cougar.

Pihi—Heart

Puuka—Horse

Sunipu—Medicine (as in strong medicine)

Suumaru—Ten

Taa Narumi—Master/God

Tabu—Coward

Tamu—Rabbit

Tasiwoo—Buffalo

Tenahpu—Man

Tomoobi—Sky

Tosa—White man or woman

Tosaabitu—White

Tumah tuyai—After life

Tuhibitu—Black

Tumhyokenu—Believe, trust

Tu Taiboo—Black man

Umaru—Rain

Unha haksi nahniaka—Phrase for *what's your name?*

Wa'ipu—Woman

Wasápe—Bear

Wutsutsuki—Rattlesnake

www.ingramcontent.com/pod-product-compliance
Lightning Source LLC
Chambersburg PA
CBHW011431240626
47153CB00011B/2942